I0612133

The Strong Dress

Meg Vertigan

PUNCHER & WATTMANN

First published in 2023
Published by Puncher and Wattmann
PO Box 279
Waratah NSW 2298

https://www.puncherandwattmann.com
web@puncherandwattmann.com

ISBN   9781922571649

Cover design by Danielle Kojic and Miranda Douglas
Photo by Gabriel Silverio, downloaded from Unsplash (gabriel-silverio-QJCtd5KGI9Y-unsplash)
Edited by Ed Wright
Proofreading by Claudia King
Typesetting by Morgan Arnett
Printed by Lightning Source International

While inspired by historical events, this book is entirely fictional and its characters bear no resemblance to actual living persons.

NATIONAL
LIBRARY
OF AUSTRALIA

A catalogue record for this work is available from the National Library of Australia

For all the Kates.

Follow me and I will take you upstairs to the reception area. Don't feel intimidated by the waiting room with its velveteen couches and the brass plaque hanging on the door. Take a seat; it will soon be your turn. The seats here are comfortable, aren't they? The magazines are fashionable? You are in good hands. Of course this doctor is the expert. He will help you. Read over his name on that brass plaque: Dr Jack Grafton. Surely you have seen him in the newspapers?

Ah, there he is now, ushering in the next patient. Look at him, isn't he everything I told you he would be? Look at his suit. Surely it was made by a tailor? He's tall, dark and handsome. He ticks all the boxes. Look past him into his office. See the leather couch? The large oak desk? All those books on his bookshelf? He must have read them all, every single one. Surely. How else would he be able to help you?

Come on, let's sneak in with this patient. No one will notice us. We will just sit quietly in the corner and watch. Maybe we will learn something? Look at this poor young fellow. He doesn't look happy to be here. No doubt he has been dragged along by his parents. Who does he remind you of? Your brother? Or your cousin? Perhaps even your son? Look at his hair, left to grow too long. Look at his clothes and his slovenly walk. He doesn't want to go to school. He doesn't want to get a job. He doesn't want to do anything. He doesn't want to be *here*, that's for sure.

Don't worry though, Dr Jack Grafton, with his nameplate in brass, is the expert. He can turn this delinquent around. A couple of sessions at 35 dollars per hour will make this young boy comb his hair and hand out the hymn books at church on Sundays. It's a bargain, really. The neighbours are starting to talk. My friend's cousin brought his teenage daughter to see Dr Grafton. She was starting to get a reputation, but now she is engaged to a nice young man with a job—and a decent haircut.

So, sit back, relax, but remember to pay attention. Watch as Dr Jack Grafton closes the door. Now we can see the doctor weave his magic. This is a private show. There is no one else in here. Just the doctor, the patient and the four walls that surround them.

There is a knock at the door, and the seal is broken.

"I'm Billy's mother." A woman walks towards the doctor, her hand outstretched in front of her. Dr Grafton stays standing behind his massive oak desk. It should be clear to this silly woman that his desk is there to create a division between the doctor and his clients: between knowledge and misunderstanding. But she doesn't understand. She grabs for the doctor's hand as if she is trying to pull some of the power out of him, but she is left with her arm awkwardly stretched across the desk. Soon she gives up and goes to sit on the couch beside her son.

"Mrs Dunbar," said Dr Grafton. "This appointment is with your son. It does not concern you. Anything that is discussed in this room is confidential and remains between your son and I."

The doctor smiles as he says this, walking around to stand in front of Mrs Dunbar who now looks like a naughty schoolgirl. He takes her hand in his and leads her as meekly as a lamb out of the room. Perhaps his words are softened by his jazz singer voice, but she does as she is told and leaves to wait in the reception area for her son. I would not be telling you everything if I omitted the tiny detail of the good doctor placing his hand on Mrs Dunbar's hip to help escort her out the door. Perhaps he holds it there for too long. And perhaps there's a pause as lets his eyes sweep from those of the desperate mother to across her well displayed chest down to her crotch and back up. Are his eyes twinkling when they return to her face, mocking and questioning at the same time? Please, don't judge the doctor for his love of women. It's natural for a man to be attracted to a good-looking woman. But once the door is closed again, with Billy on the inside and his mother on the outside, Dr Jack Grafton focusses all of his attention on the boy.

The doctor sits back behind the desk and looks across at the young man on his couch. When the doctor does not say anything, the boy volunteers his own diagnosis.

"There's nothing wrong with me," he says.

"I can see that," agrees Dr Grafton. "The problem is with your mother and most likely your father as well."

The scowl on the boy's face begins to move and change. The lines do not disappear entirely but resettle, with his left eyebrow cocked in the way that infuriates his father.

"You see," continues the doctor, as he puts his feet right up on the shiny wood and leans back on his chair. Take note of this action. Is it staged to gain the boy's trust as he says these next words? "You and I are different from them."

The boy leans forwards in his chair as if trying to draw the very words from the doctor's mouth. Then he straightens up and smooths his hair with his fingers. There's an improvement already.

"That chair really is uncomfortable, isn't it?" says the doctor. "Put your feet up, relax."

That is the magic of Dr Grafton. This boy, who will do nothing his parents ask of him, not only follows the doctor's directions, but bends down to take his shoes off first.

"No, no," says the doctor. "Leave your shoes on. I insist. Now let me tell you, Billy, just why your parents have it all wrong."

The Book of Love

Kate

Once upon a time, not so long ago, a girl was born. The doctor held her upside down, all curly black hair and thick white mucus and slapped her on the backside. She opened her red gash of a mouth and screamed. They named her Katherine, but everyone called her Kate. Except for her father; he called her Princess.

Some months passed, and her dark hair fell out and regrew in fine blonde ringlets. That is really when this story begins. When her hair became blonde, and her mother forever after burnt her own dark hair into brittle yellow straw in an effort to mimic her daughter's transformation. As a toddler this girl was the delight of old ladies in Woolies and her father's chest swelled every time someone said, *You'll have to lock that one up someday*, as if it was a strange pseudonym for those cursed by being beautiful, or blonde, or in his daughter's case, both. It could be said that she was only beautiful in a girl-next-door sort of way, and I guess this is true. But isn't that the most dangerous kind of beauty?

*

Seventeen years later this princess sat with her school friends on the netball court at school. The goal circle curved in an arc, dividing Kate and Sue from the other Kate, Kate Noble, the other Sue, and Frances. It was the year *Advance Australia Fair* became Australia's national anthem. Like the song these kids were young, but they weren't quite free. It was May, and there was still more than half a year until they would leave school and enter the real world. Then they would be free. (Or so they thought.)

They were always marking time. How many minutes could they stretch to get to French as long as possible after the bell without being deemed late? The time it took until the next six months would be over, so they could escape the nagging of their parents and the endless oppression of school. Kate was more interested in the next ten minutes of flirting and preventing the boys from playing handball than she was about the popularity of *Waltzing Matilda* versus *Advance Australia Fair*.

Kate, Kate, Sue, Sue, and Frances were the only five girls left from Kate's childhood posse still at school. Being only five of them they had free reign over the boys. But only a couple were deemed kiss-worthy, so the girls still squabbled among themselves like a gang of magpies over a couple of juicy bits of devon.

The rest of their schoolfriends had disappeared into secretarial oblivion or become shop assistants. Until they found husbands. But that is a different story. "Our" girls stuck together, so although they may have hated each other, they became friends. These girls were linked by their ambition, to be doctors, or teachers. Or because their parents were too afraid to let them out into the real world, just yet. The reason Kate was still at school with her ever-dwindling posse was due to her idol, Ita Buttrose, who at the time was the editor of *Cleo*, the most fashionable magazine of the 70s. Kate planned to go straight to Ita Buttrose's office after the final exams and beg for a job. But before that she would wear a very short dress at Kate Noble's end of school party the first Saturday night after their final exam. The girls had been talking about this party since fourth form.

So, as you can see, this group of girls sitting on the asphalt had more important things to think about than heading over to their classrooms. Being still at school had not necessarily made them more scholarly, especially seeing as they had French next, and French meant sweaty old Mr Gilmore and a mess of verbs that needed conjugating from a country where people ate frog's legs and snails and therefore were barely people at all.

If only Mr Gilmore had thought to show the students pictures of French fashion or the Alpine A110, the sexiest sports car on the planet. If only he had thought to tell them about the allure of the French accent, even a fake one. He should have hinted that his accent alone could, even still, in his fifty-second year, entice one of those new divorcees at the Epping club to sleep with him. If Mr Gilmore had let these almost-adults know that learning to speak French could lead to sex, they would definitely have practised those phrases they were supposed to have done for last night's homework.

The boys had given up on their game, their wristwatches ticked towards the impending doom of the bell. They stood back and watched the two Kates, the two Sues and Frances clapping their hands together. The girls were too old for this game, but there was something exciting about revisiting this rhyme. Their faces were flushed as they chanted. Kate hoped the boys were watching her the most. Unlike most girls her age, Kate was pleased with what she saw when she looked in the mirror. Her blonde hair reached just to the pink of her nipples, curling around them, framing them. Still wet and dripping from the shower her pubic hair curled lusciously between her legs, blonde against her tanned thighs. Her eyes were blue, her stomach flat. Long legs, tick. Clear complexion, tick. Small nose, full heart-shaped lips, tick, tick. Kate's mother may have been the best-looking woman in Sydney, but Kate was surely catching up.

That morning Kate had put on a hot pink bra so that it would show through the thin cotton of her school uniform. She dressed seductively, like a reverse stripper, watching herself as she reluctantly covered those things that marked her as a woman. Her breasts, her bottom, her hips. She didn't wear a jumper although it was still cool in the mornings. Most of the other girls wore jumpers to hide their lack of boobs, or the shape of them, or the pouches of empty wombs that had grown to betray their little girls' bodies. They couldn't wait until the endless monotony of school finished so they could get married and fill them. Those overweight, sweaty girls that hung silently in the periphery were not on Kate's radar, so she had never thought to remember their names.

The girls slapped their palms together and sang.
My boyfriend gave me an apple

My boyfriend gave me a pear

Kate loved the feeling of the boys watching her. The long shadows of the afternoon sun showed a ball on the ground, mechanically being kicked between them. The girls continued with their game. Kate was glad that she had cut nipple holes out of her bra that morning and knew that the chill of the day was obvious through her thin school dress.

My boyfriend gave me a kiss on the lips and threw me down the stairs
He threw me over Ireland
He threw me over France
He threw me over the USA and then pulled down my pants!

Kate looked across at the other Kate, Kate Noble, her long brown legs crossed with her school dress tucked up to show them off. She has to resort to that, thought Kate. She's got no tits.

Everyone knew Kate Noble's chest was as flat as a boy's. They all had to get dressed in their swimming costumes facing each other at the wooden benches. There wasn't room or time to be discreet, with their teacher barking at them to hurry up from the moment they arrived. They had barely enough time to dry themselves with hair dripping and underwear sticking to their wet legs as they tried to pull them up. But there was always time for furtive glances, and they all knew each other's bodies well enough to place them on the pecking order. Kate Noble was easily the most beautiful with sapphires for eyes and her doll's nose. Her beauty superseded her lacking chest. Sue Golding had the best tan, but her ankles were thick. The other Sue had beautiful skin, but it was too white. There was nothing wrong with Frances, apart from the fact she faded from the memory of everyone she ever met before they even thought to ask her name. She didn't even have a double to be compared with, like Kate and Sue, so her existence was limited. Our Kate was blonde with breasts that were big enough to fill a desert bowl. No one saw much past that.

My boyfriend gave me a kiss on the lips and threw me down the stairs
He threw me over Ireland

"Hey youse, get off the court," Michael Ballins called over to them. They always called him Michael Ballins because there were two Michaels as well. Beecroft parents of the 1970s lacked imagination when they were naming their kids. "Little Michael" was shorter than all the girls, which was a shame as he was good looking, with dark hair and cupid's lips. The girls had been waiting since first year for him to grow. Michael Ballins was tall enough, but he always looked like he had left Weet-Bix round his mouth.

The girls sang louder, mucking up the words with their giggles.

My boyfriend gave me a papple

My boyfriend gave me a bear

Frances did have small rose buds trying to bloom under her school dress, but she wore a tight singlet under her uniform to hide this shame. Kate watched Frances as she laughed and tugged her school dress over her knees between claps.

He threw me over France

He threw me over the USA and then pulled down my pants!

That morning Kate had loosened her top buttonhole with the help of her school compass and now she undid her top button with the flick of the wrist she had been practicing in front of the bedroom mirror. She wore a chain around her neck, the charm hidden just out of sight of the boys who stared at her chest, imagining where that necklace ended.

As the other girls fled from the ball that Michael Ballins had thrown into the centre of the group, Kate was left behind. Then three things happened very close together, but I remember. Firstly, the ball hit Kate in the face and then Mr Mason walked across the asphalt towards her. Kate covered her face in her hands to hide the snot and blood that had exploded from her nose just as the bell rang. That is how it happened. I am sure of that. The ball, then the teacher, and then the bell rang. Just like a warning that was too late.

Kate felt Michael Ballins' hand on her shoulder. "Are you alright?"

"Mr Ballins," warned Mr Mason, close to them now. Even in an emergency a regulation one-foot space must be observed between the boys and the girls. This was the teacher's favourite rule to police at Beecroft Secondary College.

Kate ran to the bubblers, her hand still covering her nose. The others surrounded her. As she washed her face, she saw the blood.

"Are you okay?" A gaggle of girls.

"Girls, the bell has gone. I am sure you have a class to go to."

Kate turned to follow her friends, but Mr Mason stopped her.

"You had better go to sickbay and get that checked out," he said.

His eyes flicked then to a place that no teacher's eyes should. But then who could blame him? Kate was the girl-next-door type remember? And she had her top button undone after all. Mr Mason noticed. She noticed him notice. He turned and walked away across the asphalt towards the science lab.

Kate sat on the bed in sickbay with a moist face washer stuck to her cheek. She thought about the look Mr Mason had given her. Or should I say, her breasts? Was he wondering what the charm at the end of her necklace was as he ate his beetroot sandwiches in the lunchroom? She reckoned that as he squeezed pink fingerprints into the white bread, he would smile just enough to show the dimple on his left cheek. She remembered how the new science teacher had stood so close to her shoulder when she had labelled her diagram of a male reproductive system.

When Mrs Blewett from the office came to check on her in the sickbay, she found Kate conjugating verbs in her French book and muttering under her breath.

Elle a chaud, C'est chaud, Il fait chaud, Elle est chaude, Mr Mason est chaud.

"That's nice to see. A student doing her homework. I would expect nothing less from you, Katherine, but it is a rare sight in the sickbay. Most of the students who come in here are trying to avoid doing work."

The bell rang then and the occasional slow squeaky shoes on the linoleum corridor turned into a stampede of giggling, shouting feet. Kate stood with her books clasped to her chest.

"You still looked a bit flushed dear," said Mrs Blewett. "Would you like a bit longer in here?"

"Oh, no thanks Mrs Blewett. I have science next. I'd better go."

Jack

I'm not sure how to begin this so I will start with what everybody wants to know. They all ask me the same questions.

"You knew Doctor Grafton on both a professional and a personal level for many years. How would you describe him?"

"How would I describe him?"

"Yes, how do you like to remember him?"

"How do I *like to* remember Jack? Well, of course to describe him fully would involve more contradictions than a Thomas Hardy novel."

They always look at me blankly then, and I know what they really want is just a simple list of adjectives. Nothing too complicated. "Intelligent? Oh yes, he was the most intelligent man I have ever met. Pompous? (I laugh at that.) Not that I would ever describe him that way, but I have heard it said. Eccentric? Maybe. Nutty? Never.

He was gregarious and elegant. He always wore a suit. He always dressed as a gentleman. He may have been one of the last true gentlemen."

"But, ah, didn't he have lots of lovers?"

"Oh yes. Yes. (I laugh again. What else can I do?) But this did not stop him from being a gentleman. He treated all of his women very well and sometimes they even became friends with each other. His long-time 'companions' Linda Pascal and Nancy Collins became good friends at the end of his life and Jack even gave them identical gifts. A pearl necklace and a Persian cat. Or maybe it was a pearl ring? I am sure about the cats though. He gave them one each. They were out of the same litter. Imagine that! Only a gentleman could get away with that kind of behaviour.

But seriously, Jack was a crusader really, for psychiatry. He was ahead of his time, as they say. It is terrible the way it all ended up. His life was a terrible tragedy. That is the only way to describe it. It was a terrible tragedy for such a talented man to end his life in that way."

People still invite me to dinner parties on occasion, and I know it is so they can ask me about Jack. I don't mind. He was my friend. I like having an excuse to talk about him. They usually wait until there are a couple of empty glasses before the questions start in earnest.

"A lot is known about Doctor Grafton's professional life, through the media and the Royal Commission. How would you describe him as a friend, though? The Jack that *you* knew?"

They might need a drink to ask the questions, but I don't need a drink to answer them.

"Fabulous. He was the most fabulous and loyal friend. Jack had many friends. He was an entertainer, you know. He loved to entertain. He entertained throughout his life, throughout everything. His dinner parties were famous. (I laugh again. I have told these anecdotes so many times now that the pauses for my laughter are built into the story. The repetition has begun to make the stories feel false, though, and that reminds me that Jack is gone.) I pause then to regain my composure before I go on, 'Or should I say infamous? Oh, the stories I could tell.'"

"Do share with us."

"Oh, well. Where do I begin? There are so many stories to tell. He was a wonderful host and Daphne, his wife, was a wonderful hostess. They always made their guests feel welcome and interesting, as if everything we had to say was important. But, of course, Jack was always the real storyteller."

"Really? Can you give me an example?"

One time I was at the Graftons' when his twin girls were still little. The family home was in Leichhardt Sydney's inner west. A group of us were sitting around their beautiful, expansive oak table, looking out the large picture window at their yard.

It must have been around October, the jacaranda at the end of the backyard was flowering. Jacarandas had excited me in my youth, as if they were announcing my birthday by flowering just for me. As I have aged though, they seem to mock me. I watched the tree out the window with a melancholy eye as the dusky evening turned the sky almost the exact purple of the jacaranda, so that it seemed as though the blooms were dissolving into the night. I was thinking of my own mortality and what I thought was my own imminent departure into the great unknown. Ha! Who would have guessed that I would be the sole survivor? It is rather amusing to me now because I was only in my forties then, but I considered myself an old man.

We were all sitting there around the table when the glamorous wife of quite a dull looking fellow said, "This apple sauce is delicious, Mrs Grafton." She had one of those seductive voices like Marilyn Monroe, half small child and half chain-smoking nightclub singer.

"Please, call me Daphne," said Jack's wife, forever the genial host. This other woman had been making eyes at Jack from the moment she walked in the door, not that this was an odd occurrence. Daphne must have been aware, yet she always behaved like a lady.

The woman had complimented the apple sauce and that was enough for Jack to step in.

"Oh yes," he said. His voice was rich as a wedding emcee's. "My dear wife went down to the market this morning and bought the apples fresh. I was barely awake, just sipping at some coffee in the kitchen when Daphne appeared through the front door with a basket of apples on her arm like Little Red Riding Hood. She had them peeled by the time I'd finished my second cup of coffee. I'm not a morning person."

Jack paused, sliced off a piece of his pork, then pushed it through the apple sauce on his plate. That is what he was like. That whole time he cut the pork, swivelled it through the sauce and chewed no one said a word. We were spellbound.

"It *is* good," he finally pronounced. "This apple sauce is part of the reason I married Daphne. We'd only known each other for three weeks when we got married, you know. And I have to tell you that apple sauce is one of the many reasons why, along with her obvious beauty. My wife's apple sauce reminds me of the apple pies my mother used to make when I was just a small boy out in Bilpin. The first time I tasted Daphne's apple sauce I knew I was home. I had to marry her immediately!"

Jack could do that, you know, make a connection out of anything. Make a conversation out of a banal comment regarding apple sauce, of all things.

Jack just picked it up and ran with it.

"My mother picked the apples herself, with us kids picking those on the lower branches from these trees that she had espaliered against the back fence," he went on. "Every single apple had a worm hole in it, they were that good. I used to wonder why the worms couldn't just eat one whole apple and then leave the rest for us, but Mum used to say, *There's plenty here for all of us*, and she spent hours in the kitchen cutting the black spots off the apples. Then she peeled them in a single peel, all the way to the end, and us kids would sit at the end of the bench with these peels hanging out of our mouths and down to the ground while we watched her making pies.

"I have to tell you these pies were very good. Perhaps it was the apples. Even my own dog Betsy, a beautiful Border collie she was, used to bite the apples off the trees and eat them.

"But those pies. I dreamt of those pies when I was at boarding school. I was only twelve years old when I was sent away, and I missed everything. I missed my family. I missed my mother. I missed running around the homestead with Betsy. But you know, when I was lying in bed in that boarding house, what do you think was the thing I missed the most? Oh boy, I sure did miss those apple pies."

Jack spoke that last sentence with the twang of an American. I can let you in on a little secret though. This story was an example of Jack's devoted loyalty to Daphne, despite everything that happened with other women. Jack loved his wife, and I will tell you how I know that. I was a good friend of Jack's and as such I had been the first to arrive at the dinner party that evening. Daphne was bustling around the kitchen getting everything ready and Jack and I were sampling the wine.

"Making sure it is respectable enough to serve to the guests," as Jack put it.

Jack was opening a second bottle of riesling from the Barossa Valley when Daphne turned around, saw that Jack was busy and so said to me, "Here, make yourself useful. Open this jar for me, will you?"

Now you can guess what the jar was, can't you? It was a jar of apple sauce. Back then it was almost sinful to buy a product like that in a jar. It was the same with baby food. You would certainly not admit to it. My own wife was ashamed if someone dropped by and she did not have some homemade treat to offer them and had to get a packet of biscuits out of the pantry. That was the whole point of Jack's story about the pies and his dog. Not that the story wasn't true, although poor Jack was prone to exaggeration. I would never be so arrogant as to accuse him of lying, but exaggerating, yes, he was certainly capable of that.

His mother would have made apple pies, of course. The odds were that the apples were homegrown. Perhaps the dog even ate them. Dogs eat almost everything. But was the dog a Border collie, a pure bred? Or does that just add to the melancholy nature of a story about a boy who is forced to leave his dog behind to go to a dismal boarding school in the city?

Now I am not going to warn you every time Jack tells his stories and point out the inaccuracies of his speech. I will, however, warn you now that his stories are at times questionable. So, keep your wits about you as I tell you about Jack, but do try to look past these slight discrepancies to the essence of my dear friend. Remember also that the only reason he may have waxed lyrical about his wife's homemade apple sauce was to save her from humiliation. He rescued her from social embarrassment, and he did it out of love. Jack was a man who did everything out of passion and love.

Well, the apple sauce was delicious, even if it was from a jar. The wine was superb, and plentiful, and the conversation was anything but bland. Doctors have wonderful dinner party conversations, especially psychiatrists. Ordinary doctors may have conversations about burst appendixes and setting broken bones, but after time these stories become little more than talking shop. Remove this kitchen cabinet to make room for a fridge. Paint the kitchen lemon yellow. She'll be right. Remove this appendix and stitch him up. He'll be right.

But the lives of the insane are infinite and varied and let me tell you this; the psychiatrist has taken over the role of the priest. It is the psychiatrist that you make your confession to, either to relieve your burden, or perhaps to boast, just a little. While the priest has no wife to pass on the titillations of his job, the psychiatrist not only has a wife, but a whole dinner table full of people washing down their pork and store-bought apple sauce with another glass of wine.

"Thank you very much, Doctor," his guests would say as Jack refilled their glasses, for he was always a generous host.

"Oh, no, call me Jack."

Ha, that's right, I remember now. It often ended this way. I would stop short of saying invariably, but only just. I liked to sit back and watch the antics of the guests after a few glasses of wine. It was better than any of those shows on the box, *Number 96* and all that. Soon the nylon stockinged foot of the beautiful woman, whose fate had been to marry that dull man, was in the lap of Jack while the private lives of crazy men and women were reduced to anecdotes served as part of the evening's flirtations, an aphrodisiac of sorts. At least under the spell of Dr Jack Grafton, this is what they became.

I wasn't the only person who noticed the stray foot on Jack's lap. The husband in question, I am relatively sure he was an accountant of sorts, had too. His face turned grey and became set, devoid of emotion. I took a sip of my wine and let it swirl around my mouth. I waited, too. I was, I am not sure, excited? Surprised? Perhaps titillated is the word? Being around Jack you felt as if something was always about to happen. I could not wait to see what this cuckold of a husband would do next. I imagined that he would either confront Jack, or else shuffle his wife straight out the front door with some poor excuse about the babysitter. But this man, small and bald as he was, surprised me.

"So, Jack," he started, in an effort to distract the doctor from his wife's ample cleavage. It was certainly not the kind of cleavage one would expect from an accountant's wife. "Craziness? Is it hereditary? Leah here's sister is as mad as a meat axe, and I have to say that I have seen that same look in the eyes of her daughter. Lovely little thing she was as a kid, and still is now I guess, except for that look in her eyes. It's like a wild animal."

"Neil!"

That's right. Neil. That was the accountant's name.

Jack smiled. He always welcomed an opportunity to give his opinion. "Yes, hereditary. Yes," he said. "There is no doubt about that. I have been in the field of psychiatry for long enough now that I am beginning to see the second generation of some families. Madness is inherent in them. Not that it can't be cured. But madness is born into their brains, I like to say. I often tell Daphne that when I start getting the third generation coming to see me, I will have to give the game away.

"Let me tell you a story," Jack continued, and the whole dinner party shifted in anticipation. I swallowed my wine and relaxed.

"I was working at a mental facility when I was an intern," Jack began. "I was green, just learning my trade and every drooling maniac made me stop and stare. Every masturbating psychopath was imprinted into my brain. I had not seen such behaviour before. On this particular day, I was in charge of walking a group of female inmates through the grounds. They were all what we called safos, meaning that they were not dangerous, either to themselves or others. One of these women kept pinching my behind. Every three steps she did it. Step, step, step—pinch. Step, step, step—pinch."

Every time Jack said "pinch" he jumped a little in his seat as if an invisible hand was rising up through it and pinching his derrière right there and then. At this his wife chortled, not an ordinary laugh, or a chuckle, both of which are spontaneous, but the practised chortle of a canary. Lewis Caroll would have been proud. The accountant blushed, his head leaned ever closer to the doctor, and yet his wife's foot seemed to lose interest, as if it did not agree with the topic of conversation.

"The other 'clients', as we called them, were following behind, shuffling along like old ladies. Some were drooling. They were heavily tranquilised. The others were distracted with small talk. But this one woman kept at it. Step, step, step and pinch. Step, step, step and pinch. Until there was an almighty crack like a car had backfired. Glass shattered and men were barking like dogs. Voomp!! A man landed on the grass next to me, grabbed one of the women who had been trailing along behind and they started copulating like dogs. Like dogs I tell you! That, my dear friend," he said as he moved his chair closer to Neil, as if he was the most interesting man in the room, "is why I have generation number two, the veritable Sleeping Beauty, sleeping her beautiful life away in bed number seventeen of Ferriby Private Hospital."

"More trifle, Neil?" asked Daphne.

"No, thank you, I've had enough."

"Jack?"

"I might have just a tiny bit more, Daphne. I must say, your trifle is irresistibly delicious."

Jack was not a man who was easily satisfied. Dr Grafton had to have the admiration and respect of *all* of his audience members. For everyone else sitting around that large oak table that night, the accountant and his wife, Daphne and I, and I am sure there must have been others, the evening may have been another respectable dinner party but to Jack, every moment when he had people in the room with him was an opportunity to be revered. He needed to be loved and admired by everyone. It was the most essential requirement of his existence.

I could see that Jack needed to charm the accountant so that by the end of the evening he would be following Jack around like a tame dog.

"Come outside with me Neil. I have something to show you. A pet little project I am working on for my girls." Jack led the accountant out into his yard as if he was making a grand entrance onto the stage. The yard resembled most of those in Leichhardt with white iron-lace garden furniture on a small porch leading onto a long, narrow block.

Jack gestured into the dim yard.

"How do you like that then? This is going to be the best-looking swimming pool in the suburb. I'm digging it out myself. The bigger the pool, the less lawn there'll be to mow."

Light from the kitchen window sent a muted glow over the lawn where the wide mouth of a crater gaped back towards us.

"Come down further and have a look," said Jack, tipping his head towards the window where Daphne and Leah were making polite kitchen talk.

"Be civilised. Bring your wine. No point in being uncouth now, is there, even if we are discussing backyard maintenance?"

Jack led the way, his sure feet confidently leading us towards the hole in the ground. As we got closer, we could see a mound as tall as a man rising out of the earth.

"Good God," Neil cried. "That hole is as deep as me. You can't tell me you dug that yourself with a shovel you bought from the hardware store. It would take ten men the better part of a month to build such a hole."

Jack laughed. "A hole isn't built though, my dear friend. A hole is dug. But apart from the semantics you are right. And I have one word to say to you, Neil. Dynamite."

"Dynamite?" the accountant repeated, and all at once his face lit up like a small boy and I could tell he had forgotten about the wife he had left in the kitchen, looking out at us from the porch light. It was as if he no longer cared that the women were probably silently comparing his short rotund frame against Jack's superior form and even more superior head of hair. For once again Neil was a boy, scrambling along behind another, larger boy, his shoes slipping on the lumpy clay soil as they made their way towards the garden shed.

I was following along close behind, of course. There was no way I wanted to miss out on anything. The night air must have excited us all. Jack emerged from the shed with a stick of dynamite in one hand and his red wine still in the other.

"You can't have too many deep ends," he announced in his best news-reader voice and led the way back to the pool.

"Jack?"

"Girls! My girls. Come on over here."

I looked up to see Daphne and the accountant's wife still hovering under the porch light. They looked as good as Daphne's trifle had tasted. For that is what I thought after all the red wine I'd had. But I still could not help feeling a little disappointed that Jack had invited them to join in our fun.

"You look like an angel my darling," called Jack in a booming tenor.

"You are not playing with your dynamite again, are you Jack?"

"Just in time my dear. Come here and hold my glass for a moment, would you? My gardening boots are over there near the door."

"I'll tell you where I got this from," Jack murmured to us while Daphne picked her way through the clumpy mounds of dirt, her husband's gardening boots covering her stockinged feet. She was a good-looking woman, a lovely woman I thought as she made her way towards us. The type of woman who looked elegant even in her husband's gardening boots. A simple gold strand glistened at her throat. Sometimes I wondered why Daphne could not be enough for Jack. Most men would be more than satisfied with a wife like her, despite her cheating a little in the kitchen.

"Well, my dear," said Jack as Daphne took his glass. "What kind of a dinner party would this be if we didn't light a candle?"

Kate

Kate sat in her backyard painting her nails. You remember, long blonde hair and curves. The typical girl-next-door. If a boy lived next door, he would certainly peek over the fence at Kate sitting on her towel in her cut-off denim shorts, painting her nails hot magenta. And there was a boy next door. A handsome young man with a good head of blonde curls. Kate visited him often and even slept with him on occasion. It was love at first sight, blue eyes looking into blue-pools of water flowing between and all that crap.

Ah now, I can see the look on your face. Tell me more, you say! I will. No point in holding out on you. His name was Scott Carroll but Kate called him Scottie and curled up with him on the lounge to watch television. His parents approved, of course. Good babysitters were difficult to come by, and it gave them the freedom to go out to the movies now and then. Sometimes to a dance.

Tricked you! Scottie was only four years old. Oh, come on. I didn't lie. All that stuff about cuddling on the lounge, blue eyes staring into blue. It's all true. If you are disappointed that says more about you than me.

Her radio was tuned to the local station. It was Saturday afternoon and 'Pussyfoot' came on. Kate rolled the volume to ten and sang along to the slow static voice. *It's not the way that you do it but how you do it to me.* The sun was warm enough for the baby oil on her legs to give off a sweet, sweaty smell. Kate put one leg onto her knee and laid back to apply a second coat of nail polish admiring the tan glistening on her legs. *One and one makes two. But you and me we make three.*

Kate heard her parents' car hum up the drive. She didn't look around when her mother slapped her door shut, followed by the more deliberate close then shove technique favoured by her father.

"Move over sweetheart." Her mum squeezed onto the beach towel next to Kate. Her belly was bigger now, and she exhaled softly as she plumped down beside Kate.

"Nice colour, where did you get it?" Polite small talk.

"Chemist." Noncommittal.

Her mother unbuckled her sandals and stretched her long brown legs out on the towel. In comparison Kate thought her own legs looked like the inside tube of Glad-Wrap, a straight line from her knees to her feet. Her own skin was the colour of cardboard while her mother had the golden tan of someone who had just returned from holidays on the Gold Coast.

"Nice, goes on well," said her mother, pinching the brush from her daughter to apply liberal strokes to her own pedicured nails.

"Mmm. Better than that crappy pink stuff you bought last time," replied Kate. "It's called Hot Magenta."

"Hot Magenta, hey," and then, "Honey?" Her mother's voice rose with the half question.

"Mmm."

"I was thinking that tonight we could spend some time together."

"I'm babysitting Scottie."

"Oh, that's good. It will give you good practice."

"Yeah, yeah, I know."

"Know what?"

"As soon as the baby is born I will be babysitting."

"Honey, I need to talk to you about something."

A quick flick and hair covered Kate's face. Her response needed to be hidden. Had they realised that she'd refilled the vodka bottle with flat lemon ade and kerosene? *It's the way you do it to me*, Pussyfoot murmured from the radio. Kate wondered what else her parents could know. Her ears listened for the invisible presence of her father behind her. He was there all right, fidgeting from foot to foot in the way that irritated her mother so much, his shoes digging at a clump of grass. This must be serious. Kate felt relieved when the song changed to 'Popcorn'. 'Pussyfoot' was way too sexy to listen to with your parents right next to you. Kate didn't mind old songs like 'Popcorn' but she didn't really see the point of songs without lyrics. Or of words without songs. She turned the volume low so she wouldn't have to listen to the announcer's smart alec voice as he talked over the start of the song.

"Look at me, Katherine."

Kate turned and peered at her mother through her fringe, blurring her image into a more refined version of herself. Her mother's nose was straighter, her skin smoother, her eyes larger and framed by perfectly plucked arcs. Her Christian Dior gave off a scent more sophisticated than Kate's Mum deodorant and baby oil. Her mother reached forward and tucked Kate's hair behind her ears. Kate turned the volume of the radio back up.

"You think you know what I am going to say, don't you?"

"No." Admit to nothing.

"Kate, I have just been to the doctor. Your father and I are expecting twins."

"Twins?"

For a moment Kate forgot what the word meant. Then in a single leap she was at her feet singing along to 'Popcorn'. It did have lyrics after all. It was obvious to her now. "I am gonna have two brothers. I am gonna have two sisters. Twins, twins, twins, twins, twins, twins, twins, twins, twins, twins, twins, twins, twins, twins-s. Yeah."

Her father laughed, and he looked like a cheeky schoolboy as he hugged her, something he never did, locking his elbows so that their bodies didn't touch. Kate pulled her mother to her feet and realised for the first time that they were almost eye-to-eye now. The three of them danced together in a circle, awkwardly, their knees clacking into each other. Kate reached out and felt the small hard lump of her mother's belly.

"I've been dying to tell you there are two babies. Today Doctor Morris said I could. Finally."

"Why did you need *him* to tell you that? Why didn't you just tell me?"

"Oh, you know Kate," and this time it was her mother's turn to hide her eyes behind her fringe. "Sometimes things happen."

"What things?" Disbelieving.

"It could be a boy *and* a girl." Sidestep. "Sometimes twins are born early. They could be born before the end of summer." Double sidestep.

"Really?"

Kate looked at her mother then and realised the flowing chiffon she had been wearing lately was more function than fashion, a first for her mother. She couldn't imagine her glamorous mother having twins. She tried to see her with strings of hair hanging around her face like the woman down the road who spent all day walking, around and around the block. The baby was often naked in the pram with just a towel around her. Two years old and it didn't even talk yet. Then on the weekend when her husband was home, they all played happy families, and no one said anything to him. No one spoke about it.

Kate imagined her mother looking grotesque, and now she noticed her puffy neck and half an inch of dark hair growing from her scalp. Her mother followed Kate's eyes and she touched her head nervously and laughed.

"Oops, just haven't gotten around to it." Giggles.

Later Kate looked in the mirror and searched for dark roots in her own hair. For some reason she was more surprised that her mother wasn't really blonde than that she was having twins.

Jack

Now, where were we? The famous dinner party, that's right. Or should I say the infamous dinner party? You can imagine us all out there in our shirts and ties. Oh yes, we all knew how to dress for dinner back then. No one would have dreamed of arriving at a dinner party without wearing slacks and a shirt, with a tie at the very least. Oh yes, I know it was the 70s and louts were getting about with long hair and denim jeans, even at restaurants, but certainly not within the social set that we enjoyed. I guess by today's standards we may have looked quite strange out there under the jacaranda, coveting Jack's dynamite in our shirts and ties all the while holding our wine in the correct red wine glasses. But that is the way it was back then, and I have to say there was something dignified about it.

Of course, Jack had to give a little speech before he threw the dynamite into the bowl of the swimming pool. He stood there with the dynamite lit and we were all mesmerised as the fuse fizzled down closer and closer to the detonator in his hand.

"Gentlemen," he said, gesturing in our direction with the dynamite as if he was giving a toast with a glass of wine. "Ladies, let us mark this special occasion with the inaugural deepening of the deep end of this swimming pool, hereby named the Grafton Leisure Centre. Let me introduce you all to the joys of landscape gardening."

I swear that just one miniscule moment before the dynamite blew up in Jack's hand, he threw it into the darkness, overarm as if he was bowling for the ashes. The dynamite exploded, dirt filled the air and rained down on our shoulders. Jacaranda flowers rained down on us as well. The little accountant was ecstatic. The blast was so loud it rang in our ears. We laughed and slapped each other on the back, congratulating ourselves as if we were all responsible for the explosion. When the dust cleared there were jacaranda flowers on the women's heads, making them look even more beautiful through my red wine tinted glasses.

Kate

Kate's thongs flipped against the cobblestones of her parents' driveway as she walked next door to babysit Scott. Grafted rose bushes lined the driveway. Kate stopped just before the footpath and held a rose up to her nose. Her mother always picked the roses when they were tight little buds and then loosened out some petals as she arranged them in her grandmother's crystal vase. Kate couldn't see the beauty in the buds, holding selfishly onto their perfume. She preferred the roses open, their yellow stamen unashamed at just that moment before a gust of wind came and blew the petals into the air. Kate grabbed a handful of rose petals in her fist and threw them up, watching them, white against the still blue sky, until they fell at her feet like confetti.

Before the Carrolls had moved in next door a string of families had come and gone, never staying long enough to make the place their own. From the outside the house looked unloved. It wasn't rundown, it just looked as if people lived in it reluctantly. The front yard was a grass rectangle mowed once a fortnight, with bull grass edges that were left to grow over the concrete path like a messy fringe.

The slap of Kate's thongs in the balmy evening must have pre-announced her arrival as Mrs Carroll was talking to her before she opened the door.

"Come on in, Kate! Can you make a cake with Scott? He knows how to do it. The recipe's on the bench. There're some lollies on the bench for you too, but don't tell Scott. He's already cleaned his teeth."

"It's almost six, love," said Mr Carroll, winking at Kate. "You'd better go and put your face on."

Mr Carroll remained in the doorway. Goosebumps hardened on Kate's thighs and her cheeks grew pink with, I'm not sure what, not embarrassment. Self-consciousness? Sure, perhaps a little, but something else too.

Kate flicked her long hair over her reddening face as she twisted past Mr Carroll and joined Scott on the couch where he was watching television. Scott ignored her greeting. Kate sat next to him and pretended she was intent on watching the television too and hadn't noticed Mr Carroll standing by the fireplace watching her.

"I'm ready."

Mrs Carroll's face looked like an alien mask floating towards them from the hallway. Her eyelids were bright green blended to a sallow yellow that went all the way to her hairline. Purple blush bruised her cheekbones, and her lips were brown. Crimped hair stuck out in tufts from behind each ear.

Kate almost laughed, but then Mr Carroll smiled and said, "You look wonderful, love."

They headed to the door in a haze of aftershave and Avon perfume. Mrs Carroll turned back and said, "Oh, I forgot to ask. How is your mother's extra special pregnancy?"

There was too much rouge on Mrs Carroll's cheeks to see her embarrassment when Kate was too surprised to answer.

"Oh," she said. "You still don't know?"

"Oh, love." Warning.

The ABC news anthem blared from the television, reminding the Carrolls of the time.

"Oh, never mind. You'll find out about her little surprises soon enough," said Mrs Carroll, and Kate was left, abandoned with Scott. They stared at each other until Kate's anger subsided. Everyone knew.

"News is boring."

"C'mon, let's go and make a cake for your mummy."

Kate turned the television down and led Scott to the kitchen. She sat him on the bench next to her. The kitchen looked like it had been copied straight from the pages of Women's Weekly. Chocolate, tangerine and cream were all mixed up together on chairs and tables and plastic benches. It was 1977. You should have seen the wallpaper in the Carroll's bedroom. But that is another story, and we are in the kitchen right now. Baking a cake. Lovely.

"Oh," Kate said, looking at the open page of the recipe book. "Pineapple upside-down cake? Do you *like* that?"

"Ye-ah." Singing.

"You don't want to make chocolate cake?"

"Nope."

"Okay then. Flour first. Does your mummy have a flour sifter?"

"Put it in the cup, then put it in the bowl."

"Sure matey," said Kate pulling a bowl out of the cupboard.

"Not that bowl. The yellow one wiv flowers on it." Sing-song.

"How about this one? It has cherries on it." Pleading. Smiling.

"No. You have to use the yellow bowl." High pitched.

Scott's blue eyes followed Kate as she opened and closed every cupboard door in the kitchen.

"I can't find it anywhere." Singing back at him.

"Up there." Scott pointed his superior finger to a cupboard above their heads. Kate flicked it open with her fingernails, her magenta polish clashed with the tan cupboards.

"Der tis." Triumphant.

"Mate, that's a cereal bowl. It's not big enough."

"Yeah tis." Voice rising.

Kate looked at the excitement in Scott's eyes and knew that no amount of wheedling or bribery would change his mind.

"You're lucky you're so cute." Kate squinted until she could see a double image of Scott sitting on the bench, twins.

Kate let Scott make the cake and her youth allowed her to laugh at flour sifted into the open cutlery drawer.

"It's a volcano." Shrieking as Kate poured the milk into the flour.

Batter spilt over the side of the too-small bowl onto the bench and floor.

"It's erupting!"

She picked eggshells out of the batter one by one and giggled as Scott sucked the cake mix off her fingers. It was a patience that she would never have with her own siblings.

"Okay, cake's finished now. Let's watch telly."

"But you forgot to put it in the oven."

Kate swung Scottie through the air.

"Wheee," she said, turning the television back up and throwing Scott onto the couch in one fluid motion.

"Eww, they're kissing."

Scott sat on the couch giggling through his fingers at Felicity and Gary kissing on *The Box*. Kate raced back into the kitchen, slapped tinned pineapple onto the cherry oven dish and poured the lumpy batter on top. Using her fingers, she scraped the excess mixture off the bench and flicked it into the dish, then pausing for less than a moment she bent down and spooned some mixture off the floor and added it to the rest of the mixture. This cake was never going to turn out like the picture. Kate realised she hadn't turned the oven on but shoved the dish in anyway.

The kissing was over by the time Kate sat down with Scott. She pulled a rug over them both and stroked his neck, until he felt heavy on her. She was about to get up and clean the kitchen when she noticed a magazine on the floor next to the couch. *Cleo*. She couldn't reach for it without moving Scott, so she carefully lay on her side, the magazine on the floor next to her. The *Cleo* was old and dog-eared as if it had been read many times. She'd heard her father telling her mother that the doctors working in his building refused to have *Cleo* magazines in their waiting rooms. *It's not suitable for our calibre of clients*. On the cover, it read *Sealed Section: Jack Thompson*. Kate opened the magazine. Mrs Carroll had already unsealed it. Mrs Carroll wanted to see a naked man! Kate opened the page and was disappointed that his hand was covering what she wanted to see. She folded the page back so she could watch him on the floor, staring back at her. Kate used a tendril of her long hair to cover Jack's hand, imagining him truly naked underneath, then she laid her head back and dreamed.

*

The house smelled of burning pineapple when an argument brought the Carroll's home early, and angry. Kate and Scott were still cuddled up on the couch, Kate's hair still hung over the edge, covering Jack's nakedness.

Kate woke to smoke, screaming, and a man's hand on her shoulder. Fingers splayed as if they wanted to touch as much of her body at once without the crime of them moving. She sat up, using the still sleeping boy to shield her chest. Mr Carroll stood before her, too close, then Mrs Carroll also. Her make-up had mostly slipped from her face, her real face, peeked out from behind. Frightening.

She was holding the blackened cherry dish. A trail of steam had followed her into the room. Her eyes were on her husband's retreating fingers as Mr Carroll backed into the hallway where the tide of beers in his belly made him sway.

"Oh, lookie here," she sneered. "It's Rapunzel. Tell me Rapunzel, why can't you make a cake? How will you keep a husband happy if you can't even make a cake? It's simple. Anyone can make a cake."

Kate pulled her coiled hair around to one shoulder and stood up, still holding Scott to her chest, his head lolling. Whimpering. Mrs Carroll's eyes fell onto the almost naked figure of Jack Thompson. Mr Carroll rolled his eyes at his wife but winked at Kate. He moved between them. Kate could still feel his handprint on her shoulder and hoped he wouldn't offer to walk her home again.

"Here, I'll take Scott." Mr Carroll's fingers scraped the boy from her chest.

"I've gotta go," Kate said as she hugged herself and pushed her shoulders forward as she squeezed past Mr Carroll who was swaying towards her in the hallway. Once outside she padded back over to her house. She thought she heard noises coming from the Carroll's. A thud. A groan. She paused in the driveway. The neglected petals that she'd thrown earlier were soft under her bare feet. She'd left her thongs beside the Carroll's welcome mat.

Fingers clamped over Kate's mouth and she was thrown off the driveway onto the grass. Rose thorns caught her arm and held her. It was not a graceful throw. It ended with Kate facedown, grass in her mouth and a weight on her back she was too terrified to recognise as lighter than her own.

Kate inhaled but before she could exhale a scream the weight shifted, and she was roughly turned over. Knees pressing down on her ribcage trapped the scream in her lungs. Kate closed her eyes. She didn't want to see, didn't want to know.

Fingers were shoved into her mouth, prying open her jaw and something hard was pushed in. A poisonous liquid was poured straight into her throat, choking her.

Giggles.

"Fuck. It's you, you mole!"

Towering above her was Frances. Her make-up had transformed her plain face into the image of Princess Caroline. Her small breasts were pressed high enough to peek out of her tank top. She was waving a pink drink-bottle.

"Give me that." Kate drank, loving how the alcohol burned its way down her throat.

"Come on. Everyone's gone to Scouts."

"Who?"

"Everyone. Your mum is asleep anyway. I already checked."

"Mum is having twins."

"Twins? How? No wonder she is so fat."

"She isn't that fat."

They continued on in silence. As they walked Frances's white sandals slid along the footpath while Kate's bare feet were soundless beside her. They walked along like that for a while, passing the drink-bottle between them. Scotch was a luxury. Usually all they could get was beer which was hot and thick by the time it had spent all day in one of their schoolbags. Kate loved the night air against her skin, tickling at her throat like fingers. Every now and then she looked over at Frances. The transformation was amazing. She wore a short denim skirt which unveiled curvy thighs. It made Kate uneasy.

"I flogged the Scotch from Mum and Dad," said Frances. "I filled their bottle back up with cold tea. Mum nearly caught me, I reckon, 'cause I was acting so weird. I haven't used this drink bottle since I was in Grade Two, but I told Mum I really wanted to use it 'cause I like the princess on it and I want to get married in a dress just like it 'cause 'it's so big. Mum kept watching me that's why I chucked some lime cordial in on top."

"Tastes pretty good actually."

"I can't believe I got away with it."

"How funny, this kiddy drink-bottle with alcohol in it," said Kate.

"Anyway," Frances paused under a streetlight, using a compact mirror to apply more mascara, "What do you think of Michael Ballins?"

"He's a bit up himself. Can I borrow that?" Kate applied the mascara to her own lashes. Christian Dior. Frances must have stolen that from her mother too.

"Yeah, I guess. Nice arms though."

Kate looked at Frances and knew that she had her. Frances had a crush, and Kate knew this, but Frances didn't know that she knew. Kate had to be very careful now and gently pull this information out of Frances so that the thread of trust was not broken, or it would snap and recoil back into Frances's mouth never to be spoken of again. Kate knew she had to get these fragile words out unharmed.

"I reckon he'd know how to give a girl a good time," Kate said.

"I caught him checking out my bum on the bus yesterday." Snap.

"Oh yeah, baby."

Kate slowed to have a look at Frances' bottom, cute and round, pushing at her denim skirt.

*

Shall we follow these kids then as the summer evening stretches for an eternity over the sky in the way it does for the young? At least in their own minds. Before they have grown old enough for their brains to be moulded around thoughts of tomorrows, headaches and angry spouses. The endless consequences of adulthood. On this first night of daylight savings, when the day finally surrendered into night, Kate met the love of her life. It was a classic hero, villain and victim story; each of them had their role to play.

Perhaps the story of Kate really began when she downed one too many swigs of Passion Pop behind the Beecroft Scout Hall and looked across to see Michael Ballins. I'm not telling you whether Frances's secret crush had anything to do with it. You can decide that for yourself. But he was the boy in Kate's immediate vision, even if the villain could easily have been someone else. Kate had drunk so much that almost any of the boys looked good to her. But whoever it was she went with, a villain they would be, because quite frankly that is what teenage boys are: villains, or else villains in waiting. Ask any parent of a female child.

As they rounded the corner of the Scout Hall, Frances and Kate could see their group sitting in a circle out of view of passers-by. The sky still held the promise of an early summer. Even though it was nine o'clock dusk was only just starting to settle in, muting the faces of those in the circle so that Frances looked even more like Princess Caroline and Kate, as she looked over at Michael Ballins, could not see or did not notice the cloying brown birthmark that looked like Weet-Bix around his mouth. For now, she was looking at his eyes. She'd never noticed them before. They were green.

There were seven of them that night. They passed the bottles round and gulped the alcohol down. Something was always coming around the circle. A warm bottle of Passion Pop. A couple of soggy joints and menthol cigarettes. And, of course, the princess drink bottle.

Frances was sitting opposite Kate, her denim skirt pushed high on her thighs, so that a triangle of peach coloured underwear could be seen.

"Hey," said Frances. "Kate's mum is having twins."

"What? I didn't even know she was up the duff," said Michael Ballins.

"Double duffed," said Frances and everyone giggled.

Frances smiled and looked up at Michael Ballins with her eyes. "How do you make twins anyway?"

"Twice as hard for twice as long makes twice as many," snorted Little Michael.

It was a lucky night for the boys. Little Michael's growth spurt over the last term had allowed him to disappear first into the mounting gloom with Kate Noble. It always goes like that in these situations, the best-looking boy pairing off with the best-looking girl. They always went first so the others know what was expected of them.

Our Kate had no initial intention of going off with Michael Ballins. She thought she'd let Frances have him. But whisky in a princess bottle can do that to a girl.

It's not like he wasn't a willing participant. She just touched the poor boy's fingers for a moment too long, holding onto the drink bottle as she passed it across the circle to him and looked into his green eyes.

She got up and moved away from the group. The poor boy, oops, I mean our villain, followed her.

What happened next is a blur of half-remembered moments that Kate would agonise over in the shower the next morning. Don't worry, you will get to know all she knows. The gaps in her memory left her a little puzzled as to exactly why she ended up alone beside the little creek in the brush behind the Scout Hall, with her mascara down her face and Michael Ballins nowhere to be seen.

But don't worry, our hero's here now. He just happened to be returning home from somewhere. Some secret mission no doubt. But that is irrelevant right now. The point is that our hero rounded the corner of the Scout Hall just in time to witness our villain scampering off (not all villains are brave) and to see our victim lie down next to her vomit on the grass, deciding that the bed of violet-coloured weeds that grew under the white gum was the perfect place to sleep. I must point out to you now that I am sorry for calling our Kate a victim (I say our Kate because I am assuming that now you know her a little you are growing to like her, despite her poor judgement at times) but we have a hero and a villain, so victim is the only label left for her. That is, unless you want to call her a princess. That would be okay too.

So, now, where were we? Ah, our hero. Our hero's name is Peter and I guess saying that he became the love of Kate's life may cause you to think of other great love matches. Real people who have died for love like Romeo and Juliet, or those that have lived together for 50 years and still look at each other's wrinkled faces with the smile of their youth in their eyes. Perhaps Kate and Peter's love would last this long?

Like many drunken unions it began sitting on the ground waiting for the sunrise. They sat in the clearing outside the Scout Hall, which had been designed for city boys to learn how to be men. And Peter still had plenty to learn about manhood. The few clouds in the sky were purple, lit orange from beneath by a sun that had not yet appeared over the horizon. It promised to be a beautiful day. Unsatisfied, but not unrequited. Was it chaste? Yes, of course. But not for want of hints from Kate. The difference between them was only a few years, but those years weighed upon Peter, making him too scared to move, while her magenta nail-polished fingers picked at the flowers in front of her. Yet the smallness of the years also made it impossible for him to leave, to stand up and to return her to her parents' house. The cockroaches were hiding for the night, waiting for the sun. The cacophony of the cicadas had quietened.

There certainly wasn't the regulation one foot between Peter and Kate. They were so close that they could feel each other's heat. But that's okay, Peter wasn't a school kid so surely different rules applied? Or perhaps no rules at all? Kate looked down at Peter's tanned forearm. He picked at a leaf on the grass in front of him. He folded it at each side of the spine and then ripped off the flesh like wings off a butterfly.

Don't read too much into this. It is not a metaphor. This is just how Kate imagined it as she watched the muscle in his forearm move as he tore at the leaf—so it probably says more about her than him if you are the analysing type. But really the thought of butterfly wings was only in the back of her mind. She was really concentrating on the blonde hair of his arms and how far she would have to move her own arm for them to touch. A few inches? Why not? Too far to move in one go.

Kate followed his direction and reached for a leaf in front of her, closing the gap by an inch and a half. He moved then, to pick up another leaf, a younger, greener one. His hand moved closer to Kate's legs, crossed like the schoolgirl she still was. Perhaps they may have stayed like that, separated, until Peter resolved to return home or until Kate's friends woke up and began to wonder where she was. (She may still have a few friends left after her unauthorised kissing of Michael Ballins). But then a mosquito interrupted their solitude.

"Mozzies just love me. Little vampires," said Kate, swishing the buzzing from her ears. The thought of vampires made Peter think of vampire movies with virgins. His fingers froze before he could tear the flesh from another leaf.

Instead he said, "They never eat me."

"Why not? Why do they love me so much? Mum says they don't bite people who eat vegemite, but it's so gross."

Peter recoiled from Kate at the mention of her mother. It made her sound so young.

"They need blood to fertilise their eggs. That's why only the females drink our blood. They are attracted by the carbon dioxide that we breathe out." Brisk. Noncommittal.

But Peter had already committed himself to this story of Kate. The moment he rounded the corner at just the right moment, the moment he decided to sit down beside her in the semi-seclusion of the urban bush, instead of doing what was right.

"Why aren't they attracted to your carbon dioxide then?"

"They are. But my smell repels them."

"I wish my smell repelled them."

"The best thing you can do to avoid being eaten by mosquitoes is to sit close to someone whose smell repels them."

"Is this close enough?" The inches between them dissolved. "Anyway, you smell kinda good."

There is no denying that their attraction was physical. Isn't it always with your first love? You know about Kate's beauty; let me introduce you to our knight in shining armour, our hero, our rescuer. For on that night Kate needed rescuing (even if it was just from loneliness) and Peter was the one to do it. He certainly had all the contradictory attributes of a hero: lean yet muscular, Caucasian yet tanned, clean-cut yet rugged and of course coarse and yet gentlemanly enough for Kate's virtue to still be intact as they watched the sunrise together.

"I should take you home… I mean, you should go home."

"Let's just wait."

"For what?"

"For the sun."

The white of the sky was turning blue, as if the colour had been sucked out of the sky during the night and was just now being spat back into it. But our lovers became distracted from the sun by the return of the mosquito that buzzed down onto the forearm of Peter.

Kate slapped at him, their first contact, and wiped a smear of blood down his arm.

"Oh gross," he said, adopting her language, as lovers do, future and otherwise. "That isn't even my blood. It probably has some kind of disease."

"It could be my blood."

"That would be alright then," he whispered, and I swear that at that moment the early morning birds began to call out for a mate, not prepared to go through another day alone. The cicadas began to chirp. Lorikeets screamed in excitement from the white eucalypt that would soon cast the only shade over the day.

They looked at each other then. Not at brown eyes versus blue eyes, or straight teeth or clear skin. Not even at each other's need or longing, but they looked at each other and they both saw the same thing: perfection. And so, they kissed. What is so wrong with that? It may mean marriage in a fairy tale or waking up to adulthood. But this is no fairy tale, and there is still a lot of sleep in store for Kate. Adulthood is a long way off. Perhaps as far away as tomorrow.

Who made the first move? Did you miss that bit? It was Kate of course, she was the one who moved her hand the remaining distance until the hairs on their arms were touching, but their skin was still apart. Now, as Kate made use of the time Scottie was pretending not to watch kissing on television to finish baking her disastrous cake, let us make use of Peter and Kate's kissing time now. You watch while he moves closer. Are you wondering whether he can taste the tang of vomit in her mouth? A hint of lime, perhaps? Oh yes, it was definitely that kind of a kiss. Watch his hands. He's older than her. Does that bother you? Peter is only in his early twenties, an innocent boy from Gilgandra. Kate is seventeen, but she is a city girl, so while we are being all mathematical let's add a few years to her age, for being a city girl. And let's take (for the sake of argument, as my mother would say) the same years off Peter's age for being a country boy.

And I'll let you in on a little secret, although Peter was always good with his hands (shearing sheep, repairing gates) he had not wiped the grease and mud off his hands and onto his moleskins—as his brother did at every opportunity and even where there wasn't an opportunity, he'd create one—and try them out on a girl. It may have been 1977 but the sexual revolution had not hit Gilgandra. Peter's mother was the type of woman who would not dream of offering packaged biscuits to a stranger. She didn't even keep them in the house as back-up, (that is what a quick batch of scones was for). His father finished each day's work knowing there would be dinner on the table and fresh lipstick on his wife's lips (she had read the 1955 "Good Wife's Guide" before she had walked down the aisle) when he routinely kissed them as he came in for dinner. It was not really a routine though. The thought of that kiss often got Peter's father through a day of shooting starving sheep in the midst of the ten-year-drought or delivering a stillborn lamb in 40-degree heat.

But what about our lovers? Are they kissing still? Oh, yes, as if nothing else matters. So, I will continue telling you about Peter. He would not necessarily have expected his own wife to behave like his mother did, but he knew nothing else so when he arrived in Sydney wearing his new polo shirt and saw girls with short hair and even shorter skirts, he felt for a moment like he was in a *Dr Who* episode and had been hurtled thirty years into a future that was expanding his mind like the universe. Well, more like an elastic band, that would eventually snap back into place. Which will happen, let me assure you, but not just yet. At the moment Peter's mind is still stretching.

Did you think I was rambling on a bit then, while more details of their first kiss should have been described to you in intimate detail? No, it wasn't idle chatter. I was just giving the poor kids some privacy.

So, what happened next? Peter put his arm round Kate and said, "You are so…" but he did not finish his sentence, leaving Kate to forever wonder what he was going to say. Yes, forever after, even now, despite everything that has happened and everything she has forgotten. She remembers his first touch, the hair on his arm glistening in the new day. The weight of his arm on her. The cicadas singing a chorus in the background, not for them but for themselves. She remembers the gossiping parrots in the eucalypt. Kate can still smell the start of an unseasonably stinking-hot day that would make her parents wake up angry and sweaty, exhausted before their arguments could even begin.

*

The next morning Kate sat at the breakfast counter watching her mother make rissoles. Canisters were lined up like soldiers in order of hierarchy under the window. Saucepans also hung in order of size, waiting to be selected. The kitchen was brown wood with liberty print curtains that blended with her mother's own liberty print blouse, tighter now. Kate preferred the tangerine and chocolate of the Carroll's kitchen and thought her mother's kitchen looked morose in comparison. It reminded her of *The Little House on the Prairie*. Not that they didn't have all the 'mod cons', a garbage disposal unit and of course a Mixmaster. But Kate wanted more colour. Like the bright red of the Carroll's oval shaped spa bath that rose up like a stage in the corner of their enormous bathroom.

Her mother cracked an egg with one hand, a feat Kate was yet to accomplish and tossed the shell into the garbage disposal in one deft movement. She repeated the process with another egg and put her hand in the bowl to knead the mixture. Kate watched her mother heave and gag into a tea towel.

"I feel really sick," she said.

"You'll be alright." Her father was hovering behind them again.

"I can help," said Kate, sliding off her barstool and around the bench to stand beside her mother.

"No, I can manage."

"It's okay. I don't mind."

"Don't you have homework?"

"Nothing important."

"She's almost a grown woman now," said her father. "She should be giving you more of a hand around here."

"No. I said I'll manage. And, so, I will manage."

"Oh look, she's almost as tall as you now sweetheart. And so beautiful." Daddy's fingers twirled in Kate's drying hair.

"Dad! Don't touch my hair! Mum, go and sit down. Let me help."

As Kate moved closer to the meat mixture her own guts heaved. She'd been feeling queasy all day as she tried to remember the night before. She remembered Peter walking her home. All the way home and kissing her dangerously close to their front fence, while the Carroll's dark, silent house watched them with its unloved window eyes.

"Help? You don't want to help. You just want to overtake me in everything." Accusation number one.

"What?" said Kate.

"I didn't mean…" said her father. Attempted sidestep.

"You didn't have to. I can see it in your eyes. You think I'm fat and ugly."

"Sweetheart."

"Mum, are you crying?"

"You are beautiful to me, and you always will be."

"To you. Puh."

"I think you are more beautiful now than ever before and no man would disagree with me."

"You don't want me anymore." Accusation number two.

"Mum, gross."

"Gross. That's it! I'm just gross."

"The doctor said."

"Blow the doctor!"

A knock at the door caused Kate's mother to spin around and dab at her eyes with the tea towel. She checked her face in the reflection of the window. The liberty print curtains hung nonchalantly in the background.

"Yoohoo!" the door opened, and Mrs Carroll was standing in the kitchen wearing an orange and green paisley kaftan. She had let herself in, and now she spread her arms and her drooping sleeves took up most of the room. "Kate left last night before I had the chance to give her any money. She did a wonderful job with Scott as usual. They baked a marvellous pineapple upside-down cake. I took it to church for morning tea. It delighted the minister, I must say. Is she here? I just wanted to thank her in person."

By this time Mrs Carroll was standing in front of her mother, and with her mother blocking the entrance to the bedrooms, trying to hide her red eyes from the neighbour, Kate was left with nowhere to hide.

"I thought it was burnt?" Eyes on the linoleum.

"Oh no. I just cut a couple of the overcooked edges off. It was perfect. You will make some man very happy one day."

"Not too soon, I hope." Kate's mother joked, recovering her dignity.

They laughed together although none of them found it funny, and Mrs Carroll handed Kate a ten dollar note.

"Oh no. That's too much. I only did three hours. You came home early."

"No, no. That's fine."

"You were actually later than that Honey. I heard you out the front talking to someone. Did Mr Carroll walk you to the door?"

"No."

"He most definitely did not," said Mrs Carroll. "But I know what you mean. I also heard Kate with some fellow in the early hours. I think she is a little too boy crazy for her own good."

"Kate!!"

"No. It wasn't me!"

"You are young," said Mrs Carroll, pushing at the flesh of her cheeks as if she could make it sit up high and firm like Sofia Loren. "It's alright sweetheart, really. You don't want to wait too long and have to grab whatever man is left over when you are twenty-five. That almost happened to me, you know."

Kate looked at her mother. There was nothing really to say. Her mother's lip quivered with the start of a smile. Mrs Carrol caught the eye contact between them.

"My husband is really quite…" with that she stopped and looked at Kate's dad as if that explained everything. Which of course it did. A full head of hair will always beat a receding hairline. Kate's dad lowered his head in recognition of this fact while Kate's mother tried to move Mrs Carroll towards the kitchen door.

"People tell you not to be in too much of a rush," Mrs Carroll continued, looking over the head of Kate's mum. "But don't leave it too late either. You don't want your body to be permanently affected by pregnancy. And imagine the shame of your children at the school gate if you are an…" Mrs Carroll lowered her voice, "an older mother."

Kate turned to see the tears crown in her mother's eyes.

"Oh no," said Mrs Carroll. "I didn't mean you. Of course not. Everyone knows you have had difficulties."

Everyone knows.

Mrs Carroll turned to Kate. "Why don't you go and put that money away before you lose it."

Kate turned to her mother. "Go on then," she said.

Kate raced up the hallway, the slurry of Mrs Carroll's words were indecipherable behind her. In her bedroom she shoved the money into her jewellery box with the rest. Her escape fund.

Her mother and Mrs Carroll sprung apart as she approached.

"What?"

"We are talking about you, not to you," Mrs Carroll said, winking at her mother.

*

Kate's father pushed past her into the lounge room, his head down, as if only memory and luck prevented him from walking straight into a wall. Mrs Carroll winked at Kate. Mrs Carroll poked out her droopy bosom and indicated back towards Kate with a tilt of her head as if she was mimicking her. The Kaftan did not hide the fact that she wasn't wearing a bra. "Maybe she is a little boy crazy. I am not sure what kind of boy you must be meeting in the street in the small hours." And with that Mrs Carroll left in a swirl of orange kaftan as if she had won something.

Before her mother had turned from closing the door, Kate said, "It's not true. I babysat Scott and then I came straight home, but I ran into Michael Ballins. We were just talking. Michael is gross, Mum. I would never!"

To her relief her mother was laughing, "Not your type, huh?"

"I am going to vomit, Mum."

"I knew you were talking to someone. I heard you outside talking to him just before the screen door went. You know I can't sleep properly until you are home safe."

Kate blushed. Her mother must have heard Peter.

"Kate! You are blushing. You *do* have a crush. Be careful of that boy. He has been making excuses to ride his pushbike past our house since he was ten years old."

"No he doesn't! I do not!"

"I think perhaps you protest too much, Honey," her mother drew her to her then and tried to hug her. Her swollen belly sat between them like a rock. "There is plenty of time for this," she gestured at herself.

"How come they knew you were having twins before me then? Why does everyone know everything before me?" Deflection.

"What? Did they tell you they knew?"

"Yes, they thought I had known for ages. Who else knows? Everyone on the street? My teachers? Everyone in the whole world?"

"I'm sorry Kate."

"Why didn't you tell me first?"

"I told you before Kate, sometimes things happen. Especially with twins. Anyway, I didn't tell Mrs Carroll. She guessed."

"How?"

"I stopped drinking coffee with her in the mornings. My tummy could only handle weak tea. I also stopped wearing my belts. They became uncomfortable very early on. Some people notice things like that."

Kate's mother had always worn belts to accentuate her thin waist between her voluptuous curves above and below. They had given way a while ago to the infernal liberty print, so many different patterns and yet they were all the same. There were no liberty prints in *Cleo.* "How did she know it was twins, though?"

"Mrs Carroll said you were looking at naked men in magazines?" Her mother knew how to deflect also.

Kate blushed. "It was on the coffee table."

"The coffee table? I really don't approve of those magazines Kate, you know that. I think it was inappropriate for Brenda to have a magazine like that in her house, and on display so blatantly."

"I just took a peek."

"Don't tell your father. He thinks those magazines make women hate men. And I have a good mind to agree with him."

"Mum, I want to become a journalist."

"Oh Kate, that's not a very becoming profession."

Her mother had resumed rolling the mince into balls and dropping them into a bowl of breadcrumbs before flattening them into rows on a baking tray. Kate watched her, wondering how she could make each patty the exact same size, perfectly round.

"Well, that's what I want to do so there."

"Kate!"

Kate sat sulking while her mother finished the rissoles. She rolled the final portion of meat into another patty the same size as all the others and put it into place on the tray, neatly filling it. For some reason this made

Kate angry, and she sat silently enjoying that her anger had banished the nausea from her guts.

Kate pulled a *Women's Weekly* towards her on the bench and flipped through it. It was full of casseroles and clothes from Sussan's. Her mother turned to face the sink and Kate watched as she slid her wedding rings up and down her finger and washed the raw mince off the claws of her sapphire. Her mother's fingers had swollen during her pregnancy and made the rings impossible to remove. "Not that I'd want to," she would laugh and pat her father's balding head. Reluctantly Kate acknowledged her mother as the winner by sliding off her bar stool and retreating to her room.

Kate spent the rest of the day hibernating. She lay on her bed trying to ignore the nauseating smell of frying rissoles that was coming in under her closed door. Again, she went through the itinerary of what she remembered. Babysitting Scott and going with Frances to the reserve. But by the time they had reached the Scout Hall her memory was hazy. She remembered sitting in a circle and Michael Ballins' green eyes. She remembered kissing him, his tongue thrusting in and out of her mouth until she wanted to be sick. Until she was sick. She remembered standing next to a tree, her hand supporting her body weight on its trunk. She remembered the dark, and then more kissing. Gentler this time. She remembered the light and knowing she would look terrible and hiding behind her hair.

Kate didn't remember how it started, but she knew who he was. She remembered his name was Peter. She couldn't remember walking home, but she remembered hiding him in front of the next-door neighbour's. They kissed again, and Peter groaned in an agony that Kate didn't understand but was desperate to hear again.

She rolled on her bed and laughed at the ceiling, feeling as if she could reach up and push it away so there would be nothing between her and the sky. The stars would reach down to dance with her. She didn't care that she couldn't remember how he got there, or how she knew his name was Peter. She just wanted to hear that groan again.

Later Kate sat on her bedroom floor with her maths book in front of her.

She flipped the book to the back and turned it upside-down. On the top of the page she wrote *Aphrodite*. Then she crossed out the *-dite*. *Cleo* was short for Cleopatra so Kate's magazine would be *Afra*, short for Aphrodite. Kate cut around a school photo of herself and stuck it underneath. With her ballpoint pen she drew herself a dress underneath in Yves Saint Laurent style. She shaded the folds of the dress so the light came from behind her, highlighting her hair. The dress was short. Scandalously short, as her mother would say. Kate enjoyed tuning out from the world around her as she crosshatched the stockings, making her legs ridiculously long, then her high-heeled boots ridiculously high.

On each side of the page Kate wrote the headlines for her feature articles: "How to Kiss your Man and Make him Groan"; "Makeup Tips from Princess Caroline"; "How to be a Sexy Housekeeper without Casseroles". "Mate of the month: Peter".

Kate read out each headline as she shaded the letters with a texta. She thrust her tongue to the front of her mouth and accentuated the 's's' to mimic Ita Buttrose's signature lisp. When she had finished, she smiled at her handiwork, turned the page and wrote her first editorial. Her magazine would be a liberty-print free zone. As editor, she would guarantee it. No clothes from Sussan's and no casserole recipes. In fact, no recipes at all.

Kate could spend the whole day like this—drawing, cutting and pasting, writing. It was so much better than maths homework. Mr Spatch loved telling them that Einstein made up the whole of what they were learning for their HSC while he was away for a weekend in Venice. Kate wished Einstein had stayed at home.

At that moment she had no idea that her future wouldn't be full of these dreams. Perhaps her picture on the cover of *Afra* was as close to journalism as she was really interested in. Or maybe not. Ita Buttrose was her hero after all. Kate stretched out on her bed then imagining Peter lying next to her. She imagined taking photos of him with the sheet only barely covering his hips. Then with nothing covering him at all. Soon she drifted off to sleep and when she woke her hangover was gone, like it does for the young, lucky things. The smell of rissoles cooling in the kitchen whetted her appetite and she jumped out of bed and went to sit at the kitchen table to wait for dinner. Food wasn't the only appetite she had whetted. Now that she was no longer feeling nauseous, she closed her eyes and replayed how Peter had groaned when she'd kissed him out the front of her house.

Jack

Mixing business with pleasure? Yes, one cannot deny that. But we all did back then. I hate this modern idea of compartmentalising our lives into working from nine-to-five, "family time" until supper and doing it all again the next day. Then perhaps if you are lucky, you may attend a social event here and there, with your wife, of course. That's no way to live. All that work-life balance hoo-hah? Fooey.

Any person who lives their lives with passion must by default mix business with pleasure. As doctors, we were always at work. Therefore, pleasure had to be mixed in, be it a liquid lunch here and there or a game of golf in between patients. Talking shop was part of business, and what better time to talk shop than over a drink at the office?

That is why, I am sure, Jack initiated the Wednesday Champagne Club. He had started up his supremely successful private practice on Macquarie Street by this stage. He told me he made $250 000 that first year, which was an absolute fortune. Back then you could have bought ten houses in the middle of Sydney for that amount of money.

We talk about the human condition. It sounds like a sickness. Perhaps we are all mad or diseased in some way. For me it's my liver. It was impossible to partake of all those Wednesdays without gaining an appreciation of fine liquor. My poison is scotch. Neat. I used to drink it on the rocks like any sophisticate, but it was too difficult to sneak past the wife. Ice cubes are such noisy creatures and retirement left us with nothing better to do than pick at each other's foibles. For her it was the scotch; for me it was her. I still had the mind of a psychiatrist. My patient list was reduced to one and that was her. Now there is just me and I cannot resist analysing myself, my every move. I can see now why Betty left me. But alas, I digress.

We were discussing Wednesdays, were we not? The day of champagne! (After lunch, of course). The rules of inclusion in the Champagne Club were straightforward enough. Each patron must bring along their best bottle of wine to be shared. This was a real leveller. Once a secretary even brought in a bottle of Moët, obtained from some conquest or other, no doubt. That day she was an equal among men. Not that women needed to bring champagne to join in. Not with Jack around. He was very generous that way. A true bon vivant.

Ah champagne! Such a celebratory drink. I suppose that is why it's so long since I have drunk it. The older one gets the less one has to celebrate. The obligatory glass and a cigar to wet the grandchildren's heads, after the first no longer a celebration but an insistence of one's own mortality.

There is a time in one's life, however, when one has much to celebrate. Your own children's baptisms, weddings, birthdays, Friday nights, Saturday nights, work functions, new houses (and mortgages). My personal favourite though was Wednesdays. All celebration with no obligation! We always began in the early afternoon. At lunchtime papers were shoved aside on desks and replaced with exotic cheeses. I can still smell the Stilton and Lancashire casting out its perfume as the room heated up. Wednesday was the day of champagne and flirting. The secretaries hitched up their skirts, sat on their desks, and smiled. There was this one little girl who used to wear fluffy knitted jumpers over short dresses, her hair was as red as the sunset. Oh dear, I digress again. I don't know what possessed me. Perhaps it is the memory of the champagne, or the scotch that sits even now beside me as I write, alone in my study.

You would think that under this premise the champagne would start off respectable and decline as the weeks went by. But that's not how it works in Jack's world. The grade of champagne started beautifully, a wonderful way to celebrate the beginning of the easy end of the working week. From there the quality simply skyrocketed. Sparkling wines from Adelaide gave way to Moët as everyone tried to outdo one other. To bring an outstanding bottle of wine served to draw the focus away from the hierarchy created by our professions, the cut of our suits, and even the relative beauty of our personal secretaries. It was like the wedding feast when Jesus turned the water into wine much superior to the wine first brought out. Jack was like Jesus. He created Wednesday's Champagne Club and the wine just got better and better. Oh dear, I think I am repeating myself. It's the drink, you know. It does terrible things to one's head; terrible and wonderful at the same time.

The dinner party where Jack threw the explosives into the swimming pool hadn't been the first time I met that bald little accountant. He had arrived one Wednesday with a bottle of 1959 Dom Perignon and even Jack stepped aside. Perhaps so he could step closer to a cute little piece in a twin-set, but that is another story. The accountant bore his 1959 champagne like a trophy, which it was. Everyone in the know had their eyes locked on that golden crest on the label and the unknowing eyes soon followed as unknowing eyes do. Ah, that wonderful Dom Perignon crest, so much more significant than most family crests. The little bloke walked straight to the centre of the office and stood on a chair and then stepped up onto a desk. The lovely little redhead with the sunset hair had to slide sideways, a beautiful thing to watch in itself. For the accountant, standing on the desk wasn't a bad idea due to his small stature. When he started shaking that bottle, that exquisite bottle of bubbles, the room turned into a crazy house. Honestly, it was a crime to lose those bubbles in a spray of froth but Jack stood in front of this crazy little man with his glass held up like he was ready to take communion. I threw three quarters of a glass of quite a nice riesling into a pot plant. It was a sacrifice, but it would have been greater sacrilege to mix the two.

There was a pop and that 1959 vintage went to the few of us who were there first. A set of boy-girl twins were the cause of this man's celebration, an event that bonded him to Jack, whose twins, Susanna and Donna, were lovely young ladies by then. Everyone thought their friendship was rooted in the fact they both had twins, or the years of childlessness which had preceded them. But it wasn't just that. There were other matters that bonded them.

If I had the chance to go back to that day I would drop to my knees and suck that spilt froth from the carpet just for the chance of savouring the essence of that champagne once more. Even if it has been mixed with the scum and grit from a hundred madmen's feet.

I sit here with the infernal footy on in the background. Australian winters are all about footy. It is unavoidable, but I keep the television on to keep me company and it does its job well enough. It annoys me as much as real people do, so I do not feel quite so lonely. I sit here and flagellate myself with cheap scotch. The rim of the glass is chipped so I must be careful where I choose to sip, but to tell the truth, as the night wears on I bother less whether the broken glass scratches my lip. I will never choose another glass, though, or another scotch for that matter. It is not that I cannot afford Glenfiddich, or some other fine whisky, but when I come to understand why Jack chose beer, of all drinks, for his final toast to the world, then cheap scotch it is for me also.

I rather feel as though I am gaining a taste for it, so much so that even a Glenfiddich feels almost precocious (in the most vernacular sense of the word) with its malt and smoky undertones. When I drink quality scotch on those rare occasions an old colleague has a dinner party and I am invited, I yearn for the dirty steel taste of my Johnny Walker Red.

Oh dear, I can only laugh at what I have become: a melancholy bore. Jack would never have allowed it. Not for a second. I guess I have always been prone to melancholy, and most likely I have always been a bore. Both of my wives thought so, and they were right about most things. I think I most likely skipped my teens altogether and headed straight for middle-age. I am not sure what would have happened to me if I had not been rescued by the outrageous and extraordinary Dr Jack Grafton.

Kate

In science the girls sat up the back and revelled in the luxury of watching Mr Mason. A science teacher without socks and sandals is a bonus even today, but back in 1977 it was a sheer miracle. They watched Mr Mason ruffle his own hair when he was thinking, and their knickers got wet as they imagined tousling it themselves. They watched his muscular forearm extend towards them with handouts and the farmer-boy muscles of his bum gyrate under the fabric of his pants as he wrote on the board.

When the chalk broke and he bent to pick up the broken piece, the room went silent as the girls, and one of the boys, feared to inhale or exhale. Quite an achievement for a young teacher with his back, or in this case backside, turned towards his pupils.

This particular Monday the class were dissecting mice. The pissy smell of them leaked out of the box at the back of the classroom as they squeaked and ran over each other. Being in the back row, Kate was closest to them and thought anyone who got a good nose full wouldn't care about cutting them up. She didn't believe Kate Noble and the Sues who said they'd refuse. Sue Golding wanted to be a doctor, for heaven's sake.

It had been the same on the Grade 5 camp when they had watched a lamb get slaughtered. Kate Noble had refused to watch then too. She'd stood at the back with her eyes averted. The lamb had dead fish-eyes anyway well before the thin red slit appeared on its neck and the farmer let it slump to the floor. Some of the girls had shrieked and gagged but it seemed to be all a show to Kate who was sure they felt nothing. Except for Frances who went white—Kate envied her that. When they went back to their cabin and the colour returned to Frances's face, Kate had stood in front of the mirror, breathing slowly and imagining the image of her grandmother's coffin being lowered into the ground in order to make the colour drain from her face. The mirror was pocked with fly spots but behind the spots Kate could see her own face, white, but with red cheeks from all the outdoor activities giving her away.

Every mouse looked the same. Little brown rodents the colour of Frances's hair. Nothing to get attached to. Each pair had to gas their own mouse. Kate and Frances's mouse ran around and around the perimeter of the bell jar, unable to breathe. Soon it lay on its side, its stomach moved in and out as it struggled for air. Kate watched its heartbeat and knew it was a creature. It seemed to her like it knew it was going to die and Kate wondered why it bothered to struggle on when death was imminent. Why didn't it just close its eyes against the ugliness of the science lab, with its brand new but dreary Laminex desks? All dull green and grey like the rest of the school. Who would want to look at that in the throes of death?

Finally, the mouse closed its eyes. Kate watched as its panting slowed. Frances lifted the jar whispering, "No, it's terrible. It's simply a terrible thing to do. Let's save it."

But it was too late. The mouse was dead. Its blue eyelids were closed in its final sleep. I imagine there isn't that much difference between the two when all is said and done. The Greeks called sleep the little death, after all. As she picked up the scalpel, Kate felt no remorse, but she did hope that her mouse's last thoughts had been sweet.

"Girls up the back. What's going on?"

"Nothing, Sir." Two girlish faces. One pink; one white.

Each of them had a board and pins to hold back the mouse's tiny pelt. Kate knew she would be doing all the work while Frances sat all floppy and pale. Kate laid the still-warm mouse on its back and splayed its feet to each side. She took the scalpel and, imagining she was a surgeon, cut the mouse from its little scraggy neck all the way to its tiny penis and engorged balls. Next, she cut the two horizontal lines forming a capital "I."

"Be careful not to tear the skin. Use the tweezers to pull the skin off the mouse and pin it to your backing board with your drawing pins. Don't breathe in when you do this. Your partner should be waiting with paper towels ready to clean up any blood or other bodily fluids that leak out."

Kate looked down at the mouse splayed on the board in front of her and thought it had a look of such complete boredom on its face, as if death and dissection was something that happened to it with regular monotony. She looked at the perfectly displayed organs of the mouse and was surprised that they were presented in exactly the same way as Mr Mason's chalk diagram. She was sure that her own organs would be all over the place. Her heart enlarged with love and her stomach shrunken with nerves and her intestines twisting around her lungs like lantana until she could hardly breathe. Kate wondered whether if she pushed on its heart its little mousy secrets would be revealed.

"You must have been a very organised little dude," she whispered to the mouse as she took up her pencil to draw and label a diagram of him.

She barely noticed the light tap on the door until the collective, "Ooh," as the class announced Miss Leach (aka Bubble Bum) standing in the doorway, her round blue eyes searching the room for Mr Mason. There had been a rumour circulating that Miss Leach and Mr Mason were getting it on.

Some kid in fifth form said he'd seen them at the ten o'clock session of *Star Wars* in the city on Saturday night and Little Michael reckoned he'd seen them coming out of the science lab late one afternoon.

They were both tucking their shirts back into their belts, he had claimed. Probably rooting on that bench right there, and from that moment rumour became fact, in the minds of the students at least.

Mr Mason reddened as he faced his class just in time to catch Michael kneeling on his seat to try to see out of the window.

"That's enough class, sit down. I have to step out for five minutes. I expect you to carry on with this lesson as I have explained to you. I know that mouse dissection is exciting for you, but I expect you to behave in the mature manner expected of the young adults of Beecroft Secondary College."

Kate decided she definitely hated Mr Mason when he said that. Well, you all know what happens as soon as a teacher leaves the classroom, despite any threats or warnings given moments before they do so. A cheer echoed through the lab as the students became one in their freedom. Even the fat girls and the sweaty girls and that scrawny girl with too many teeth. The boy with BO and a bowl cut. Michael Ballins stood on a bench to look out the high window (designed to let light in but stop the students looking out) at the private conversation between Miss Leach and Mr Mason. Michael gave an authoritative commentary back to the class.

"They look like they're having a fight." Excited.

"She gave him something." Suspense.

"She looks like she's going to push him off!"

Kate ignored him. She knew he was full of it. She looked up and watched the boy with the bowl cut and the redhead with the gingivitis gums stretching mouse intestines between them like they were Italian chefs making spaghetti.

Frances was engraving the initials M.B. on her thigh with the same scalpel Kate had just used to cut open the mouse. She could be such a dork. Kate wondered at Frances's ability to cut into her own flesh and yet be unable to look at the dead mice splayed open on the desks around her.

It must be love, she thought. She should cut her own flesh for Peter. As she sketched the dead mouse in her workbook, she imagined cutting Peter's name down the length of her arm, dark red blood curving out of her veins and collecting in a pool at her fingertips. She knew she could cut deep into her inner arm and feel no pain as she carved the letters. She would only feel love. Love that would flow just like her blood until the two mingled together and the blood dripping down into her hand formed a heart. And that's when Kate knew it for sure. She was in love. And after school finished. After the stupid exams. After speech night and Kate Noble's graduation party, she would walk down the street arm in arm with Peter and people could say what they wanted. It wasn't that big a deal. He was only a few years older than her.

Kate looked at the pale flesh of her inner arm and could see the carved letters. She ran her fingertips from the inner elbow to her wrist and felt the raised scar of his name. Just seventeen days to go until the end of all this.

She smiled to herself as she shaded the heart of the mouse and laughed at the antics of her classmates. Little Michael was feeding bits of his mouse to the goldfish. Michael Ballins was fingering Frances in the corner, even while blood dripped from the freshly carved M.B. on her thigh. Some redheaded girl was up the front flicking mouse intestines at Sue while she squealed and tried to hide behind the teacher's desk. And just for that moment Kate loved them all, even the smell of burnt flesh as some kid burnt the tail off his mouse with the Bunsen burner.

The screaming started just as Mr Mason returned to the classroom. First it was Frances and then both the Sue's were next to her screaming until Kate was surrounded by the cries of the whole class.

"Its heart. Its heart." High-pitched wail.

"It's alive. It moved." Hysterical.

The fat, sweaty girls and the girl with too many teeth joined in the chorus.

"There, over there. I can see it."

"It moved."

"It moved again." Chanting.

"What's going on here?" Mr Mason's calm voice of reason.

Mr Mason walked towards her. Little Michael tried to shove some intestines back into his mouse as he flung himself back onto his stool. Frances couldn't stop screaming. Not even for the teacher.

"Heart!!"

As Mr Mason got closer Kate looked at her mouse, its closed eyelids were blue under the fluorescent lighting. And then she saw it. The slow rolling heave of the creature's heart. Frances's head cracked the side of the desk as she fainted, exposing red panties trimmed with black lace.

The class went quiet as Kate reached over and flicked the mouse's heart with her chipped magenta nails. The class crowded behind her, pushing her into her desk. The mouse was still. No flicker of its blue eyelids or twitch of its curled-up toes.

"Thank you, Katherine," said Mr Mason as he dropped to his knees to open the top buttons of Frances's school blouse, exposing more red satin and black lace and then, "Kate, take Michael Ballins and go and inform Mr Guard, will you? Tell him what's happened. Don't mention the mouse. Just her." He gestured at Frances's fluttering eyelids.

Kate couldn't believe Mr Mason had picked Michael Ballins to go with her. They hadn't spoken since the previous weekend when he'd gone off with Frances. Not that she cared. She had Peter now. But she still walked ahead of him, so she wouldn't have to look at his ugly mouth, all soft and wet with spit.

"Full on, huh?"

"I guess."

"Hey man, your mouse was alive. That's full on!"

"I'm not sure that it was."

"Dead set man. I saw its legs going like the clappers like it was trying to run away—until you smashed it in the heart."

Kate didn't say anything. She was thinking about Peter again. She felt the need to touch him so acutely that she almost closed her eyes and reached for Michael, right there in the middle of the quadrangle, as a substitute.

"What happened to you on Sat'day night anyway?"

"Felt sick and went home."

"You sure about that?"

Hair over her face to disrupt eye contact.

"Yep."

They walked on with Kate lengthening her strides and Michael shortening his, trying to slow them down. Forcing her back. He had more to say.

"Fran reckons she saw you rooting some bloke behind the Scout Hall."

"Frances is nuts. She thought my mouse was alive. She didn't see anything."

"Your mouse was alive."

They were at the deputy's office now and stopped before knocking. Kate pulled up her socks and Michael puffed out his tie, so it looked like it had been tied with a Windsor knot and not the banned *round and round, up and through.*

"Frances was stoned. I went home."

"Sure."

"Maybe it was ghosts. She seems to see dead things moving."

"Yeah, rooting ghosts."

Kate knocked on Mr Guard's door.

"Sorry I nicked off with Frances. I'd rather go you any time. I was just pissed. And you did throw up while I was kissing you."

"Frances was wearing her mum's undies just then, in class."

"Come in." End of conversation.

Jack

I remember that Jack went overseas for eighteen months fairly early on in his career. He went to study in one of those prestigious Scandinavian university hospitals where brain research was so far ahead of us here in Australia. I must admit that it looked great on his resume. He was in one of those cold countries where everyone is educated and has a wife that looks like a model. On his tour he met the esteemed psychiatrist Dr Masters. This was where he witnessed firsthand the trials into Slumber Therapy. Doctor Masters was his mentor of sorts, I guess, and they kept in contact after that. Jack was good at that sort of thing. They would call it networking these days, I suppose. He had contacts all over the world from that one trip. Was I jealous? At first, I was to a degree, when Jack came back home giving speeches to the press. Jack loved the press and the press loved him right back.

Jack was a good-looking man back then. He was probably in his mid-thirties and he always wore a well-cut suit, with his dark hair swept up into a coif like Elvis. He was extremely articulate and, with his small goatee style beard, was sometimes compared to Freud himself. He was psychiatry's golden boy. Not to take anything away from him, but I did feel a tinge of jealousy. I had the better academic record, Jack had the gift of the gab and the WHO (nor anyone else for that matter) never awarded such a travelling scholarship.

My wife was the one who put me straight in the respect of my jealousy. "Darling," she said. "You don't like to go more than two hours away for your holidays, you don't even like to go up the street if you can help it. You're a homebody, my love."

Her exact words. This must have been in the beginning of our marriage for her still to have called me darling and love. She was right, though. I had no real ambition to travel around the world, much less be in the spotlight. Standing up and speaking in front of an audience was something I cowered away from, and still do. I thank God for that talking to she gave me now, I can tell you.

"Besides, you have something he doesn't," she said nodding at our children playing in the sandpit. It was true. While most of our contemporaries were building families and houses it appeared that Jack's wife remained as slim as the day they had married. We all speculated on Jack's failure to reproduce. Back then being childless was a failure, never a choice. I think it made our cohort feel less jealous, even superior in that respect, due to the fact that we had children and Jack didn't.

That's just it though, isn't it? People carry on with their accusations, but most of the time they are simply envious. Jack was given a grant to open a new psychiatric centre. He ordered state of the art equipment he had discovered on his tour overseas. Some of this equipment is still in use even today. That just shows you how ahead of his time Jack really was. The equipment was based around the theory that physical treatments can cure mental ailments. This was a long time before Ferriby and Slumber Therapy. People always want to know about Ferriby, but they forget about Jack's other accomplishments.

One time I was at a luncheon for some hospital benefit or other. I can't remember what for, all those events seem to have rolled into each other in my memory. I was sitting at a table with a couple of dreary looking fellows and I was sure the conversation was going to go nowhere. One of them was a teetotaller and the other was a drunken bore. What a combination, and with poor old me stuck in the middle! The alcoholic went to the bar for beer before our orders were even taken. His fingernails were bitten to the quick, so it was obvious that his alcoholism was simply a symptom of his oral fixation. His mother must have weaned him too early and no amount of alcohol could ever make up for her selfishness.

The teetotaller looking disapprovingly at me and waited for me to raise my eyebrow in agreement, which I regret to say I did. I had no problem with this fellow ordering a drink, for heaven's sake, it was simply his choice of beverage which was a bit much for me to handle, as well as his obvious eagerness for it. He took such a great swig from his glass that he had to wipe the froth from his moustache.

We were overlooking Sydney Harbour and I must say that is a view that no one could possibly tire of. The Opera House was being built, its outline like the crest of a growing wave. Ferries were chugging underneath the Harbour Bridge, taking tourists across to Luna Park and the zoo. Personally, I caught a ferry some days when I worked in the city and every time I did, I thought of how lucky I was to be able to do that. A million-dollar ride for just a few bucks. On that day, however, I must admit I was less than happy with my luncheon companions and imagined the drunkard was going to get louder with every course and soon enough I would be shying away from the attention our table would attract.

Midway through the entrée, though, I thought that I had judged the situation too soon. He simply repeated the phrase, "Can't complain," whenever he was asked anything and that was that. The teetotaller, on the other hand, was a smug man, not a character trait I admire. He smiled knowingly when I ordered a glass of Moselle, even though I had waited until the main course was served and didn't order the house wine.

When my wine arrived, I took a sip. I didn't lunge at it like the other fellow had at his beer, although I must say I was relying on that glass to alleviate some of the awkwardness at our table. I restrained myself, and despite my usual reserve I tried to make conversation with the others.

"What do you think of that monstrosity being built over there?" I asked, indicating our view of the construction, the Opera House looking like a cluster of upended boats. I detest making small talk.

"It's a wonderful boon for our country. It is a fantastic for Australia to be able to host many of the world's greatest performers," said the teetotaller.

"Can't complain," said the drinker. He had shifted to rum by this stage, although we were barely halfway through our main course. The waitress came and leant straight across the table to serve the rum, although we were in an upmarket establishment. The fumes coming from that glass were enough to make me want to follow suit instead of drinking my moselle like a woman.

"I believe it to be a hideous waste of public money and a hideous design, if you can even call it that," I said.

It wasn't a sound argument, I know that. All emotion and no logic, but I gestured to the dazzling harbour and thought that must surely tell the rest of the story for me. "My friend," said the teetotaller. "This building will have acoustics that will make the violin move from the silence to something that moves your soul with nothing in between. Imagine the ballet. The Opera House will put Australia on the map as more than a prison overflow for criminals and runaways. We will become a sophisticated part of the international community."

"Can't complain," said the whisky drinker and being the weakling I am I agreed with them, at least verbally, although I was still looking at the view in silent rebellion.

"You are a colleague of Jack Grafton's, are you not?" he asked me. I'm sure he had known this as soon as I sat down, perhaps even before. He seemed like the type of coward to lay in wait and I suspected that he had delayed his questioning of me until the waiter had filled my glass of wine several times.

"Friend first, perhaps, and colleague second," I said to alleviate his embarrassment when he, as many invariably did, tried to pump me for incriminating information about Jack. It was beginning to happen to me often when people realised who l was and my connection with Jack. Clarifying our relationship caused men to swallow their words and listen to me, to what *I* wanted to say about Jack. Not necessarily what they wanted to hear. They wanted to hear nasty little titbits that would fuel their self-righteousness and their jealousy. Well, they weren't going to get that from me.

As I said before I had already come to terms with my own professional jealousy regarding Jack and was happy with my place in the world, beside him but invisible, except as Jack's friend and colleague. The teetotaller didn't hear or didn't want to hear, and I had to remind myself that he was sober and that I should be aware of how much wine I had drunk.

"How is the new section going?" he asked.

"Can't complain," said the drunkard, thinking the question was for him. The teetotaller raised his eyebrow at me once more.

"Oh well, as you have probably heard it is a state-of-the-art new facility,"

I said. "It may have cost a million pounds, but this is an amount that needs to be spent if we are to be competitive in the world market. The budget of your Opera House was seven million dollars, and we all know how much that continues to expand. That is a lot of money to pay for violins and ballerinas. You cannot compare the arts to science, to medicine that saves lives. The equipment that Doctor Grafton has sourced is world class as far as the community is concerned." I let my Moselle tongue loose for a moment. "It will be the best centre for psychiatric research and treatment in Australia, and the southern hemisphere."

"Is it true that Doctor Grafton installed fly repellent tiles in the operating theatre?"

The teetotaller was laughing at me now. I could see it in his eyes, along with his sober superiority. I was livid.

"Well," I took a sip of my Moselle.

"I have never seen flies in an operating theatre," he continued. "I heard that Doctor Grafton ordered them simply because they were the most expensive."

"Well, a fly in an operating theatre would be a sanitation risk."

He laughed then, right in my face. "Who has ever heard of flies in an operating theatre?"

I wanted to ask him then how many operating theatres he had been in, but I don't like confrontation and besides my drunken friend stood up for me.

"I have," he said. "It was in Bougainville near the end of the war. Used to happen all the time when we were trying to operate in those tents. Stinking hot it was and flies coming in for the blood. Fat with it they were. Before those poor bastards' stitches had healed, maggots would be crawling their way out through the wound. Most of them had no hope anyway. Or if they did, they were better off dead. They say a woman is attracted to a man by his personality. I used to say that to those wounded soldiers who'd lost their legs or half of their face. One of them turned on me after I said that. He was only a young feller too. Probably lied to get his conscription in. He'd lost his left arm and left leg and for some unknown reason God hadn't struck him down with blood poisoning, like he did for most of them.

I told him, you will find a woman who really loves you and she won't care what you look like.

"Well, this young bloke got real angry and waved the stump from his amputated arm so closely in my face that I thought he was going to slap me with it. Then he started talking, real slow, probably the morphine."

"I've never heard of a woman walking down the street and saying oh my goodness. Look at him. What a lovely personality."

I had no answer for him and before I could come up with one, he said, "I've got three sisters Doc. Don't even bother trying to think of some other lie to tell me. My sisters would all run a mile from this." He shoved his arm at me then and this time I felt the soft crepe of the bandages under my chin. "And this," he said and tore the sheet off his leg, amputated below the knee. "And I wouldn't blame them neither."

"He killed himself, that one. Saved up his morphine. Can't say I wouldn't have done the same thing under the circumstances. Poor sucker."

The drunkard waved at the waiter, who brought him another rum. I could think of nothing to say. His drink arrived and he took a big swig. "Maggots only eat the rotten flesh anyway, so probably no harm done. But who wants maggots growing out of their guts?"

"Australia is a first world country," said the teetotaller. "We don't have flies in operating theatres. We don't have maggots in wounds."

"Because of the tiles!" proclaimed the drunkard as he clicked his fingers again at a passing waiter.

"Cheers," he clicked his almost empty glass with mine. I felt a real solidarity with him then as we swilled the last of our respective beverages. The teetotaller did not give up so easily though.

"Alright then," he said. "Forget the tiles. Apparently, your Doctor Grafton had a door fitted to the operating theatre with a 'seeing eye' motion detector so that if someone wants to enter or exit then they can do so without touching the door with their hands."

"Of course. That eliminates the spread of germs," I explained to him.

"Except for the problem of roaming patients. You know those postlobotomised drongos wandering around like ghosts. Or the dribblers. Every time one of them walks past the operating theatre the door opens. That's what I've heard."

"Yes, that is what you have *heard*," I said and left it at that. The drunkard laughed. He was clearly enjoying this.

Then the drunkard spoke up. "Apparently Grafton has a hidden compartment in his desk with a gun in it. Good idea I say. Who knows when you are going to need one? Especially with crazed lunatics wandering in and out of the operating theatre. Much worse pests than flies, I reckon." He laughed then and so did the teetotaller. Were they secretly on the same side? When you are changing the way your medical specialty works, your peers cannot be trusted.

"The new state-of-the-art treatment centre doesn't even have bars at the windows," he continued. "Oh, no. That would not be good enough for Doctor Jack Grafton. He has instead ordered armoured glass so the patients can't escape."

Ah. I had him now. As I said before I am not a man used to confrontation but when I am right and I know I am right and when I am three glasses of Moselle in, I will on occasion speak up.

"It isn't armoured glass," I said. "It is anti-suicide glass."

Another Moselle arrived for me. Ignoring the look from the teetotaller I took a deep mouthful. I knew I could beat him at his argument now, and the story I was about to tell was more horrifying than a few maggots crawling out of a wound.

"When I was doing my internship," I said softly enough that the others had to lean forward to hear me. Ha! I thought to myself. I have been listening to Jack tell stories for long enough to have learned a few tricks. "A young girl was brought in. She wouldn't have been more than twenty but already she was an alcoholic. She wasn't brought in for her alcoholism though. This girl came in sporting two matching bandages on her wrists."

"Cutter!" the alcoholic's arm flew into the air as if he was playing bingo. People looked over from nearby tables, but I was rather enjoying myself by now.

"Yes," I pointed at him. "That's what everyone thought. She was bought into the ward still stinking of alcohol. She was aggressive and had some good-for-nothing bloke with her. You know the type, too skinny and with broken teeth. This girl must have been dependant on the alcohol or she wouldn't have let this bloke walk on the same side of the street as her.

"Anyway, we got rid of him and she really went pear-shaped then, hollering obscenities that I was surprised someone that looked like her would even know."

I could see that I was losing my audience by then and so I described the girl. That sure brought them back. Even the teetotaller with his wide polished wedding band looked like he was salivating.

"She was a little blonde," I said waving my hands to indicate an hourglass. That is all that was needed to regain their interest. "Only a small thing. She would have fitted snugly under my armpit, and I am not the tallest bloke in the world. The alcohol may have destroyed her vocabulary, but her face was like that of an angel. She was perfect."

I paused then for effect, and Jack would have been proud of my performance, I am sure.

"We gave her something to calm her down and the next morning it was my job to dress her wounds. Being an intern, we had to do all manner of odd jobs like that, I am sure you remember.

"I was shocked when I undid her bandages. Her wrists didn't have the little scratchy marks of your usual cutter. Her wounds were deep. Ugly black stitches had pulled together a slash in a straight line up her right wrist. Her left wrist started off straight and then curved across like a question mark."

"She was a left hander." The alcoholic said as matter-of-factly as you do after a few years in the profession.

"Yes, apparently she was having a fight with the goon that brought her in. She wanted more alcohol, but the shops were closed, or some such thing. That is the story he told us anyway."

"Bullshit."

Although I didn't like to acknowledge the drunkard's language, I had to agree with him. Husband's and boyfriend's stories are most often that, just stories.

"She had grabbed a piece of glass and threatened to end it all. Well, more than threatened as it turned out. She was out on the street yelling and screaming. My point is that these wounds were vicious. There were not created in a superficial manner. There was nothing hesitant or attention seeking about them. Whatever the circumstances this girl had intended to do herself in.

I went immediately to my supervisor with this information. This girl was in a low security wing. She could walk out at any time.

"Let me guess, your supervisor didn't give a rat's arse?"

"No, he accused me of having a crush on her. A crush, of all things. I was simply concerned about my patient's welfare. The whole situation made me feel embarrassed though, and so I left it at that. The nursing staff found out about it and took to teasing me about my supposed crush during the day. I was trying to keep an eye on her, that was all. I didn't want her leaving.

"She must have realised that I had taken a special interest in her though because she waited until my coffee break. A few minutes, that is all it took. She grabbed a chair and smashed it through a window. A window with no bars, you will note, or armoured glass." I paused and looked straight at the teetotaller.

"At first the nurse on duty thought she was trying to escape but this poor girl just wanted to die. She thrust her head through the hole in the window and forced her neck onto the broken glass, slashing her way back and forth."

"Oh, oh,"

"Two nurses restrained her before she got to her jugular."

"Sometimes you have to wonder whether it's best just to let them go," said the drunkard.

"How can you say such a thing?" asked the teetotaller.

"If they really want to die? Why not just let them? *C'est la vie*, as Ned Kelly would say."

"The point is," I said. "Anti-suicide glass could have prevented this incident." I again looked pointedly at the teetotaller, waiting for his acknowledgement that I had won.

"Until she found another broken bottle in the gutter," he said.

"She was a very beautiful girl," I said. "It didn't have to be like that."

"Not with that scar on her neck she wouldn't be," said the drunkard. "I often say that. Someone thinks they have troubles, so they get their shotgun and put it to their temple. Then they wake up in hospital. Now they have troubles. Now they have no face and they dream of the life they still had when they had that shotgun to their temple."

"It's not about troubles," I said. "It is about mental illness."

They seemed afraid of me after that. The conversation became awkward again. Only I didn't feel awkward. I was thoroughly enjoying myself.

Kate

Kate stood with her back to the white trunk like it was an extension of her spine and grew straight up into the heavens. The tree glowed pink in the moonlight. Peter pressed her further into it, nuzzling her neck.

"Come over here," Kate said and pulled Peter along behind her. They scratched their way through the brush. The lee of a retaining wall protected them from the gossiping eyes of dog walkers and kids who had come to smoke behind the Scout Hall. The grass was soft and the native violets had modestly closed their petals for the evening. To Kate this was the perfect place. She remembered the lantana flowers that they used to pick in primary school when the only thing they knew about weeds was that they wouldn't get into trouble for picking them. This had enhanced, rather than diminished, their beauty.

Kate pulled Peter to the ground and the warmth from the day that had been stored in the wall rose out to meet them. They kissed, and it was the first time Kate had ever kissed anyone when she was sober. She smelt Peter's clean smell and felt the breeze caressing her bare arms. She felt nervous, unsure of what should happen next. What she should do? She moved her hand to his fly and pulled down his zipper. Every feeling rushed to her groin then. Her inner thighs. *Between your legs*, as her mother would whisper as she handed Kate the face washer in the bath when she was little. Kate forgot the smell of him then, the wind tickling at her elbows and the cicadas screaming under the ground, desperate to come up and reproduce. Her fingers probed behind his underpants and teased at his pubic hair. Peter pushed her hand away and stood up.

"I know a better place," he said. "But no one can see us."

He hastily picked a flannel flower and bent down over Kate who was still panting on the ground. He slid the flower behind her left ear, grabbed her hand and pulled her up. And that is how Kate ended up riding in the boot of Peter's blue Mazda to a hotel in Pennant Hills, in the opposite direction to the city. It was not a direction Kate had ever intended on travelling, but her groin was on fire as she counted the corners like a hostage.

Kate covered her face with her hair as she entered the hotel ten minutes after Peter. The barren smell of the room flushed the heat from between her legs and back to the extremities of her body where it belonged. She wished she was back on the grass, the violet flowers tickling her arms. The white gum watching above her, supporting her. Peter's arms encircled her waist like an octopus, pulling her close.

"This is better, isn't it?"

"It's nice." Liar.

They lay in the double bed afterwards, playacting at being adults. Kate nervously smoothed the creases from the bedspread while Peter lay on his back with his arms under his head, just as his father always did. And Kate's father did. Arms that should have been cuddling. Kate imagined for a moment that Peter was her father. She curled up into foetal position with her back to Peter so she couldn't see his tentacle arms.

Peter of course mistook this as regret and rolled towards her—unfurled his arms and touched her shoulder. Kate shuddered, and Peter, thinking she was crying (he was right about this at least) said, "Katherine Louise (many girls born in the 70s have the middle name of Louise, as if it was a name not deemed worthy of first-name status. It was never at the top of the list of baby names and stayed stuck between the first and the last).

"Are you okay?"

For what else could he say? He thought he knew what was wrong. Did he really need to hear it?

Kate rolled tighter into a ball.

"Katherine? Louise?"

Finally Peter relented. He'd have to hear it and he regretted everything at that moment.

"What's wrong?"

She turned to him then, tearful, and said, "This bedspread is the ugliest bedspread in the whole world."

"What?"

"It's stale, and ugly, and feels gross."

Of course, she was right, our Kate, our heroine. Even now some such bedspreads have survived in hotels around Australia, their surfaces both scratchy and slimy. Always cold. They still disappoint lovers that have imagined lying with their lover on a bed of rose petals with soft orchestral music playing somewhere in the background.

"Katherine."

"Don't call me that. I hate it. And Katie too. Mum always calls me Katie when she wants something."

"Kate then."

"Yes, Kate. Just Kate."

"Not just Kate. Kate full stop."

"My grandmother called me K—that's okay."

"You really do have a versatile name." Laughing.

"Peter. Pete. Peter Rabbit."

There were kisses now, punctuating the pauses between his name.

"Can I call you Kay?"

"Yes."

"Kay, those curtains look like vomit," he said, tickling her, "but at least they match the bedspread."

"No, that's too weird."

"What?"

"You can't call me Kay. Nonna called me that—just her."

"Kate then."

"Kate. Full stop."

"Everyone calls you that though."

"So?"

"You are special. I want to call you something special."

"Special K? You make me sound like a retard—on the special bus. Or a breakfast cereal."

"Kat."

"Cat?"

"Yes, Kat. Like, meow, you know. Is that okay—Miss K?"

"Cat? Only if you can make me purr Mr Peter."

"I can certainly try."

"Meow."

"Kat. You are my Kat."

"Purrrr."

Of course, it was terrible and lame. The things we say in bed usually are—especially if you are in love. The ugly nylon bedspread was cut out of Kate's vision as she closed her eyes against the world of her hotel room and imagined them as they had been behind the Beecroft Scout Hall, with the cicadas, the occasional scuffle of a lizard, and the grass tickling her back.

"Mmm, my Kat. That is my name for you. Not your mother's or your grandmother's. Mine. You are mine."

In the chaos of her imagination, Kate purred. But Peter was young and soon changed his mind. He hadn't considered what a liability his Kat could be.

Jack

There were fifteen of us who took LSD that day. We all sat around waiting for our turn, each trying to hide our nervousness from the others. I kept my head down and doodled in my notebook. I did not particularly want the others to recognise me, yet that did not stop me from making sly glances at them. I knew a few of their faces and I was hoping they would not remember me.

It was a night of epiphanies for all of us, but especially for Jack. It cemented the ideas he had been introduced to overseas. He became even more convinced that mental illnesses were as much physical complaints as other illnesses and for that reason they required physical therapies rather than the traditional talking therapies to cure them.

"The talking cure," Jack used to say. "What a ridiculous waste of time. Imagine if a patient was brought into hospital suffering from a heart attack and some fool tried to talk him out of it. It is just as ridiculous to try to talk a woman out of post-natal depression or a man out of schizophrenia. Imagine a man is in your office. He is not sitting on the couch telling you about his childhood. He is hiding behind the couch. What is he hiding from, you ask me? Well, who knows? Maybe he's hiding from the dragons breathing fire on him? The point is, discussing the terrible sandwiches his mother packed him in his school lunchbox when he was five years old is not going to help now, is it? Anti-psychotic medication on the other hand will get him out from under the couch at least. His brain is an organ much more sophisticated than the heart. Now if the heart needs physical treatment, it follows that the brain must also."

I used to wonder why Jack chose psychiatry over cardiology or surgery. Back then psychiatry was the underdog of medical specialisations. The people of Sydney were lucky that Jack did chose psychiatry, though, because he did so much for the field in Australia, especially through his development of Slumber Therapy. Perhaps this is the brain's equivalent of open-heart surgery or heart transplants. Jack would of course have been accepted into

cardiology, but it didn't interest him. Why, you ask me? Because for someone like Jack, the heart is too simple.

"The heart is just like a big pump," Jack would say. "Blood in one tube,
pump a few times and then out the other. Something goes wrong and you
fix it just like you fix a bicycle valve. It takes about as much expertise. Even
those transplants. Those heart surgeons are just like glorified mechanics,
replacing an old part with a new one. Nothing difficult about that."

Jack considered heart surgery to be something of a triviality, and I must
say that I agree with him. The brain, on the other hand, is much more
complex. Even in dissection it is not as simple as valves and tubes. Without
a brain we cannot survive. Without a heart, these days, it seems as if we can.

It was Jack's mission to educate people in the field of psychiatry, to raise
awareness in the minds of the general public and to build psychiatry into
a worthier profession. He succeeded in this of course, or psychiatry would
not be what it is today, despite the attempts by the Scientologists to debunk
our work and keep it in the realms of myth. Despite what people have said,
despite the bitter envy on show at the Royal Commission, the people of
Sydney were lucky to be treated by someone of Jack's calibre. In the future
Jack will be recognised for the leading light he was, just like Hofmann and
the rest of them.

Jack believed he could fix the brain using physical methods such as medication, electroshock therapy, and surgery. A patient need not be any more
afraid of it than getting their appendix out, or their tonsils. Jack was great
at reducing complex medical procedures for the average Joe Blow. I guess
he was using the KISS principal, Keep It Simple Stupid. I am sure that
compared with Jack, most of us were. He was fantastic at reassuring the
families of patients about to undergo brain surgery.

"Don't worry," he'd say. "The surgeon will simply insert a thin gold pipe
into the brain." Even a plumber could understand that. Although I have
often wondered whether Jack's explanation would have gone down as well
if the tubing wasn't made of gold. *A rose of any other name*, as they say.

But I digress from the LSD experiment I was describing. I guess I am putting off writing about it, even now. There were fifteen of us, Jack included. We weren't like some bunch of hippies sitting in a park taking drugs. This was a serious scientific experiment and we all treated it as such. Doctors trying out treatments on themselves have been a phenomenon since the Middle Ages. Where would we be today if Isaac Newton had not stuck a chopstick into his own eyeball? Where would we be if Jonas Salk had not used himself and his family as guinea pigs for polio vaccines? We can thank Salk that we no longer see little children in callipers or dragging one foot behind them.

I know, I know. We were doing drug experiments. Everyone gets so moralistic about that, don't they? Nevertheless, I ask you, where would we be today without psychiatric medication? Before that, patients just got shoved into a strong dress and were left to rot. Plenty of credible scientists have tested drugs on themselves. Let me think, there was August Bier. He injected cocaine into his assistant's back and then, to make sure it worked he kicked him in the shins. Oh, it makes me laugh just thinking of it, this scientist kicking his assistant in the shins and burning him with matches. He even pulled out his assistant's pubic hair and crushed his testicles in his fist. Although the image is hysterical the end result is that all those Mrs Robinson types on the north shore of Sydney get to breed without feeling a thing. The baby goes straight from the womb to the nanny with minimal disruption to mother dearest, easily defying God's punishment for the Eves of this world.

I do concede that John Hunter and good old Stubby Ffirth got it wrong. Everyone knows about John Hunter rubbing gonorrhoea pus onto his own John Thomas. He wanted to prove that gonorrhoea turned into syphilis and he thought he had proved that when he contracted both diseases. The problem was the donor of the gonorrhoea pus also had syphilis. It was the same with Ffirth. He was a cocky fellow. He was so sure that yellow fever was not contagious that he rubbed the black vomit of a patient into open welts on his arm. He drank their vomit and rubbed it into his eyeballs. He basically swam in the stuff. To be honest, I think there was a bit of showing off involved in this case and yet again, I believe that it was his lack of doubt in his hypothesis that was his undoing. Ffirth may not have contracted yellow fever but he did not cover all the bases now, did he? He conveniently forgot about, or worse, dismissed the notion that yellow fever could be contracted through blood, by mosquitoes. That Ffirth was such a dill, and while I laugh at his lack of systematic research methodology, I do admire his tenacity.

As you can see, I have a particular interest in medical scientists that have practised self-experimentation, and it was in this vein (literally!) that I agreed to take part in this experiment. We were meticulous in our research methods, sitting in a room with our notepads ready to write down any phenomena we might discover. We had all had our heart rates and blood pressure taken and were ready to roll, as the kids say.

We were all to be injected with LSD by the nurse. She was well endowed and my heart rate must have gone up as she leant towards me to measure my blood pressure. I still remember who a few of the others were but we were all volunteers of sorts and I am sure that the few that I did know would not appreciate having me name them now. I tried to make small talk with one fellow while we waited for our turn to be injected.

"I rode my bicycle in," I said.

"I drove," he said. "I'll catch a cab home if I need to. Leave the car here overnight."

He obviously wasn't getting my joke. I thought it was my deadpan expression, so I raised my eyebrows a little and said, "Pity it is not April the nineteenth."

I know that it isn't considered kosher to laugh at one's own jokes but sometimes the other party needs a heads up.

"You know, bicycle day, April nineteenth."

This fellow did join in with my mirth eventually, but you know what they say, "He who laughs last, laughs loudest," or something to that effect, but to give the poor fellow a break, he was probably just nervous.

The nurse came over to us then, so I didn't have time to explain it to him. I have always thought there is something intimate about injections, whether I am penetrating a patient's skin, or as in this case a nurse is inserting a needle into my own bloodstream. She was skilled enough to pinhole my vein on her first attempt and I held my breath as she drew out the plunger and I watched my blood ejaculate into the yellowish liquid in the syringe. The injection worked almost immediately, and I had the distinct impression that I was made out of that black and white static we used to have on our televisions. That is what it felt like, yet it is hard to explain. I could not talk because of my static mouth but this did not bother me, the feeling was not unpleasant. By this time, I was staring at the wall, a common mint hospital shade of green. Yet it was moving. Paint was running down the wall. I reached out to touch the wall, but it wasn't wet. The paint flowed over my hands, but no matter how many times I took my palm out of the paint, there was none left on my hand.

Further up the wall there was a painting of a sailing ship. I say a painting, but I definitely do not mean art. It was one of those mass-produced and characterless prints that are found in offices in equally uninspiring frames. The print had probably always been there but now I noticed that the sea was moving. The waves were crashing. The ship started to roll and toss on the ocean waves. The bow came right out of the frame.

"Look," I said to those around me. I was completely unaware that I was watching a hallucination. I really thought the boat was coming out of the picture. "That ship is moving. Look."

"Shh," said Jack pointing to the light. "There's a palm tree."

I looked at the light then, and sure enough beaming down from its centre was a palm tree. I knew it must have some kind of significance. I tried to ask Jack what this could mean but I could only say, "Oh." That was the only utterance that would come out of my mouth although my mind was making a lot of connections between palm trees and love and Palm Sunday and Easter, but I could only say "Oh," so I think I said it over and over again. "Oh, oh, oh, oh, oh," but nobody reacted so maybe I said nothing at all.

This sort of thing went on for hours and I think that we barely uttered a word to each other. Maybe we communicated solely with guttural utterances, yet I felt that we all understood each other. We all had a connection. I have heard people describing taking these hallucinogenic drugs as taking a trip, and that is exactly what it felt like, but at the risk of sounding crass it was a trip to another world where time stretched and contracted at will.

A pot plant was on the side table and I sat for some time watching it grow. It was one of those office plants that grow in trails around curtain rods and hangs down over cupboards. Its leaves stretched out towards me and I knew instinctively that I was the one making the plant grow. The leaves were gaining their power from me and me from it. We were connected somehow. It was then I noticed that the leaves were heart shaped and I felt the urge to undo my tie and unbutton my shirt, which I did, and wrap the tendrils of the plant around my naked torso.

The feeling was indescribable, the closest I have felt to ecstasy, even in that fevered anticipation of sitting in my underwear on the edge of a hotel bed waiting for my new bride to come out of the bathroom. The plant hugged me; it grew into me and we breathed together. She fed me her oxygen and I gave her my carbon dioxide. I revelled in the co-dependence of our relationship while I fondled her rubbery leaves. I was happy. That is the only way to describe it. I was simply and deliriously happy.

Writing this takes me back to that rapture, to some extent, although I cringe at the fact I am even writing this at all, even if I am alone in my study and nobody will ever read it. I have never told anyone of this. There was no one, I guess, to understand.

By this point some hours had gone by. Someone pulled at my sleeve and said, "Come on, I want to show you something," but I did not want to leave my plant. We needed each other. I remembered her Latin name then, *Epipremnum aureum* and the name flowed through my mind.

At some stage I believe I got distracted by the grey and green mottled linoleum. It was that same stuff that was laid down for miles in every public building in the early 70s so that there was some kind of strange cohesion between schools and hospitals, universities and doctor's surgeries, and even protestant churches. (Of course, the Catholics kept themselves apart with their plush carpets, and I cannot say that I blame them.) At this point, though, I watched as the green and grey floor bubbled over my shoes like a foamy bath. I unravelled myself from my plant then and followed Jack. He was staring at the floor too and we raised our feet and splashed along the corridor, laughing like children. He held my sleeve and took me to an office. We stood and looked out a window at the sky. It was the most marvellous scene. I guess in our profession, working as we do indoors, looking into the depths of people's minds, we psychiatrists too often forget to look outwards.

The Southern Cross shining out of the darkness was a beacon that made me proud to be Australian. I could see lines joining the stars together and even now when I look up at the sky a part of me wonders whether I was hallucinating back then or whether the universe was just showing me the connections that really are there for those that can see them. Whatever the case I felt privileged to be in that state of mind and even today whenever I am outside at night, I take the opportunity to look up at our Southern Cross. Even now it gives me a connection to this planet. Ever since that night, when the family went skiing in the northern hemisphere, I would look up at a sky devoid of the Southern Cross and feel deeply that I did not belong.

After some time, I began to feel weak and a little unsure of myself. I needed my plant. If I found her, I knew everything would be alright, and my strength would return. I stumbled back into the unfamiliar corridor and walked for miles. The mush of grey and green linoleum was hovering around my calves and rising, threatening to choke me with its poisonous gas. I had no option at this point but to cover my mouth and nose with my naked arm and push on. I reached a doorway just as the linoleum gas began irritating my eyes, making it difficult to see. I thought I was safe at last but as soon as I stood in the doorway, I realised that something was wrong. The room looked the same, but I knew it was not the same room. My notebook was sitting on a coffee table, open and face down just as I had left it. Someone must have moved it to this strange room. A feeling of dread came upon me and I knew that if I went inside the room, I would be walking into a trap.

Then Jack was beside me, but it was not Jack, just an imposter wearing his white shirt and tie. A strong breeze whipped across the room then, dissipating the gas and causing this fake Jack's shirt to ripple across his body.

"Come in. Sit down," he said. I stayed in the doorway, my arm still across my face in case the gas came back. I did not trust this man.

"Where's Jack?" I asked.

"I am Jack."

"You're not Jack. You are just wearing his clothes. Where's Jack?" My voice was rising like an angry wife.

"Come in. We are all going to talk about our experiences now."

"I'm not telling you anything," I said, and this man laughed. It sounded like Jack's laugh. I realised then that the CIA had infiltrated our experiment. Everyone knew that the CIA were the owners of LSD. I looked into the room again and realised that the window on the other side was a two-way mirror used to spy on us. The wind calmed down, but Jack's shirt was still rippling.

"They are watching," I whispered to him.

"Indeed," he announced loudly, and I knew then that he was one of them. Jack had definitely been replaced and this person was a poor substitute. This Jack motioned to someone in the room and the nurse that had injected me was holding my hand. She was wearing too much eye shadow; it drowned the natural blue of her eyes. Did she think that I was that stupid? A hold of the hand and a hold of the wrist are the same thing. I was being restrained. I looked into her face and a skull with blue eye shadow smiled back at me. I gripped the doorframe with my free hand.

"Come on Doctor," she said in the sweetest melancholy voice. "Come and eat something."

The nurse took me into the room then and there was food on the table. My eyes were drawn to a round cake with bright pink icing and sprinkles. It was the most beautiful cake I had ever seen. Jack stood over the cake wielding a knife. He handed me a slice on a napkin as if I was a child at a birthday party. I bit into the cake and I cannot explain to you how repulsive it was. It was as if my tastebuds had been removed and I could only feel the texture of sand and sawdust. I thought of Rasputin and cyanide as I retched into a napkin and threw the terrible cake onto the ground where it was sucked under the froth of the linoleum. The eating of that cake was a big mistake, I even feel that now, as ridiculous as it might seem. Rasputin was right to avoid the cakes with the pink icing. I have never eaten pink desserts since.

"Don't do that," the nurse reproached me. "At least put it in the bin." But it was too late. The napkin had been sucked under the floor.

I was still retching, and I knew the nurse was mocking me. Jack was also grinning down at me as he stood there in front of the poisonous cake. He held the knife loosely in his hand, pointing it ominously at my groin. It was obvious to me that I had to kill him then and I knew that I could. I would play by their rules for now until the opportunity arose. I looked at Jack then to make sure he wasn't onto me. I looked into his eyes. His face looked like Jack, but he had the cold grey eyes of my father. It struck me like an epiphany. My father was wearing Jack's clothes. That is why they were too big for him. Yet my father was dead.

"Father?" I said.

"Son," he said. I heard a laugh track and looked around the room. It was an exact replica of the room we had been in before. I looked at the picture of the ship on the wall and although the waves were still pitching the boat around in its frame enough to make me feel seasick, it was obvious now it was just my mind playing tricks on me. The wall was fuzzy as though I was just very tired. I pushed my fingers under my glasses and rubbed my eyes. I looked at my watch. It was ten minutes to ten.

I walked towards my plant, but she was not pulling me anymore. The plant was wilted, and I knew that she too had been replaced. I would have gone closer but I knew that her nasty tendrils were waiting to strangle me. I remembered her common name then, the name my wife used for her: the Devil's Ivy. The symbiosis of our relationship had disintegrated. I sat in my seat and pretended to look in my notebook. I had not written anything. I decided to write, but I knew it was not really my book and I could not trust these imposters not to remove my secrets from my heart as I wrote and then use them against me.

I couldn't let them know I was onto them though, so I pretended to write. I would write nonsense. That would get them. They'd know nothing. Hours went by and I wrote and wrote until my wrist hurt. At some point I looked up and everyone else had gone except for Jack and the nurse. They were watching me from the other side of the room, just in front of the two-way mirror. Other people were watching me, and it was not for the good of science. Jack touched the nurse's pockets and I saw that she had a syringe in her hand. They were going to do me in. I started writing for real then. I knew I was going to die. I could not get away fast enough and even if I did, I had no idea where my car keys were. I could run but they would easily overtake me in a car. Any car. Jack's car. His midnight blue Jaguar.

I looked at my watch. It was five minutes until ten. I became scared then. Really and truly scared. I did not look at anybody. I would write until my notebook was full. The night would surely be over by then. I wrote about where I was and the imposters that had taken over Jack's experiment and the two-way mirror and the CIA. Finally, I looked at my watch again and it was still not yet ten o'clock.

People started wandering into the room, but they weren't the same people we had started the experiment with. I knew that much. Or maybe they were. Maybe they were starting the experiment again. I searched for Jack. He was standing by the doorway ushering people in. They began to take their seats around me in slow motion and it was still not ten o'clock and I did not know how I could possibly live a life where time went so slow. I could not do it. I understood now the drag of immortality. And suddenly, an epiphany. I knew what this was about. It was a conspiracy to make me kill myself, just like Socrates. I looked for Jack again, but I couldn't see him.

I decided to make a break for it. I ran for the doorway, but the lino floor sucked at my feet like quicksand and those five steps took so long I felt as if I was in a slow-motion film. Jack blocked my path. It was the real Jack. It had to be. The other Jack was still in the room putting objects into the nurse's pockets.

"What's going on?" I asked him. But his face kept changing into my father's and my brothers' and I didn't know who I was talking to. Jack took a step into the threshold of the room and turned back to me.

"It's okay," he said as the deepest darkest terror gripped me. I stared at Jack's face and a skeleton stared back. I could see the tendons gripping his bones and the blood pulsing through his veins and I could see what he was thinking. I was still holding onto the doorway and so now I sat and gripped the wall between my knees. That room was a bad room. The nurse was behind me. Jack held my arms and she shoved the needle into the back of my thigh. I could have resisted but it seemed pointless. I wondered whether some of the fabric of my pants went into my body then like the Jesus of Nazareth film when Christians were shot with bows and arrows and I had watched as a piece of one man's shirt was driven into his heart by the arrow.

*

I woke up in bed at home. Jack came to see me still wearing the same white suit, but it was unmistakably him. He had my notebook that I had written in for hours. I opened it with rubbery velum fingers and scrawled across one page in five-year-old handwriting was the date of my father's death. Just that and nothing else. I flipped though the blank pages just to be certain.

As you can see LSD is a very powerful drug, psychologically. It unleashes your unconscious mind. It plays with your beliefs. Obviously, I had become obsessed by my father's death. It was an unexpected heart attack. The brute felled. Not that it helped me a lot. I think that is what was subconsciously bothering me at the time. His death was what was holding me back. LSD is a very mysterious drug... it opens doors to the unknown... to the insane... to the corners of the human mind. It is very difficult to explain in words.

Since that day, however, I have understood the mind of the schizophrenic, because I have been there. I understand the paranoia and the attachments to certain objects that become very important to some patients. I understand that because I have experienced it, both the terror in a familiar environment and becoming afraid of loved ones. It has made me a much better physician. I am now more sympathetic to the fears of my patients.

I am writing about this but let me tell you that I have never spoken of this experience to anyone, not even my wife. Jack and I had an unspoken agreement not to discuss my behaviour on this night with other people. Yet the amazing aspect of that night is that when I woke my mind had returned to normal. I still felt a bit strange; my world was a little grey for a few days, but my mind had returned. Time had gone back to normal. I had gone back to normal. I felt as if I had been cured. This experience taught me that Jack was right. Schizophrenia is caused by a physical complaint, albeit in the brain, and a physical treatment is needed for the cure. Schizophrenic brains just need to be reset, like mine was by artificial rest. Reluctantly I left Freud behind to be used as a diagnostic tool only and bravely followed Jack in the only direction he knew how to travel: forwards.

Kate

The demise of Miss Leach, although not planned, was probably unavoidable. Who knows what got into those teenagers as the smell of summer got closer? Those gifted kids that had stayed at school. The ones that hadn't gone off to become plumbers, clerks, hairdressers and shopgirls. The best of the bunch. Or so their parents thought. Perhaps it was because the cicadas' love songs screamed into their brains and left no room for learning, only further surging of their hormones so that the girls walked around the school with wet knickers and the boys with books hiding the front of their pants. Anything could set them off, the toss of hair, the glint of an earring, shiny blonde hairs on tanned knees. Or the underwear lines under Miss Leach's slacks. Perhaps it was simply just the greenness of the grass and the blueness of the sky. Stuck together in a classroom, it was impossible for the students to concentrate. They sat staring at the back of each other's necks while gently grinding on the edges of their seats. It hit the HSC students the hardest. The possibility of sex hung in the air. Between friends, between best friends' boyfriends. Even between students and teachers. By the time the HSC trial exams had finished, and the students were on their final dash to freedom, frustration formed the core of their lives. And who did they take this frustration out on? Miss Leach. She never had a chance.

On one fatal day, Miss Leach heard the students discussing *The Crucible* as she led them into the classroom. Perhaps she thought they'd turned a corner together. That she'd finally gotten through to them, and that the next forty-five minutes wouldn't be like the usual slow battering of hell. The students sat outside the classroom waiting for the bell. Their sloping backs were propped up against the brick wall as if they had no spines at all.

"John Proctor is sooo sexy."

"John Proctor is weak. That's not sexy."

"Yes, yes he is. He's my dream man. All muscles and yum."

"He's a pervert. He had sex with a sixteen-year-old girl."

"So? I'm sixteen and if John Proctor leapt out of my book right now, I'd do him in the dunnies!"

Miss Leach opened the classroom door and as they all filed in behind, eyes turned to her round bottom. She was wearing white linen slacks. Kate thought she had probably chosen those pants to show her bottom off. The students always joked that Miss Leach's bottom entered the classroom five minutes after her. That's why they called her Bubble Bum. Never to her face, of course.

"Actually," joined in Miss Leach as she sat at her desk, "John Proctor might not have been much older than Abigail even though he was married and had children. People got married very young back then. Perhaps even as young as thirteen or fourteen."

"Oh gross." Disgusted.

"John Proctor would have been in his early twenties at the most."

"He was still taken."

"That's true."

"Twenty is still old, no offence Miss Leach."

"He was probably gorgeous then if a sixteen-year-old wanted him. Like Mr Mason, huh Miss Leach?"

And with that the tables turned on Miss Leach. Her blush didn't help. It was as simple as that. The boys were mesmerised by Miss Leach, the best-looking teacher at the school. She was fresh out of teacher's college, with cheeks that glowed hot when she was questioned. She had blonde hair and small high breasts not dissimilar to the students. Unfortunately for Miss Leach, their obsession with her did not make them behave.

"Students, turn to the last scene of *The Crucible*. We will continue to read from where we left off yesterday. Michael Ballins, you can be John Proctor. Kate Noble, you can be his wife. Read from the top of the page."

Michael started, "*I hear nothin', where I am kept.*" Sexy voice.

The class laughs.

"I'm not just John Proctor's wife. My name is Elizabeth," said Kate Noble, her lower lip pouting in just the way all her friends copied. Trying to be her.

"Read on Kate."

"Me?"

"No. Kate Noble."

"*Giles is dead.*" Kate Noble.

"*When were he hanged?*" Michael's sexy voice. Wolf whistles from the back of the class.

"Now this is a very important section for you Kate. If this man admits to the crime he will be hanged and if he doesn't he would be tortured until he dies," cut in Miss Leach.

"I'd rather be hanged," said Michael.

"If Giles admits to anything the family farm will be taken and his wife and children will be destitute. Read on Kate."

As the stage directions suggested, Kate Noble gave her lines factually, if not quietly.

"So boring." Our Kate's rolling eyes.

As if in response, Little Michael, who had not yet gotten over his short stature and still needed to be the class clown to get attention, jumped onto his seat and screeched, "Shake it up baby now."

The rest of the class sang back, "Shake it up baby," even Kate Noble, Then returned to their books as if this outburst had been rehearsed. Michael Ballins continued reading before Miss Leach could comment. Perhaps moved by the madness that was taking over the classroom, or simply by oratory delight, Michael Ballins almost shrieked his next line in a flourish of over-acting. "*Then how does he die?*"

"Twist and shout." Little Michael on his desk this time.

"Twist and shout." Dancing. Wolf whistling.

"That's enough!" Miss Leach.

"*They press him, John.*"

"Press?" Giggles.

"Class!" Miss Leach attempted to regain their attention. "This is where they torture him by putting heavy rocks on his chest. Imagine the willpower of this man who is slowly being crushed to death, and the moment before he dies, he just says two simple words. "More weight."

Little Michael left enough time to pass for Miss Leach to relax. Perhaps she even thought the class realised the gravity of the scene instead of just waiting for the inevitable next line from Little Michael. It came soon enough.

"C'mon shake it, shake it, shake it baby now." Face screwed up like a rock star. Perhaps this moment is why they say the school years are the best years of your life? Surely the rest of his life was not this memorable? A couple of kids, a mortgage and a steady job?

"Shake it up baby." Class chorus.

"Michael, outside now! Go and see Mr Guard."

Little Michael dropped to his knees in front of Miss Leach and implored. "But, but, Miss Leach," his large brown eyes pleaded with her. His lips were a perfect cupid's bow. Did she smile? Almost? "I wanna work it all out." It was his best performance yet.

"Work it all out." The entire class stood to deliver this line. The best time of their lives.

Miss Leach strode out of the classroom. In the teacher's absence Frances became magnetised to Michael Ballins lap, as usual, while he stared over his shoulder at our Kate.

"She's going to get Mr Guard." Announcement. "Sit down everyone. Quick, before she gets back."

"Kate, keep reading the book."

"Shit. What were we up to? *I want you living?*"

"No, *Giles is a fearsome man.*"

"Giles is the sexy one." Our Kate.

"He's an old man. Really old. Maybe even forty or something like that."

"Maybe, but he's a real man. The way he made them put more stones on him instead of betraying his family."

"More weight." Michael Ballins.

"Would you take more weight for me?" Frances asked Michael.

"Sure babe. Put the whole of Ayers Rock on me and I will beg for more weight." Winking at Kate over Frances's shoulder.

"So sweet." Pale blue fluttering eyelids.

"Can you imagine Little Michael taking that pain?"

"No way, man. I'd give you all up in a heartbeat. Get those pebbles off my chest. They are all witches, the whole lot of them." He threw his arms around the classroom, stopping only when his pointing fingers stretched towards Kate Noble. "Sorry Kate."

"I reckon Mr Mason would take more weight," said a girl with too many teeth, who should have known better than to join in the conversation. They pretended not to hear her.

Miss Leach didn't come back to class, not then or ever. A couple of students found her hyperventilating on her office floor. An ambulance came. Miss Leach looked thin lying on her back on the stretcher, her bubble bum hidden from view. She would never know her students had actually gone back to discussing *The Crucible*.

Kate

Adulthood sat just out of Kate's reach. The end of school equalled, to her, the start of her life. To Kate this could only bring about good things. She had always wanted money and a career, but more and more she dreamt about her relationship with Peter being visible. She sat at her bedroom window and reached out her arms towards the city, breathing in deeply. Her usual musings about working with Ita Buttrose became entwined with her daydreams about Peter. But it was Peter she dreamed about the most. She imagined going to Kate Noble's party with him. It would be the first time they would be in public together. In front of her friends. She imagined holding his hand as they walked in together. She couldn't wait to see the shocked looks of her friends when they realised that she went out with a man instead of a mere boy. As the school term ground on her mother's stomach got bigger and her movements became more awkward. A woman started coming over to clean the house.

Kate's dalliance with Peter continued and very early on they discovered that they lived close enough to each other that if Kate looked through the branches of the jacaranda tree in their neighbour's yard, she could just see the light shining from Peter's bedroom window. Although they had professed their love to each other in the first three days, they continued to find new ways to do this. Peter would flick his light on and off. Short, long, short, short, long, long, long, short, long, short in Morse code for *love* and then long, short, long, short, long, short, long. *My Kat.* She would flick back long, long, short, long, long, long, short, long, long. *Meow.*

Their love was a bright shiny thing that even when hidden under a bushel managed to cast light out from underneath. Kate's skin glowed even more than her pregnant mother's. Peter's step was light, his head fuzzy. People notice these things. This was not helped by the fact that our young couple let their guard down. It was inconvenient and costly to smuggle Kate into the hotel in Pennant Hills. They could never have met at Kate's house with her mother laying bloated on the couch, her engagement and wedding rings grinding on the swollen flesh trapped between them. In this state Kate's mother's sixth sense was heightened so that Kate's every move was known. Even too many trips to the bathroom were commented upon as her inevitable time of the month threw the household into turmoil.

Peter's rented flat upstairs in the house of a family friend became their refuge. At first careful to show up just as dusk dimmed her features, but her need for privacy was never as strong as his. There were no consequences for her, or at least she thought there weren't, until one day she was fronted up brazenly in her school uniform and sat on the footpath outside waiting for him to come home.

Peter's bed was all dark wood with a zigzagged bedspread in shades of green. Whenever they lay in it Kate imagined she was in a boat, floating on the sea unable to see anything but water all around. That was the way she liked it. If Kate saw any obstacles, like Peter's shirts all ironed and hung up in a row, her boat could move forward and create waves to capsize those shirts and they would float on the surface of the sea, destined to wash up then dry, crinkled with salt, on some distant shore.

One day they were lying on the bed, watching as two flies had sex in their love puddle. Peter was twisting her hair into a coil like a snake. He reached for the necklace that she always wore, pulling the charm from the back of her neck around to the front. He leaned up on his elbow to get a better look.

"It's an apple?" said Peter. And if it had been anything else he could not have sounded more shocked.

"My grandmother gave it to me." Kate said it defensively, as if excusing the small gold charm that hung between her breasts. She hid it in her fist, embarrassed about the cheap Avon necklace. She didn't realise that Peter was not shocked about the gold, but that he had always imagined it to be a locket shaped like a heart with a picture inside. Perhaps one of him.

"Did you hear about what happened to Anna?" Peter was learning to sidestep also.

"Who's Anna?" Jealous.

"You know Anna. She teaches English, or taught English…"

"Miss Leach?"

He laughed. "Yes," he said tickling her nose with her hair. "Miss Leach."
"It was the funniest thing. Our whole class went crazy. Little Michael was
singing 'Twist and Shout' and we all got up and danced. Michael Ballins
and Frances were all over each other, even though Michael is really in love
with me, of course. And then Bubble Bum just walked out of the room."

"Bubble Bum?" Deadpan.

"Yeah," Kate laughed. "Have you seen Miss Leach's bum? We all call her
that. Anyway, she completely flipped her lid. She's gone for good. Everyone
says so."

Peter sat up then, dropping Kate's hair so that it unravelled from its coil.
He sat with his back to her on the bed.

"What?" What?

"It's not funny," he said, standing up and pulling his pants back on. For
a moment he reminded Kate of her father. "You should be ashamed."

Kate shoved her school dress over her naked body and left. More than one
curtain shifted to get a better view of Peter chasing Kate down the street.
For he was young too, remember and, like Kate, younger than he knew.
She heard his footsteps behind her and slowed, letting him catch her. She
knew how to exploit being a damsel in distress. Perhaps it came naturally
to her? Perhaps she had learnt it from the fairy tales her father read her as
a child, sitting beside her on the pink bedspread. She heard Peter's breath,
ragged with emotion, and when he gripped her shoulders and turned her
around to face him, his chest rose and fell more than the short run up the
street warranted.

The neighbours watched him say something, begging with her perhaps?
They saw her straighten her collar, never taking her eyes of his. She did up
her buttons. Pulled up her socks. He handed her something. Was it an elastic
band? Kate pulled her hair into a swift ponytail and then finding nothing
left to do with her arms she tried to hug Peter right there on the street. He
took a step back, avoiding her arms. But the neighbours saw. They saw her
trying to hug him and they saw him avoiding the hug. That is all they saw

but not all they knew. From those two simple actions, the lean in of the hug and the step back from Peter they knew. And they were more than willing to share their insights with anyone who would listen. People listened and added their own opinions, then generously passed the story on. Precious snippets of Peter's private life had trickled back to his bosses by the time he finished work the next day.

But we are racing ahead of ourselves now, aren't we? Tomorrow is such a long way away. Tomorrow never comes or so they say. Let's follow Kate for a while, shall we? Let's follow her as she runs back to her own house, past her fat mother who was taking up too much of the hallway for Kate to slip past unnoticed.

Let's watch Kate standing in the doorway, scanning her bedroom. Her white wooden bedhead matched her bedside table and her dressing table. Chosen for her when she was a baby. A picture of a ballerina hung on the wall. It had been there forever. Next to it was a wall hanging that showed *Little Bo Peep* feeding chickens. It said, *the nice things you do return to you a thousand-fold.*

"Bull crap," Kate said and ripped it from the wall. She threw it out into the hallway where it landed with a soft plop on the carpet. The ballerina followed. That was better.

"Kate, what's going on?"

"Nothing, Mum. Just cleaning out my room." Voice steady. Good.

Kate pulled open the top drawer of her bedside table. In it was the *Cleo* she had stolen from the Carroll's, a Bible, and her copy of *The Crucible*. She tried to slam the drawer shut but the high-quality woodwork slid neatly and silently back into place. She wrenched open the next drawer and started pulling out her underwear and throwing it on the floor.

"Here, use these. Don't just throw everything out into the hallway. It is too difficult for me to bend down now," her mother said, rubbing her huge belly as if Kate was so stupid that she wouldn't realise why her mother couldn't bend down.

Kate snatched the rubbish bags from her mother and started shoving her underwear into one of them.

"Don't throw out all those. They still fit you, surely."

"I'm not a little girl anymore Mum. Or haven't you noticed?"

Her mother sighed and left Kate to banish anything that reminded her of her suddenly departed childhood. Her favourite Barbie doll, which had survived a previous childhood cull, was rammed head-first into her childish underwear. Photos with her friends on her dresser were ripped in half. Her favourite picture of herself dressed as a princess for her seventh birthday party was crushed and trashed. Everything pink. Everything fluffy. She pulled clothes out of the wardrobe and books off her shelf. Every book with a pony on the cover had to go.

When she'd finished Kate stood in the centre of her room. The flannel flower Peter had given her stood everlasting in a china vase her grandmother had hand painted. Kate wondered what her grandmother would think of her now. On her bed was her old teddy she had slept with since her dummy had been taken from her on her first birthday. At first Teddy had been a poor substitute, but now he was worn thin from Kate's love. Teddy was hardly pink anymore; his colour had been washed out then faded by the sun when he was pegged by his ears on the clothesline to dry. He was barely even fluffy. Kate picked him up and squeezed his chest. He still squeaked softly if she put her thumbs in the exact right spot.

Kate threw the bear into a bag and dragged the two bags, one with each hand, out through the lounge room.

"Leave that Kate. Your father can carry it out for you."

"I can manage."

Kate dragged the bags down the kitchen stairs to the bin at the side of the house. There was no way the bags would fit inside so she dumped them on the ground and headed back inside. Kate stopped with her hand on the screen door and went back to the garbage bags. She looked at them sitting on the ground for a moment before dropping to her knees and retrieving her teddy. She pulled him so that his nose was just out of the bag. Even discarded teddy bears need to breathe.

Back inside her mother was watching TV and Kate was pretty sure it was going to be cheese on toast for dinner again. She was hungry so she sat down in front of the television to wait, staring at the screen. The news was on and they were showing Elvis's grave. This was the first time the public were allowed to see it. People had brought wreaths shaped like lightning bolts and guitars. Crowds of people were crying. Kate looked at her mother and saw snail trails of tears running down her bloated cheeks. Kate let out a sob, but she wasn't crying for Elvis. She was crying for her mother's lost beauty. She cried for her own wretched childhood that clung to her and refused to fall. She cried for Teddy out in the garbage bag, scared of the dark. Kate ran outside and rescued Teddy, and if she hadn't run back through the lounge room so fast, she would have seen her mother smiling through her tears as she watched Kate run past with Teddy under her arm, just like she had when she was a little girl.

Kate didn't turn the light on as she stumbled to her bed across the piles of junk on her floor. She lay on top of her bed, still in her uniform, and looked at the ceiling. She was too scared to send the signal to Peter in case he ignored her, so she hugged Teddy to her to protect him from the night. As her eyes adjusted to the dark, she held him out in front of her. Teddy's orange eyes glistened in the darkness as if he had been crying too. Kate threw him across the room where he lay, like her, staring at the ceiling.

That's when she saw the light in her peripheral vision. Short, long, short, short, long, long, long, short, short, short, long, short. Morse code for love, and then long, long, long, short, long, long, long, short, long, short, long, long. My Kat.

Kate jumped from her bed to send her own signal, flicking her lights back. Short, long, short, short, long, long, long, short, short, short, long, short. Love.

Kate laid smiling at the ceiling in the dark. She fell asleep still in her uniform and dreamt of running through a maze, up and down tunnels until she woke exhausted and sweaty before another school day had even started. Kate didn't feel like showering, so she just put her socks back on that she had thrown behind the door the day before. Kate looked in the mirror and wished she could throw the uniform into the rubbish too. Not long to go now, she thought, as she pouted at her reflection. She pulled the dress behind her, trying to give it some shape and then gave up and let it hang limp as a rag to her knees. Kate looked at the schoolgirl in the mirror with envy. Her reflection was beautiful and innocent. She never said the wrong thing.

"I hate you," Kate told her, but her reflection merely mouthed the words in response. Kate could tell that her reflection hated her back and she wished this quiet version of herself would come out of the mirror and take over her life, go to school for her, all quiet and diligent while Kate stayed at home and read magazines and dreamt of Peter. Her reflection wouldn't cause any trouble. She'd go to class and sit with Kate's friends and then come straight home leaving plenty of time for her homework.

"Come on. Just for a day. Do it for me?" she asked of her reflection and then Kate pounced on the glass and kissed it with such passion and ferocity two circles of steam showed where her nostrils had been. Her mouth was open, and her tongue warmed the glass in circles until she pulled away and kissed her own mirrored lips as if it was her first time.

Finally, Kate stepped away from the mirror and picked up her necklace from the dresser and put it on, hiding the apple pendant, as always, in the left cup of her bra.

*

That day Kate played at being a good girl. She was a good girl, wasn't she? She sat up straight in class. She didn't giggle with her friends when Mr Gilmore got so excited by his verb conjugations a spray of spittle flew in a lovely arc though the air and became lost between the freckles of a girl in the front row. She ignored her peers and listened to her teacher. That was the mature thing to do in such a situation, wasn't it? She did up her top button and straightened her hated Peter Pan collar. Her pulled-up socks showed stripes of dirt that had collected in the creases. She hoped Mr Guard would not notice when she went through the gate on the way home. If he looked at her closely, she didn't notice. She may have been wearing the same clothes that she had slept in, but her hair was neat. Her shoes had been shined. She was invisible. Or so she thought.

That evening Kate was in her bedroom when the phone rang in the hallway outside. It wasn't safe for Peter to call her and Kate had no interest in anyone else. Not that that stopped other boys from calling. Pestering her when they were drunk. Even the kid with the bowl cut had dared to call her house. Once. She heard her mother groan as she hauled herself off the couch. Her heavy footsteps came closer.

"Hello. Minola residence. Leah speaking. Who? Michael?"

Kate stopped cutting a yellow chiffon dress out of a Cleo magazine so she could hear.

"I'll just get her." And then, "Katherine, it's for you. I'll lay out the fabric. Don't talk for too long."

"Who is it?"

"They just said Michael. I am not sure which one," her mother whispered then, "if it is Little Michael be nice to him. He is a nice boy."

Kate rolled her eyes. "With a rich daddy."

"Katherine!"

Katherine took the phone from her and held it to her ear.

"Kat, is that you? It's me. Peter."

"Oh!" He was ringing her at home!

"Kat. I need to talk to you. The party at Kate Noble's. I know I promised I'd go with you, but I think it's too soon."

Vomit rose in Kate's throat. "Too soon for what?"

"For us."

"What do you mean?"

"Kate. You will have only just finished school. You won't have received your results yet. You won't have graduated yet. Let's wait until you are eighteen." Prepared speech.

"What? For what? Why?"

100

"It's better that way. Listen Kat, I know it is ridiculous. But once you are eighteen the rules change."

"I don't care about the rules. I care about you."

"I care about you too and that's why we need to wait. It's only a couple of months Babe. It's only until your birthday. By Easter we will be together eating Easter eggs in the main street of Beecroft."

"Mmm." Tears.

"Listen Kat. I know you're disappointed. I can't make it up to you, but I can make it not seem so bad."

"How?"

"I give you permission to go to the party with Michael Ballins."

"What!! He's gross. And he's going out with Frances."

"But he loves you … you can tell the way he looks at you." Sidestep. "It makes me jealous as hell."

"Really?"

"Sure thing, babe. I will know you are at the party with him and it will break my heart."

"Aren't you coming at least?"

"I'm not sure I could handle it. Watching you two dancing together."

"I wouldn't do anything with him!"

"You'd better not. I love you so much it is not funny. Just having this conversation makes me feel sick and I promise that once this ridiculousness is over, I will shout it from the rooftops that I love you."

"The rooftops of Beecroft?"

"Yes. If there was a bloody pub here, I would sing about it at the main bar. As it is, I will sing all the way down the arcade and past the library and past all the manicured bloody gardens right up to your parents' house where I will knock at the door and tell your father that I love you and there is nothing anyone can do about it."

"Lights at nine?" Stay calm. Act mature.

"Yes, lights at nine. My Kat."

Kate went to the bathroom to wash her face. She looked at herself in the mirror. That made her cry again, so she scrubbed at her face until she was sure there was no evidence in the mirror of her crying. Adults don't cry.

The news was on in the lounge room. A plane had crashed near Mexico killing all thirteen people on board. Kate reminded herself never to get on a plane with thirteen people on it. She wondered if it was a sign. Her mother sighed as she eased herself onto the floor, bending herself backwards until her huge stomach triangulated into a hard lump. She panted. Kate imagined sitting on a plane next to Ita Buttrose. They would both be wearing white pantsuits.

"Which Michael was it?"

"Ballins."

Kate's mother frowned. "That's the third time that boy has rung tonight." Kate raised her eyebrows.

"He rang when you were on your way home from school. What's wrong? Have you been crying? What did he want?"

"He wants me to go to Kate Noble's party with him after speech night."

"Isn't he seeing Frances Reynolds?"

"Not anymore because I said yes." Deadpan.

"Frances is your friend."

"I need a date. He asked me. I said yes. It's not my fault he asked me." Don't push it.

Her mother just patted at the fabric again until the edges met horizontally.

"Are you sure you bought enough material Katherine? This doesn't look like much."

Her mother's fingers were like rakes, clawing at the fabric. And then before she could answer, "I think we should pin the selvages before we lay the pattern out."

Her mother filled her mouth with pinheads and Kate couldn't help but imagine kissing her and being stabbed by all the points sticking out from her mother's mouth. "It will make the fabric easier to work with this way. Satin is so slippery." Her mother spoke out the side of her mouth like a cowboy smoking a pipe and one by one took a pin from her lips to pin the holey edges together.

"Oh no, I should have come with you to get the material. This is nowhere near enough."

"Yeah, I got a yard and a half. That's what it says on the back of the pattern. I can fit a front and a back across."

Kate grabbed at the tissue paper and threw it roughly onto the satin. See, it all fits."

Kate handed the pattern envelope to her mother which showed three versions of the same dress. Dress A was long with puffed sleeves. Dress B was short and with puffed sleeves. Dress C was both short and sleeveless.

"You are doing dress A." It was a statement not a question.

"No, dress C."

"Oh," her mother paused, searching for tact but not finding any. "It's not really very nice."

"Why?"

"It's just not really suitable…" Her mother's vocabulary was twenty years behind Kate's.

"Why not?"

"Well, it shows your legs." Flustered.

"That's okay. I shave them."

"Since when?" Voice rising.

"Since I was twelve." Kate delivered it like the punchline to a joke that wasn't funny.

"Mrs Noble won't appreciate you dressing like that, especially if the boys start carrying on. She is already going out of her way to have the party at her house."

"It's fine. I'll wear stockings. Don't worry."

"Maybe we should add a few inches, just in case."

"In case of what?"

"Michael might try to take advantage."

"That's what I'm hoping for." Singing.

"Kate!"

"I'm joking Mum. I don't even like him, but Kate Noble is going with Little Michael, of course. I need to go with someone. I'll wear tights. Thick tights. It'll be fine."

She didn't tell her mother about the high-heeled boots she had saved her babysitting money to buy. Or about the day she had wagged school and Peter had rung in sick to work and they had caught the train to the city together, holding hands all the way. The freedom of it all. They pretended they were married.

"Oh, you really do like the other Michael? Now that he is all grown up?"

"Sure," said Kate to appease her mother.

"He seems like a nice boy. His father is a dentist."

"If his father was a garbage collector, would he still seem like a nice boy?" Look me in the eye.

"It's so hot in here," said her mother. She pulled the buttons of her blouse open and sat cross-legged on the carpet. She looked like a fat primary school child with her huge belly obscuring her lap.

"Mum!"

Kate looked up at the television. They were playing a rerun of *Number 96*. Abigail leaned forward and her boobs looked like they were going to explode out of her blouse. And the telly. *Je t'aime,* thought Kate.

"Are you sure you don't want me to add a little to the hemline? Maybe some pale blue lace? That would look nice? Just to cover the knee. I just think with this length you are putting yourself in a possible situation, you know."

"You want me to look like a tablecloth? Besides, you're the one with no shirt on."

On the television, Abigail provocatively unbuttoned her blouse and dropped it to the floor. Kate stared at Abigail's body. I look exactly like that, she thought, and knew then that everything would be alright. Kate's mother rubbed her fingernails over the huge mound of her stomach and left jagged white lines scratched into her red flesh.

"Let this be a lesson to you." Wink.

"Yeah, thanks Mum." Eye roll.

Abigail and some bloke were in bed together. Kate saw herself in Abigail. She looked at her mother, her fat neck and the blue veins that ran all over the place just under the skin of her breasts and stomach. She looked at the blue fabric of her dress and thought about what Peter had said about her going to the dance with Michael Ballins. Abigail sighed *darling oh darling* and Kate felt like she was surrounded by sex, in her mother, the consequences of sex, and her dress, which was the promise of sex. She vowed to herself she would never have children. She would never allow her body to become distorted like that, with her veins showing as a map to nowhere just under her skin. She remembered what Little Michael had said that night behind the Scout Hall, "Twice as hard for twice as long makes twice as many!"

Kate let her fringe fall over her face. Abigail was panting and tossing her head from side to side until her face couldn't be seen and she could have been anyone. She could have been Kate.

Her mother pinned the pattern to the fabric, measuring and remeasuring to ensure that the centre line was perfectly on the grain. Both of them pretended not to notice Abigail groaning on the television.

"You don't want the fabric to swing at the wrong angle," said her mother, "or you'll be picking the dress out from between your legs all night." Kate only heard *between your legs*.

Abigail's groans turned to whimpers. To kisses. *Touch me, darling. Touch me.* Kate tucked her hair behind her ears and said in unison with her mother, "You pin it. Then you tack it. Then you sew it." They said it loudly, in the exaggerated nasal tone of the sewing teacher at school, trying to drown out the television. Miss Fance was an old maid who had taught Kate's mother and was now doomed to teach the next generation, the students always being worse than the ones who had preceded them. She often advised the girls that they should be "working on a little something for their glory boxes." Kate imagined Miss Fance's glory box, big enough to fill her bedroom. It would be overflowing with doilies smelling of mothballs that had never shown their glorious selves to the daylight, rather had lain pristine in their virginal state all these years, just like Mrs Fance herself.

Miss Fance had a trim body, trim meaning older lady for slim, with breasts that looked like they'd been carved from stone. Kate imagined Miss Fance's body under her clothes as a hard, petrified version of a young Miss Fance, with only the crêpe skin of her face and neck hanging like old lace above it. Kate hoped that time would petrify her own body also. It was better than the alternative. The television seemed silent. Kate relaxed.

"Penny for your thoughts?"

It was more of a demand than a question and Kate knew she had one of two choices, either not to say anything and to endure relentless prodding and poking through her mind by her mother, or to make something up. Abigail gasped. Usually, Kate was good at this but today something wasn't right. The television and her mother's stomach had put her off and the words just slipped out of her mouth before she could stop them.

"I want to go on the pill."

Abigail gasped again. Louder this time. Her mother shrieked and started scurrying backwards with her arms on the carpet behind her like a crab. Kate realised that the bond of sewing together did not bind them in all things. But she had already known that, yet her mother was still shrieking, and her father came running in from the study. Kate realised that the blue satin that matched her eyes had become stained under the mass that was her mother, with liquid fingers spreading across it.

The slow motion of Kate's mind did not keep up with what was happening in front of her so when her mother shouted, "It's time," to her father and her father squealed, "But it's too early," she thought for a moment they were discussing her intended use of the pill. The stained fingers on the fabric moved towards her.

Luckily for Kate her accidental words were lost in the commotion. But they would be remembered later.

Before Kate knew it, her father was backing the Volvo out of the driveway. Her mother lay on the back seat with a towel *between her legs*. Kate was left alone in the house that, except for the television, was silent. Unsure of what to do she studied for her science test, remembering stamens as flower penises and the stylus as the vagina. So easy, she thought. With no one to tell her to go to bed she changed the channel to catch the end of the *The Box*, half watching and half reading her mother's *Women's Weeklies* and *Women's Days*, wishing she had the latest *Cleo*, or even a *Dolly* magazine. Her mother disapproved of both, of course. Kate read an article in *Women's Day* about sex at work. She was surprised people had sex at work. She thought of her father going into the office every day and coming home so late. "Lots of numbers just begging to be added up," he always said to her mother. She would go quiet on him sometimes. Surely her father couldn't be doing *that*? Who would want to do *that* with him? In his office with the lights on? He was short and bald. He had a patch of hair on the back of each shoulder. A shiver ran down her spine.

"Gross." Aloud. Alone.

The article said that women were more likely to get the sack when their workmates found out about the affair and men were more likely to be congratulated. She wondered then whether the rumours were true about Mr Mason and Miss Leach. She had left the school. He was still there. She breathed in and found that she couldn't breathe back out. Was it true? Could it be?

She read on: *"Women are placed on the marketplace with fixed physical values—so much for good legs, so much for good breasts, so much for long blonde hair."*

Kate smiled. She had all those, so she thought she'd be fine. She was wrong. Women are also judged by their behaviour. And Kate's behaviour wasn't quite right. She thought she was being so sophisticated by sleeping with a grown man, but she was just a silly little girl. Silly and naive. This would be her undoing.

Kate flicked through the rest of the magazine. There was an article on exercise for lazy girls but didn't bother to read it. Another article was on four minutes that could make or break a marriage. She started reading, thinking of Peter. It said to be nice when your husband comes home from work.

"Boring." Loud. Alone.

She flipped through the magazine and stopped at a Bonds advertisement. There was the usual Bonds guy, all muscular and blonde on the beach. He reminded her of Peter. There was a crowd of other blokes behind him. Dark haired, blonde, light brown hair, and white hair. All tanned, all muscular. But the first Bond guy, the real Bond guy was the one looking at her. Kate knew she could have any of those blokes, but she would have the first one. The original. That's the one she wanted.

She picked up the scissors from her unfinished dress and cut him out, not caring that she was blunting her mother's good fabric scissors on paper. He looks like Peter, she thought.

"No. No. Your name is Brad," she said stroking his face. She looked then at the blokes in the background. They held a banner that said six colours. Six colours. Six men, thought Kate. Six men all for me. One of them was wearing sunglasses and a pink singlet. She cut him out. "You can be mine too sweetheart," she said.

Kate tossed the other men aside and stood up then and went into the hallway. She pulled the Yellow Pages out of the drawer of the telephone table and opened it to the B's. She found his number easily.

"Hello." Tired.

"Can I speak to Michael please?"

"It's late Frances." Irritated.

"It's not Frances. It's Kate Minola."

"Oh? Kate?"

"Sorry I'm ringing so late. Mum just went into hospital. I wanted to tell Michael."

"Oh Kate. That's lovely news. Make sure you keep us posted. I'll call Michael." Then louder, "Michael it's Kate. Her mother has just gone into hospital to have the babies. She wanted to tell you."

"Hi Kate." Surprised.

"Hi. Do you want to come to Kate Noble's party with me?"

"Yes. No. I mean, I'm going with Fran." You know that. What's going on?

"You are coming with me now."

"Will you tell Frances for me?" Voice rising.

"Sure."

"You wanna go out with me?"

"Maybe. I've got to go. Mum's in hospital. Thanks Michael. I really like you, you know." Voice flat.

"I really like you too. So much!" Excited. Sucking in air.

The poor boy had no idea he was being used, even though Kate barely spoke to him in the lead up to the party. He walked around the school with a smile on his face and such twinkles in his eyes that he didn't even see Frances's hair turn greasy and her face spotty as she pined for him. But I am jumping ahead of myself, for Kate is still home alone and the night is still young. She picked up her two paper men and went into her room, almost missing the light show. She got to her room just in time to see the final flashes. Long, short, long, short, long, short, long. My Kat.

She flicked back long, long, short, long, long, long, short, long, long. Meow.

Kate kept her light on after that. She couldn't sleep. She imagined babies emerging from her mother. The excitement gave her energy. She thought about ringing Frances, but it was late. She couldn't risk going over to Peter's. He'd made that clear enough. She would have to wait for the morning. Kate went back into the lounge room, tiptoeing as if afraid of waking someone up. She pinned the pattern to the fabric and cut it out, even shorter now to avoid the stain. She looked at the clock and it was only ten o'clock, so she pulled her mother's heavy sewing machine out of the laundry and put it on the coffee table. The television was replaying the plane crash in Mexico.

"Stuff Miss Fance, she thought and committed the cardinal sin of sewing without tacking. The dress didn't take long to make. There wasn't much to it, after all. Kate pulled her school uniform off in the lounge room and without the distraction of her mirror it didn't take long for her to undress. She pulled her new party dress over her head but then as she struggled with the zipper, she caught her reflection in the lounge room window and that slowed her down. She ran up the hall to her bedroom with delight. She pulled the white leather boots out from under her bed and fingered the buttons that ran from her ankle almost to her thigh. She forced her feet into them, buttoning them up high.

In front of the mirror, she saw that her dress was so sexy that the sun wouldn't rotate around the earth at the party, it would rotate around her dress and as the night came the moon and the stars would follow it. Peter would look up into the night sky, wondering what she was doing, and he would see the shifting universe and know that he had to come for her. He would carry her out through the doorway in front of her school friends, just like the Bonds men carried the banner. Everyone would be gobsmacked. What a wonderful word.

"Gobsmacked," Kate said out loud. Alone.

She turned around to see the back of the dress and did the arms in the air test. The satin just covered her bottom cheeks. Perfect. Kate unzipped the dress and took it off, laying it over the chair next to her bed. She hummed, *It's not what you do. It's the way that you do it to me.* There was a knock at the door. Kate looked at her watch. It was past midnight.

"Ah!" Shrieking. She had two brothers. She had two sisters. She had one of each. Two baby siblings to love, love, love. She ran in her underwear and boots to the door and flung it open.

"Kate." Softly.

"Mr Carroll!" Hiding her body behind the door.

"I saw your light was still on. Are you okay?" Eyes sucking her in.

"Yes." Closing the door.

"Are you sure?" Shoulder in the doorway. "I saw your parents leave hours ago." Mr Carroll was standing in the kitchen.

Kate ran up the hall to her bedroom and pulled her nightie over her head. Too short. Mr Carroll was standing in her bedroom doorway.

"I was just going to bed. I'll turn the lights off." Crap. Did that sound like an invitation?

"People who leave lights on are usually scared. Are you scared of the dark Kate?"

"Please go away."

"Your father rang. He asked me to check up on you."

"I'm fine." Kate flicked her light switch. On and off and on and off. How do you ask for help? Long, long, short, long, long, long, short, long, long. Meow. Long, long, short, long, long, long, short, long, long, long, long, short, long, long, long, short, long, long, long, long, short, long, long, long, short, long, long, long. Meow, meow, help!

"I think you should come and stay at our place."

"I'm fine."

"Or I could stop here."

"No."

The phone rang.

"That's Dad."

Kate ran for the hallway, but Mr Carroll didn't move. Her body rubbed against him, only her thin nightie between them.

"Kate. Are you okay?"

"Peter?"

"It's your father, Kate."

"Mr Carroll is here." Come home. I need you.

"Why?"

"Checking up on me."

Mr Carroll disappeared down the hallway.

"Dad, wait a second." Running to the kitchen door. Turning the lock.

"I'm back." Panting.

"Kate, what's going on? Do you have boys over?"

"No." Not yet. She smiled at the thought of Peter naked in her parents' bed. "Are they boys or girls or both? Like all mixed up? One of each?" Sidestep.

"The twins haven't been born yet."

"What? Why not?"

"Sometimes it takes a long time. It's Sunday. The doctor will be in early in the morning."

"Don't they just… what?"

"Kate. I will call in the morning. I'm going to stay here. I'll sleep in the Volvo. Are you all right there by yourself?"

"Why aren't you with Mum?"

"She's resting."

Kate felt tired. She leaned against the hallway wall.

"I want them to come out. Can I come to the hospital soon?"

"Tomorrow. I will come and pick you up. Goodnight Kate. Go to bed now."

"Goodnight Daddy." She hadn't called him that since she turned thirteen.

Kate looked into her bedroom. Teddy was back on her bed. Waiting for her. She wondered who had put him there. Peter hadn't flicked his light when she needed him. She went back to the lounge and picked up her Bonds men and ran back to her parents' bedroom, diving into the bed from the doorway. She hid under the heavy bedspread like she had when she was five. She closed her eyes and imagined all the Bonds men lining up for her.

"Take your turn guys." Peter hadn't flicked his lights back. "No queue jumping." He hadn't protected her. But Brad would. She was sure of that. The real Chesty Bonds man. He was her hero.

Kate slept then. She dreamt of a creature with four arms and four legs that slithered out of her mother like an octopus. It slithered off the hospital bed and onto Kate's lap. Kate tried to hug the creature thinking, "I must love my child," but the creature's arms grew tight around her body so that her arms were pinned to her sides. She twisted and kicked her legs until her mother yelled at her, "Kate, you can't hold the babies like that!" Kate wedged her toes in under the creature to pry it off her and it slid to the floor. There was a sound like glass shattering. She heard a baby's cries then and looked down onto the floor to see a tiny naked baby crying and bleeding in a bed of broken glass.

"Where's the other one?" her mother yelled, and Kate looked under the bed, but she couldn't find it. She woke up with a thin film of sweat on her skin. She picked up her Bonds men and tiptoed down the still-dark hallway and perched on the edge of the couch in the lounge room waiting for the day to begin. She kept the lights on and the television off so that Mr Carroll wouldn't notice that she was awake. It was cold and the Bonds men became limp in her sweaty fingers. She waited as the furniture in the room became more than dark shapes and the roses on the upholstery bloomed again. Kate waited for the hum of the Volvo, but it didn't come. The phone didn't ring.

*

At school, it was her second day without a shower and a clean uniform. The two Sues twisted into the science lab, arms around each other, singing, "It's the way you do it with Mr Mason. How do you want it with me? Do it. Do it."

Frances tried to put her hand in Michael Ballins' hand, but he pretended not to notice and fell to the back of the line with Kate. He didn't seem to notice Kate's matted hair and unironed uniform that she'd pulled from a pile near her door. He tried to put his arm around her, but Kate twisted out of it.

"I haven't told Frances yet."

"She doesn't know about us?"

"I'll tell her at lunch. Just act normal with her for now."

Kate sat at her usual desk next to Frances.

"What's going on with Michael?" The heart on Frances's sleeve was already broken.

"I dunno." Voice rising. Liar.

"He wouldn't hold my hand."

"Mr Mason was watching. Michael's already in trouble for having his hair too long." Cover up.

Kate looked up then at Mr Mason on his raised platform in front of the class, like a priest at the pulpit. He looked too sure of himself up there. Kate felt a desperate need to go up there and slap him in the face. Wipe off the half-smile that made all the girls fawn over him.

Mr Mason handed the test papers out himself instead of giving a bundle each to a couple of nobodies up the front to hand out like he usually did. Kate knew all the answers. They were somewhere in her head, but she was finding it hard to concentrate. She'd hardly slept. She kept thinking about the octopus-baby. She could still feel its tentacles on her skin. Kate wondered if the dream meant that her mother would have Siamese twins, stuck together by the bottom like those girls in Mexico. But even the thought of those twins couldn't get the feeling of Mr Carroll's slimy fingers off her chest. Or his eyes off her groin. And Peter, of course. Peter. She'd flashed the light when she needed a lifesaver, and he hadn't even noticed. Or had he? Had he noticed and ignored her? He didn't want to go to Kate Noble's party with her anymore. She realised then that Peter was weak. He couldn't take the weight.

Next to her Frances was drawing buds and leaves onto the flower diagram on page three of the test. Kate fell into a trance as Frances's test paper bloomed with flowers and tendrils of ivy wove their way around the caption boxes left for the answers.

"Kate, keep your eyes to yourself or you will find yourself with a fat red zero at the top of your page." Serious.

The rest of the class turned to stare. Kate looked up at Mr Mason. She looked him in the eye and raised her eyebrows. Up there on his teacher's platform like some kind of a god he should be able to see that Frances had just drawn flowers all over her test. Kate's face reddened.

"Carry on," ordered Mr Mason and Kate scratched *stamen* on the flower where the *stylus* should be. Her mind was all messed up. As she looked up at Mr Mason all she could see was Peter. The line of his bicep pushing its way through his shirt. His hair, just a little too long. The labels in front of her remained blank. She tried to draw a cover for *Afra*. She drew a belted jacked on her test, so the flower ended up on the lapel. But she couldn't even concentrate on that. Her pen began to draw fish. Elaborate angel fish with tails that curled and swirled about the page. She shaded the bubbles that floated from their mouths. Wistfully—that is the only word to describe it.

"Kate. Bring me your paper at once." Now.

Kate stood up, sweat sticking her school dress to the backs of her legs. She stumbled forwards, the desk in front of her crunching into her groin, causing pain that was surely as intense as a boy's. She pretended nothing had happened and continued up the front, her fish-covered paper in hand waiting for Mr Mason to show it as an example to the class. A bad example. But Mr Mason simply took the paper without a word and put it into a manila folder waiting on his desk. Kate stood there in front of him. They stared at each other.

"Return to your desk Kate. Obviously, you are having difficulty with your test. Perhaps you would like to finish it in here at lunchtime?"

Kate turned and walked out of the classroom.

"Kate." Come back.

Mr Mason footsteps were right behind her. Kate turned on him. She didn't want him to say anything, to ask anything.

"Mum's in hospital. I have to go." She ran. She ran past the safe places. The girl's bathrooms. The library. Sickbay. She didn't know where she was going until she had fled the gates of the school and continued down to the main street of Beecroft. Soon Kate found herself at a bus stop fingering her babysitting money in her pocket. She would go and visit her mother.

*

The modern buildings of the Northshore Private Hospital impressed Kate. She imagined Ita Buttrose had her babies there. Kate stood in the entrance and redid her ponytail and wrapped a piece of her hair around the band to cover it in case she ran into Ita in the corridor. Her father was in the foyer waiting to use a public phone.

"Dad?"

"Kate, I've been trying to ring you all morning." He looked at her unironed uniform and matted hair. "You went to school?"

"I had a science test."

"How did you get here? Did Mrs Carroll drive you in?"

"No, I caught the bus. Bus and train. No train and bus." Laughs.

"You are so grown up. So responsible and independent. You are going to be a great help for your mother." Proud.

"Where is she? Did they come out yet?"

"Kate, you have one baby brother, and one beautifully sweet baby sister."

"Are they, you know, okay?" See she *was* growing up. "Do they have names?"

"Not quite yet. We weren't expecting them for quite a few weeks."

"Can I name them? I'll call them Jack and Jill. Jack and Jill went up the hill!" Excited.

"Come and congratulate your mother." Laughing.

"You can name them whatever you want. I'm still going to call them Jack and Jill."

Kate's father led her into a room where everything was the same sick green. The walls, the cotton blanket. Even her mother's face. Her mother was lying on the bed with her eyes closed. It all came back to her then. Mr Carroll in her bedroom. Peter wanting her but not wanting her. Inviting Frances's boyfriend to the party and stuffing up the science test. Lying to her friend. Becoming a sister, not once, but twice. Kate flung herself at her mother.

"Don't jump on her Kate, she's resting. She's had a difficult night."

Her mother's eyes rolled awake.

"Ah Kate, that hurts!"

Kate moved back. Hurt. She looked around the room for the babies.

"Where are they?"

"Take her. I need sleep." Slurred words.

Kate followed her father down the corridor an impossibly long way from her mother's room. They looked through a large window into a room lined with babies trapped under tightly tucked white blankets. They were all asleep. Some had crazy hair like clowns and others were bald. They all had red screwed up faces, some like old men and others like pixies. One poor thing already had a beaked nose that outweighed all of its other features. Nose first. Baby second.

A nurse looked up when she saw Kate's father and wheeled two small cots to the window so they could get a closer look. Cardboard labels stuck to the head of each cot said Minola male and Minola female. Two perfect, pure cherubs.

"Oh Daddy. They are so cute. Can I hold them?" Jumping.

"Oh no. It's their rest time. Your mother hasn't even seen them yet. You are lucky. Come on. I need a shower. I'll take you home and we can eat ice cream for dinner."

Kate held her father's hand as they walked out to the car park.

*

The next day Mr Guard was waiting for the students as they filed into the school gates in their gender coded uniforms. Grey for males. Green for females. As soon as the students got off their busses, or for the lucky ones getting out of their parents' cars, saw him they stopped and hitched up their socks and did up their top buttons. Boys trying to get away with hair that covered their collars walked bravely forwards with their chins pressed against their chests to make their hair appear shorter.

On any normal day Mr Guard fulfilled his Deputy's position with vigour while the principal sat in his air-conditioned office. On any other day Mr Guard forced students to do push-ups in the dust for these indiscretions, but today was different. Today Mr Guard was in his element. He was hunting for someone. Kate walked towards the gate and stopped when she saw Mr Guard waiting for her. It was the third day she hadn't showered. She had avoided the mirror that morning like an enemy, knowing her reflection would show blotches and blemishes that she didn't want to see. As Kate joined the huddle that were pulling up their socks and smoothing down their collars, Mr Guard's gaze honed in on her from the gateway and everyone knew that today she was his prey.

"Katherine Minola. I *want you* in my office immediately." No nonsense.

"I…" What?

"Now." Now.

And so, poor Kate was forced to follow Mr Guard around the quadrangle to his office. She kept her eyes on the back of his square head, thinking of Miss Leach and the ambulance. Mr Guard opened his empty office door and waited while she stepped inside, her stomach watery. She had expected others to be there. Little Michael at least. He had started the whole thing.

"Take a seat Katherine."

Kate sat opposite Mr Guard waiting for him to speak. Everyone had sung. It wasn't just her. Was Mr Guard interviewing them one at a time, so they'd dob each other in? He twiddled a pen in his fingers.

"Close the door, Katherine."

Kate got up and closed the door. Mr Guard kept his eyes on her chair and so didn't look at her again until she was seated back on it.

"Katherine, it has come to my attention that you have been frequenting the Epping Motel late at night for the purpose of experimenting with sex." He delivered that line in the same bland style he would a dictation.

"I thought..." Flushed face. Sick stomach. Silence.

"You thought what?"

"I thought this was about Miss Leach. Is she alright?" Attempted sidestep.

"This is about you Katherine. What do you have to say about these allegations?"

"Allegations? You mean accusations?" Smart arse.

"If you like."

"I don't know what you are talking about."

"Do you have a boyfriend, Miss Minola?"

"I don't know. Do I?" Oh Kate. Shut up!

"I think you *think* you do Miss Minola, but I am here to advise you that you don't."

"I don't have a boyfriend?" What?

"No, you don't."

Be the girl in the mirror Kate. For once. Please. "That's right. I don't."

Mr Guard was still playing with the pen. He slid it through his fingers and then tapped its end on his desk, clicking the point in and out before letting it slide through his fingers again. Kate picked up a pencil from the desk in front of her.

"Who were you at the motel with Katherine?"

"When? I wasn't?" Voice rising.

"Which one is your answer then?"

"What?" Higher.

"Pardon me."

"Pardon me." Echo.

"It depends on when? Or you weren't at the motel at all?"

"I weren't. I mean I wasn't."

"Why did you ask when, then?"

Kate held the pencil under her palms, rolling it backwards and forwards on the desk. She stopped talking.

"Miss Minola? You haven't answered the question. It seems as though you were at the motel, it is just a question of when." Statement.

Silence

"Miss Minola?"

Kate smiled slightly. Her mother played this game with her father all the time. Refused to talk. It sent him off in a fit, slamming coffee mugs on the kitchen counter and shoving the leftovers into the garbage compacter. She picked the pencil up in her fist and let it fall through her fingers before tapping it on the desk and pushing the pencil back through. A parody that caused Mr Guard to grip his own pen tighter.

"You think you are very clever, don't you, Miss Minola. So far you have avoided answering these allegations."

Silence.

"I will ask you one more time. Have you been frequenting the Epping Motel with a male?"

Silence with a smile.

"That motel has a reputation that can easily transfer itself onto a young girl."

Silence.

"Alright then Miss Minola. Have it your way. I understand the delicacy of the situation. We have your best interests at heart. If you have been to the motel with a man, then put down the pencil. If you haven't, then keep holding it."

Kate remembered sitting next to a boy in primary school when another boy had leant over the table and stabbed him in his pudgy hand while they were colouring in. Kate had been surprised at the redness of his blood. He was too smelly to have such nice red blood.

Kate looked at Mr Guard and gripped the pencil in her fists until she was sure that the lead was going to break her skin. The pencil snapped. Mr Guard shifted in his seat and Kate knew that she had forced him to try another tack.

"Kate," he said. "I have just been speaking with Mr Mason. He is under the impression that you have a crush on him."

"Hah?" Her silence broke.

Mr Guard took a single piece of paper out of a manila folder and placed it on the desk in front of Kate. It was her science test. She saw the blazer with the flower on the lapel. The name *Afra* pencilled on the top. And the two angelfish. They were kissing. She hadn't thought about it when she had drawn them. But there it was right in front of her next to her flower with the stamen and the stylus in the wrong places. Mr Guard pulled the test away from Kate as she attempted to redress her mistake. Kate felt the overwhelming need to sleep. She imagined curling up under Mr Guard's desk next to his brown brogues and going to sleep.

She yawned. "Every student has a crush on Mr Mason."

"You admit to it then?"

Kate put both pieces of the pencil on the desk in front of her and closed her eyes. She was back in the hotel room, lying on those stale sheets.

Can I call you Kat?

"Mr Mason is very embarrassed by this situation. His professionalism is beyond compare and as a student of this school we expect the same courtesy from our students."

Make me purr Mr Peter.

"I don't have a crush on him," said Kate, her fingers playing with the pencil, trying to connect the halves together like a jigsaw puzzle.

I can certainly try.

"You are not to approach Mr Mason out of class, or talk to him at any time, except in class where you will behave appropriately at all times. You will only answer a question if it has been asked of you."

"I don't have a crush on Mr Mason."

Meow.

"Kate, Mr Mason is an attractive man, but he is your teacher. You will meet someone soon enough, get married and have children."

"I'm not going to have children." Disgusted.

Meow.

"You think that now but when the right man comes along you will see it differently. You cannot imagine how many young girls I have had sitting right where you are now, declaring that they won't marry or have children. Within two years of leaving school, they have all done just that."

"I'm going to be a journalist."

Prrr.

"Let me give you some advice. Educating a girl, beyond a certain point of course, is like pouring water into a good pair of shoes. Either the water runs out and it is a waste of water, or the water stays in and ruins the shoes. Don't get me wrong. I can understand why being at school at your age must be difficult. You are obviously more than ready to be a homemaker." Did he look at her boobs then? Surely not. Perhaps just for a fleeting moment. Showered or un-showered Kate's chest was certainly impressive. Who could blame him? "Now, head off to class. Try not to distract the boys and keep away from strange hotels." Case closed.

Kate stood up. She was amazed that she hadn't needed to cry. Mr Guard didn't care about Miss Leach and she seemed to have gotten away with being in the motel. She smiled to herself. Silence was her weapon, much better than crying. As for having a crush on Mr Mason. What a joke. As if? Besides, if she wanted Mr Mason, or anyone else, even Mr Guard, she could have him.

Kate made a mistake then. She flipped her hair at Mr Guard and coiled it over her shoulder to show off her high cheek bones. Her hip jutted a standard pose. Kate didn't realise that Mr Guard was immune to 16-year-old girls, no matter what they looked like or how they flipped their blonde locks. He'd gotten over that about six months into his teaching career. Quickly and painfully.

My Guard looked up from his desk.

"It goes without saying," he said in response to Kate's posing, "I will have to inform your parents."

"Of what?"

"The motel room, Katherine."

"No, no, please don't. My dad will kill me. Anyway. I was never at the Epping Motel."

"Your inappropriate behaviour with Mr Mason." Mr Guard tapped at the kissing fish. "Your unwillingness to discuss this matter in a mature manner forces me to act Katherine. You have left me with no other option than to call your father into this office." He paused for long enough for Kate to imagine her father standing beside her, the vein ticking in his neck. "I understand this is a very busy time for your family, however," his thick fingers tapped at the fish again, "I think your father needs to see this in person."

Kate froze. Her hip still jutted out and her hair was still flipped over her shoulder exposing her swan's neck. Her swan's neck that displayed a perfectly rounded and perfectly purple love bite.

"Sit back down Katherine. I think we have a lot to discuss, don't you?"

Mr Guard had the last laugh, as he always did. He always cracked the code of these kids. They had a fear and tapping into that fear was the way to break them. Not being Daddy's little girl anymore was Katherine Minola's fear. So simple it made him want to laugh.

Jack

I am still prepared, even today, to say that Ferriby Private Hospital was a unique facility. Jack built that place himself. He really pulled himself up by the bootstraps as they say. Critics have accused Jack of using the place as a money-making operation. I am here to tell you that those people know little about either making money or about Jack Grafton. There were fifteen beds at the hospital, hardly enough to make a fortune. Not that that is proof of Jack's intention, but I can offer you proof. Jack only prescribed Slumber Therapy for those patients he truly believed would benefit from it. Those fifteen beds at the hospital were not always full. If Ferriby was a money-making exercise the place would have been full.

Ferriby was truly a lovely little place, a redesigned old cottage. I am sure the look of it put anxious patients at ease when they first arrived. It didn't look at all like a hospital. There were white roses out the front as if it were someone's home. I think the premises went well with Jack's philosophy that Slumber Therapy was a holiday for the brain. He knew how to relieve patients' anxiety. We were colleagues, you see, as well as good friends, so I know how Ferriby worked.

"Don't worry," Jack would say to new patients when they arrived. "You just need a good rest."

It is true that Jack was building his own hospital. He was one of those amazing people who are gifted academically but also practically. Often when one of the nursing staff needed to ring Jack at home his wife would say, "Sorry, Jack is up a ladder at the moment rewiring our electrics," or, "Sorry, Jack is in the middle of re-tiling the bathroom."

Jack was of the belief, as were many of his colleagues, myself included, that mental illness was a physical condition. We met many patients who had been through the 'talking cures' for years with no results. You can't talk somebody out of a broken leg, so what makes psychoanalysts so sure they can talk their patients out of mental disorders? You cannot talk a teenage girl out of anorexia any more than you can talk a young man out of depression. It is a physical problem. Slumber Therapy can restart the brain, just like rebooting a computer. We had some fantastic results. That is what everyone forgets.

Jack might not have done everything by the book. Unless it was Dr Grafton's book, of course, but that doesn't diminish what he achieved. In any other profession he would have been labelled as a larrikin but applauded anyway.

The problem people had with Jack is that he was a medical trailblazer. He was prepared to go where other doctors were too scared. But it wasn't as if he just made it all up. There was science behind it. We learnt about insulin coma treatment for curing schizophrenia at Broughton Hall, for instance. Everyone knows that during a coma the body heals itself. Everyone knows our cells regenerate when we are sleeping. If we initiated a coma in the same way as for a diabetic, through the oversupply of insulin, then it would only take a quick injection of glucose for the patient to wake up. They come back from the dead. As Jack said in one of his famous lectures at Ferriby, "If they went into coma, say, six hours, then you got them out again. When you woke them up, they were no longer schizophrenic. No thought disorder. No disease of the brain. No sign of the illness. They had come back."

I remember him saying this and it shocked people. It was unusual back then to hear a professional using such language, but Jack liked to speak in a way that the average person could understand. I distinctly remember him saying something to the effect of—*The only reason there is opposition for my coma clinic is because they have had the shit scared out of them.* Now while I personally would never use such colourful language, I did enjoy the looks on the faces of some of our colleagues when Jack, on occasion, did.

Kate

Kate took the towel off her curlers and applied foundation to her face in small brown blobs, as she had seen her mother do a thousand times. Two blobs on her forehead, one on each cheek, her chin, and the tip of her nose. She smoothed them across her face in a circular motion with her fingertips. She covered the tiny freckles that kissed her cheeks. She covered the pink tip of her nose. Kate poured some more foundation out of the glass jar and rubbed in another layer. If it could work for Frances, it could work for her. She covered the dark smudges under her eyes and then added a final layer until her features melted together in the mirror. Kate liked the monotone complexion that stared back at her. She scrolled open her favourite lipstick, frosted pink, but stopped short of applying it to her lips. Too girlish. She needed red.

Kate walked naked to her parents' room. She swung her hips like Abigail and sang softly to herself. Why won't you do it with me? *Je t'aime.* She stopped in front of her mother's dresser and sat on the stool. She said the words this time. She opened the top drawer and opened a lipstick, trying it out on the inside of her wrist. Too pink. Another. Too coral. Red, but not red enough. There were slashes of colour halfway up Kate's arm before she found the one that she wanted. Kate twisted the lipstick until the tip came all the way out and traced her lips. Blood red. Kate looked at her reflection in the mirror. She looked like herself, but not. Perfect.

It doesn't take long to get ready when you are young and confident and have a clear canvas to work with. Kate's skin was clear, no real blemishes of youth or wrinkles of age to disguise. No sunken flesh to hoist up into the silhouette of a mannikin and hold in place with elastic and straps. No witchy hairs to pluck out of her chin.

Dancing back to her own room Kate began taking the curlers out of her hair. She untangled it from the curler spikes and fluffed it around her face and then fluffed her pubic hair in front of the mirror. Reaching under her bed she took the heeled boots she had bought in the city with Peter when they had been Mr and Mrs. She took the flannel flower Peter had given her from the small vase of her grandmother's and put it behind her left ear.

Kate's dress fit perfectly; the inbuilt boning was unnecessary for her 17-year-old chest. She hadn't sewn the hem yet and fluffy strands clung to her bare legs. Kate twirled in front of the mirror, enjoying the satin against her skin as much as her performance of cover-girl perfection. The hem didn't matter. There was plenty of time. This was just a dress rehearsal. Kate Noble's party wasn't for another ten days. Kate imagined discussing her dress with Ita Buttrose.

"Oh yes, satin-backed crêpe," Ita would say. "A timeless choice."

"I chose the shade to match my eyes and enhance my skin tone." Self-satisfied.

"Those simple rules that so many forget," Ita would reply. "We must run a formal dress story in next month's *Cleo*."

"I have some ideas. Strapless pencil dresses with a cinched waist. Lace inserts. Gemstone colours."

Kate struggled into her boots. Ita helped her zip them up.

"You truly are an inspiration. It is wonderful to see such a confident young woman on the cusp of a very bright future." Hold the 's' on cusp.

"Well, I'd best be off," Kate said, pushing her tongue forward to emphasis the 's' on best.

Kate blew a kiss towards the mirror and headed out the door and up the hill to Peter's place. By this time the light was muted, and the blue satin of her dress shimmered under the streetlights, whispering secrets to the trees. When she got to Peter's house, there was a yellow car parked in the driveway with its nose almost kissing the bonnet of Peter's blue Mazda. Kate's mind reached for a thousand explanations; visiting brothers, cousins, mothers, old mates from school, but her clenching guts told her the truth.

Kate hesitated. She looked up at Peter's bedroom on the second storey. The curtains were parted. Peter was watching her. Or was it someone else? Who else was in there with him? Kate could see only that there were two of them and that their bodies must have been close together. Too close together for visiting mates or long-lost cousins.

Kate's body became a statue of salt. Sweating, disintegrating salt, until Kate felt like she would become a pool of brackish water, a melted witch. The downstairs curtain moved, and Kate looked at a phantom in the window with a pale, ghostlike figure. She felt dizzy. She stared at the figure in the window until she recognised her dress, her leather boots. She saw then that it was herself that she was staring at. She looked at her reflection and saw that she was beautiful. Everything would be alright. Yellow car or no yellow car, whoever was at the upstairs window would be no match for her.

Kate imagined Peter's whispered lies, secrets, and platitudes as she walked towards the door. She was ready to believe them all. Because they would be true.

Peter opened the door before Kate could knock. No need for the wooden door to graze her pretty knuckles. She stood for just a moment, letting him take her in before she leapt through the threshold and sunk her fingers into his hair, drinking in the smell of him. She brushed his neck with the butterfly kisses of her eyelashes and pressed her chest against his. Her groin.

Peter's hands touched her waist and an involuntary groan escaped his lips, like the three small groans of his orgasms. It was then that Kate saw a pair of white linen pants behind him. Miss Leach's white linen pants. Miss Leach in Peter's hallway. Anna. Anna wearing a flannelette shirt. Peter's flannelette shirt. Her hand was touching the small of Peter's back so that the three of them were connected like some kind of badly organised train. Miss Leach's hand touching Peter's back. His hands touching Kate's waist. Kate's hands wrapped in Peter's hair.

They all said—even those who knew the *truth*—that Kate chased after him. That she imagined Peter reciprocating. But Kate had kept the flannel flower from behind the Scout Hall. His love bite was still a faint purple on her neck, not covered by foundation or powder. They said it was her word against his. But Kate did not imagine the flies playing in their love puddle, his hands gripping her thighs so hard they left bruises. She didn't imagine the five o'clock shadow that left stubble rashes around her lips.

And in between her legs.

Kate broke free first. She ran down the road, the satin of her dress bunched up until she had to hold it down to cover herself as she ran. The frayed threads of the unsewn hem wrapped around her fingers. She didn't run home, rather straight down the main street of Beecroft. She thought she could so fast that people wouldn't be able to recognise her, especially in her outfit. She underestimated gossip's speed of recognition. As she ran down the street, she imagined herself as if watching from above and saw herself as a distraught Rapunzel, thrown from the sanctuary of her tower into the brambles. She held the flannel flower to her left ear and felt the wind flow through her curls as she ran down the hill. Her dress and hair shone in the moonlight.

The tears rolling over her cheeks were crystal drops that stained the bodice of her dress darker. She saw herself against the backdrop of staid Beecroft houses with manicured hedges. It was a romantic image and Kate played her part well as the suffering heroine. Surely under the circumstances someone would come and rescue her?

As Kate ran, she listened for Peter's voice. For his footsteps behind her as he called her back to him. Nothing. Perhaps he'd gone around the other way, cut through the arcade to catch her as she ran towards the station. She ran faster; ready to run into his arms. Those golden muscular arms would surround her again and she would sail away on his boat-bed into a world where she was Kat and he was Peter and nothing else mattered. And she would say *"Darling, oh, darling, oh darling, oh,"* and toss her head just as Abigail had shown her on *Number 96.*

Kate's heel slid on a mess of frangipani petals at the mouth of the arcade and the footpath came up to meet her, as they say. It slammed itself abruptly into her cheek. The rough concrete neatly grated her left arm from her wrist to her elbow. Her skin hung from her flesh in strips and small bubbles of blood formed on the surface.

Jack

I love the burn of the whisky going down my oesophagus first thing in the morning. Once again, I am drinking from the green glass. Green is possibly my least favourite colour. As a doctor one sees too much green where it shouldn't be. There is the endless green of mucus, which of course should be clear. Then the gangrenous feet of diabetics whose love of cigarettes outweighs their love for their wives (I am not being judgemental here—I fully understand this conundrum). You never forget the green-bruised skin of a beaten infant. They say that the grass is greener on the other side of the fence, but I am quite content to stay where I am, in the fading hues of my old age. Ha! Surely you can tell I am getting drunk now as I drink now from my green, green glass of home. Oh! How I amuse myself!

Yes, as a psychiatrist I must wonder whether I chose this green glass to punish myself somehow. At least the green will match my bile in the bathroom sink.

These infernal questions I ask myself over and over. If only I was asking myself something profound. Such as the meaning of life? But I already know the meaning of that. Life is just one long miserable fight against decay. Those young people searching for eternal truth just haven't begun to decay yet. They should just enjoy being young while they can still look good wearing rags and no bras. Who was it that said youth is wasted on the young?

Oh well. You know what they say? Old psychiatrists don't die, they just shrink away. My children love that joke, they are waiting for me to shrink away entirely so they can pounce on my estate. Real estate has been good to me. What am I supposed to be talking about? Ah, Jack, I am supposed to be talking about Jack, leaving behind a treatise of his life. His real life. Not the muddled-up mess it became.

"There are crazy people and there are stupid people. Sometimes stupid people are crazy and sometimes crazy people are stupid, but this is not always the case. Some crazy people are the most educated people you can meet." Jack loved to say this, and he loved to tell jokes. He was a much better joke-teller than my own children, and that's a fact.

As Jack said it is simple to presume crazy people are stupid, but it is not clever. This reminds me of my favourite joke. I do not think I have shared it with you yet, but if I have, simply roll your eyes when you think no one's watching and skip to the next page. I apologise in advance if this is the case. It goes something like this— I will attempt to tell it as Jack did. He was the storyteller amongst us, as you well know.

Just imagine Jack at the Champagne Club. He would probably be sitting with Linda, as they were seeing each other by then. Everybody knew that, even his wife, so who were we to judge? It was later in the afternoon. The secretaries were getting squirmy at the thought of getting off work early. Jack pulled out a sly red from a drawer and Linda poured it for us. Jack swirled his red and sniffed as he passed the glass under his nose, then began.

"As a young doctor I was driving along in the country when I realised that one of my tyres was flat. I was driving an old FX Holden at the time, being fresh out of medical school and already married. Anyway, I pulled over and saw, to my embarrassment, that I had gotten a flat tyre just outside a mental asylum. A group of inmates catcalled and whistled at me as I strug-gled to jack up the car. I must admit I did not have much experience with that sort of thing.

I was trying to loosen the wheel-nuts so I could wrench the offending wheel off and replace it with my spare. The whole time these kooks were watching from across the road. This one young fellow kept calling out, *Mate, it's anticlockwise. Push your wrench the other way.*

The other way, chorused the others.

I ignored him until I realised, he was right. I pushed the other way then, not acknowledging that the kook's comment caused me to change direction."

Jack paused for a sip of his wine. We all sipped our wine, as if we were following a toast.

"This guy really gave me the creeps," he said. "He looked like he was smiling even when he wasn't. Such a joker. There was a huge black fella standing right next to him. He was as big as a tree trunk and I thought he must have murdered someone for sure. Probably more than one person. He could have crushed someone in each fist." Jack held out a clenched fist and sang, *Fee-fi-fo-fum* in a deep baritone. He took another sip of his wine, "But neither of them scared me as much as their little hangers on, half-human, half-beasts that grovelled around slobbering at the other's feet.

"There was no fence between us, just a giant ditch like they have for animals at the zoo. There was a real move for that kind of thing at the time. It made the place look more like a sanctuary, less like a jail. I felt like that big black guy could have skipped over that empty moat like he was doing a barn dance. It didn't give a fellow much of a sense of security. *Fee-fi-fo-fum.*"

Jack shivered. I thought it was him shivering at the memory the first time he told the tale, but now I know it was part of the performance, just like the lilt of his voice and the dramatic pauses when he poured more wine. It got me every time though. I would shiver too, and that shiver would pass through the room as we imagined lunatics slobbering at our feet like rabid dogs, ready to crush our bones to make their bread.

"I tried to perform the task of replacing the tyre gracefully, even if it was in front of a bunch of loons. They were putting me off my game. That big black fella kept staring over at me and I swear he didn't blink once. I was thankful in a way that my clumsiness made the task last so long the dusk began to dim the afternoon, hiding the dust and grease that now covered my neatly pressed shirt. Most of all I was glad that I couldn't see the ominous smirking face of the ringleader.

I wasn't about to give up my dignity for those loons. I pretended not to hurry. I sat on my haunches, keeping my trouser knees at least up away from the death sentence of grass stains. I was eager to get home to Daphne and didn't need to be late and have grass stains on my trousers."

This exacted an obligatory laugh from the group. A few of the more sensitive among us snuck a glance at Linda and noted her discomfort. Jack continued, seemingly oblivious.

"It was at this point I realised I had misplaced the wheel nuts. I was aware of the inmates' giggles directed at my back and I knew it was impossible to find them gracefully. I felt that the black giant had silently leapt over the canal and stolen them from me. Either way I had become free entertainment for them. Lost something? called the ringleader, as if he was secretly fondling the wheel nuts in his pocket.

"I ignored him and nonchalantly felt around with my fingers in the fading light before finally surrendering my trousers to the tufts of grass and reaching around blindly under the car.

"Finally, this black giant called to me in a voice so soft that if there hadn't been a breeze to carry it across the ditch his words may have been lost before they reached me. Hey! Just take one nut off each of the other wheels and use them on your spare. That will give you three nuts for each wheel. Should be fine until you get yourself to a service station."

Jack stopped then and topped up everyone's drinks. "Well, you know, I was suitably astonished and turning to the black man I said, what a clever idea. But I must ask you, if you can think of that, why are you in there? I indicated the sign for the asylum with my thumb. The man with the smirk replied, that is because we are mentally deranged. Not just plain stupid like you."

At this Jack's audience realised the whole story was a joke. A joke or a parable, one or the other. And it's a pity Jack didn't learn more from this lesson. He underestimated his patients and what they could do to him.

Kate

Kate sat in the gutter, a broken princess. Down the hill a train had just pulled into the station. It stood waiting. Someone dashed across the road to the station steps, close enough that if Kate called out they would be able to hear her. She wondered whether they would stop their race for the train if she did. Would they come without seeing her face? Her blonde hair? Without seeing her in her dress? Or the blood that was trickling down her arm, thick like honey? But if they did stop, what then? They couldn't give her anything she wanted.

Kate put her hand to her face. She checked her teeth, did an inventory of her injuries. A grazed knee. Her arm. The bone in her jaw was tender to the touch. She pressed it harder, enjoying the pain. One of her boots was grazed all up one side until the white sheen gave way to raw hide underneath. It was uglier than the graze on her arm. It couldn't be fixed. Kate unzipped the boot and yanked it off her foot. Her fingers worried the white leather. Irreparable. A car drove towards Kate, slowed down at the sight of her, and then sped off. Kate threw the boot in its wake, then stood up and limped towards home in her remaining boot.

When she got to her house the Volvo was in the driveway. Mum must be home, she thought. She didn't want her parents to see her like this, so she went through the front door instead of down the side of the house and through the kitchen door like she usually did. She needed to change.

But her father was in the hallway talking on the phone. He held out his hand to stop her as she slid through the front door. "Stay there Katherine. I need to speak with you."

Kate thought about running. But where to? With one shoe on and one shoe off? Not to Peter's house. She couldn't go to Frances's house. Frances probably wouldn't even open the front door now that she knew about her and Michael. Kate Noble lived all the way up the hill and our Kate was so tired. She just wanted to change and watch something on television to take her mind off everything. Maybe fall asleep on the couch when the channels closed. You can understand that, surely, can't you? We have all been there. We have all felt that tired before.

"Yes," her father said into the receiver. "She just got home. We will come in now. Thank you so much for everything. Goodbye."

He hung up the phone then and looked at Kate. She could imagine what she looked like with her bloody arm and hair everywhere. She saw herself as her father must have seen her, with her dress too short and the hem frayed. Her body bulging out inappropriately. He didn't say anything. His long fingers stroked the receiver of the phone. He looked tired as well.

"Katherine," he said. "Go and get changed, we are going to the hospital. Wear something comfortable, it might be a long night. I'll be waiting in the car."

Mr Minola took a long look at his daughter standing in front of him wearing only one shoe and believed that everything he had been told was true. He rested his head against the wall for a moment, trying not to think of alcohol, then went outside.

Kate tiptoed into her room thinking that the twins must be coming home, but she didn't care. And her mother. She didn't care about that either. She just wanted to sleep. She wanted to slide in under the weight of her blankets and sleep for days.

Inside her room clothes lay in piles on the floor. She pulled out a dusty-pink lounge suit that her mother had discarded as her stomach expanded. Kate held the plush pile against her cheek. It smelt like her mother the way she used to be—the most beautiful woman in Sydney. Her mother who had worn denim shorts and tank tops, before the liberty print spread through her wardrobe. Kate sat on her bed and unzipped her remaining boot. She pulled the velvety pants on under her party frock. With her back to the mirror, she put the jacket on over her dress, rolling one sleeve up against her stinging graze.

Then she saw it, the light flashing. It was Peter. *Short, long, short, short, long, long, long, short, long, short.* Love. *Short, long, short, short, long, long…* Then it stopped. There was no finish. Kate sat on her bed. Kate looked out the window. It was five past nine. She waited, then seeing nothing she got up and flashed her lights at Peter. *Long, long, short, long, long, long, short, long, long.* Meow. There was no response. She tried again. *Short, long, short, short, long, long, long, short, long, short.* Love. Darkness. *Long, long, short, long, long, long, short, long, long.* Meow. Nothing.

Teddy was back on the bed. Staring at her. She picked him up and smelt him. She sat on the bed and held him. The Volvo's horn sounded outside. Kate waited. She heard Mrs Carroll's high-pitched chatter and then her father sounded the horn again. Kate grabbed her schoolbag and headed barefoot into the kitchen. She stuffed Teddy headfirst into the garbage disposal on the way out.

Kate opened the door to the back seat. She didn't want to talk. She wanted to sleep.

"Come into the front seat, Princess. I need you to talk to me."

"What about?"

"About nothing. Just keep me awake. I am tired from the new babies, and work." Over-explaining.

Kate closed the back door of the car. She stood outside for a moment breathing in the frangipanis that perfumed the air. The smell of summer. If she had still been in her room, sitting on her bed, looking out her window, she would have seen the light of a certain young man's bedroom go on and off seemingly randomly. But if a tree falls in the forest and nobody is there to hear it, does it make a sound?

Kate opened the front door of the car and sat next to her father, pulling her schoolbag onto her lap for protection. She closed the door and leaned heavily against it as if she was testing the strength of the lock. Kate looked out the window as her father reversed the Volvo down the driveway. She stared in the direction of Peter's bedroom window. It was too late. The car smelt like stale cigar smoke.

"You looked upset when you got home. What happened?"

"Nothing."

Her father waited for the truth.

"I fell over."

"Yes?"

"I lost my shoe."

"Mmm."

There was silence for a while. The car hummed along and Kate reached for the dial on the wireless.

"Leave it off Katherine."

"Why?"

"Your principal rang me today. "

"About what?" *It has come to my attention that you have been frequenting the Epping Motel late at night for the purpose of experimenting with sex.*

"About you."

"I am studying Dad. I promise. My marks are good." Thinking of the fish pictures on her science test.

"Your marks are not my major concern right now."

Thinking of Miss Leach.

"Apparently you have developed an unhealthy attachment to one of your teachers."

"Oh, you are joking! Mr Guard said that? It's so stupid. I hate Mr Mason. I hate him so much!"

Kate's father wound down his window with more muscle than required. The wind whipped in and clipped Kate across the ears. They drove on. Kate reached for the dial again to take the whistling out of her ears and this time her father didn't object. Kate rolled the dial between stations until she heard ABBA's 'Dancing Queen'. Kate remembered her phone call with Michael Ballins. The hopeful looks he had given her at school. Her father was driving away from Beecroft and Kate imagined her boot sitting lonely on the main road. She almost laughed. I will have to run and get it as soon as I wake up tomorrow, she thought. Maybe she could cover the scrape with white paint. No one would notice. They'd be too busy watching her dancing at Kate's party. With Michael Ballins. With Little Michael. She'd dance with both of them together. Frances and Kate Noble would just have to glare at them from the sidelines. Kate saw herself twirling in the middle of the Noble's largest lounge room. Spun around and around by the Michaels. She saw Peter in the doorway. Coming towards her. Kate's father leaned forward and turned the music off. Kate's dream went with it, but she was smart enough not to object.

"Mrs Carroll also paid me a visit today."

"I know what she thinks. That's not true either. Why does everyone think I have a crush on them? Mr Carroll is so gross Dad. Even you can see that. Surely."

"Katherine that is not a very nice way to speak. Now Mrs Carroll just has her concerns. The night I took your mother to the hospital for example." Her father waited for a confession.

"Mr Carroll came over. I told you that on the phone."

"Apparently you were undressing with the lights on. With the windows open. Dancing naked in front of him. Mrs Carroll sent her husband over because she was worried about you and she said you tried to seduce him. You tried to get him into your bedroom."

"Seduce? What's that?"

"Katherine! She said you have been flashing your bedroom light. Signalling him." Between clenched teeth.

"Dad! I did nothing. Mr Carroll came over. I did nothing." I promise.

"Now tonight Katherine. You go out looking like, well—I don't know what you looked like. You return looking like you've been in a fight." High-pitched wail.

Her father almost cried then and slapped his hand against the steering wheel. Kate wondered whether it was all for show. She looked back out the window. Her father was weak. She saw it clearly now. He was a weak man. She couldn't look at him.

He pulled the Volvo over next to a house on a suburban street. There were rosebushes in front of the windows. Purple jacaranda flowers had fallen into drifts next to the footpath like melancholy snow.

"Why are we parking here?"

"This is the hospital."

"No, it's not."

"Come inside, Princess. We will talk in there." Unusually soft.

"With Mum?"

"She's not in here."

"What do you mean? Aren't we here to bring her home?"

"She's still resting, Katherine."

"We can't bring Jack and Jill home without her. Can we?" Feeling the need to run.

"The doctor is going to have a look at your arm." Obvious lie.

"It's just a graze." Shredded tan. Hours gone to waste with baby oil in the backyard.

Her father opened his door and headed towards the lit doorway of the house with the rose bushes in front. There was a sign. *Ferriby Private Hospital.* But it looked like a house. What could Kate do but follow her father? Even if he was weak? Inside a nurse was waiting for them.

"The doctor will see her in the morning."

"Oh, ah. I was under the impression he would be here tonight."

"He was called out on an emergency. Go home Mr Minola. We will take good care of your daughter. If Doctor Grafton doesn't come back tonight, he will see her first thing in the morning."

"It's not that bad," said Kate, showing the nurse the graze. Lipstick marks mixed with blood. Pink and red and black drying blood.

"Oh, that does look nasty." Then to her father, "I see what you mean. Let's get you into a bed. Come with me Katherine."

Kate felt acutely aware of the mascara that must be bleeding down her face. Of her pink nose shining through clotted foundation and powder. The nurse walked off into the corridor and what could she do but follow? Kate realised that she couldn't hear her father behind her. She looked back in time to see him walking briskly towards the exit. He wasn't looking back at her to see if she was alright. Her father shoved open the door as if he was trying to escape. Kate followed the nurse's white shoes. She walked too fast and the green linoleum was cold under Kate's bare feet. Her arm hurt. Perhaps it was broken?

Kate trailed the nurse into a room, still in her mother's velour tracksuit with one sleeve rolled up. She held her arm to her chest as if she was wearing an invisible sling. While she was here, she may as well make the best of it. There were two beds next to each other facing the door. A woman was sitting cross-legged on the one nearest. She was naked from the waist down. Kate couldn't help staring. The woman looked exactly like Farrah Fawcett from *Charlie's Angels*.

"Kylie!" Appalled.

"Jo-anne!" The woman mimicked the nurse's tone as she resumed cutting her pubic hair with a pair of nail scissors. Kate could see the pink tongue of her clitoris. It looked like a jelly baby. A tiny pink promise.

"Kylie!"

"What? We are all girls here. Anyway, this is how Jack likes it!" Laughter in her eyes.

Kylie deposited a pinch of hair on the small table between the beds, rubbing her fingers together backwards and forwards like she was adding salt to a stew. She looked at Kate then and glared at her like women do when they realise their beauty has been trumped. She held Kate's eye like a warning.

"We are all *women* here."

"Katherine here is just seventeen years old," the nurse snapped. "Show some dignity."

Kylie's glare relaxes. Perhaps she is thinking that Jack wouldn't like someone so young?

"Put your clothes in here. Put the gown on and get into bed." Her nurse put her back towards Kylie, blocking Kate's view. Out of sight. Out of mind.

"And then what?"

"And wait," Kylie laughed, depositing another pinch of hair on the table between them. "Too late for dinner. Jack will see you tomorrow." *Might* see you tomorrow.

"*Doctor* Grafton," said the nurse.

The nurse left them then and Kate was left standing next to her bed, hesitating about getting changed in front of Kylie. There was a curtain that could be drawn around her bed, but that seemed rude, prudish, as if she was a little girl. Kate thought about taking her clothes off in front of this woman to show that she wasn't a child. That she had the body of a woman. But instead, she draped the gown at the end of the bed and climbed up onto the bed in her clothes.

The high bed reminded Kate of the high beds at the Epping Motel. The stale feel of mass-washed sheets.

"So, Katherine, *are* you a girl, or *are* you a woman?" Kylie almost sung the word woman, so it came out as woo-man. Her hips gyrated into her mattress.

"I'm seventeen. I can't drive. Or vote." Leave me alone.

"Or go to war? Or so they tell you, huh? It's all war really, isn't it? This life? You gotta fight or you'll end up face down in the mud. Looks like that has already happened to you tonight." Kylie clicked her fingers like she'd made a joke.

Kate said nothing but kept watching as the woman continued clipping her pubic hair and adding the clippings to the pile. Eventually the woman got up and put on a pair of white cottontails like Kate's mother wore. Kate was shocked. They weren't sexy at all.

"Seventeen, huh," the woman laughed. "That is the legal age for sex." Her voice was loud, and Kate's eyes jumped to the door in case the nurse was listening.

"So, I repeat. Girl? Woman?" Teasing.

Kate smiled.

"Ha! I knew it," said Kylie. "That's what you're in for, isn't it? That's your crime." Confident.

"What?" Kate whispered, hoping the woman would quieten down also, but it was as useless as whispering at a crying baby. Kylie's voice was rising again as she bounced on her bed in her cottontails. Then she stopped and looked straight into Kate's eyes like she was trying to steal something. She began again more quietly. "Being a woman. Being a seventeen-year-old woman? I know. Got it in one. You must be crazy, letting some bloke do *that* to you."

The woman's eyebrows flicked up and disappeared under her fringe and then she sat straight back on her bed, kicking her long legs up in the air and laughed out loud. The kind of laugh born out of the need for attention. From anyone. As Kylie pumped her legs into the air, her pink toenailed feet hit the lamp on the bedside table so that it fell over and her pile of pubic hair floated up into the air like confetti. The woman jumped up, righted the lamp and brushed the rest of the hair off the table where it became lost on the pattern of the mottled linoleum floor. Kylie clambered back on the bed then and sat cross-legged, hugging her pillow to her chest like a self-conscious adolescent. This woman didn't seem to be sick or injured at all.

"Guess we are roommates," Kylie said, pulling a pillow onto her lap.

Kate copied the woman, shoving her own pillow onto her lap so that they were both sat there like that, cross-legged on their beds. Kate held her grazed arm straight out in front of her like it was in a cast. They were in secret-telling stance (as they were still both at the age when secrets could be shared—and let's face it—Kate had been holding onto hers for months now.) A nurse rushed past and flicked off their light, barely looking into the room.

"So, what do they call you?"

"Who?"

"What do you mean, who? People. Surely not Kat-er-ina?" Singing again.

"Kat," Kate blurted. "People call me Kat."

"Ah, Cat. I like that. Very cute. I have a cat. I'm Kylie." And so, their friendship was born.

"Roommates, roommates," sung Kylie. Kate watched her flipping her Farrah Fawcett hair in the dim light from the corridor. She swung her slender legs over the bed and jumped the gap over to Kate's bed, her eyes popping. "When did you get your first period? Have you ever let a boy touch your boobs? Touch you down *there?*" Pointing with her finger. Stroking the velour of Kate's mother's pants. Touching her. Kate couldn't move. "Have you been drunk? Smoked pot? Kissed a married man? Been pregnant? Had an abortion? Had sex with your sister's husband? Fantasised about having sex with your father? With your mother? *Murdered* someone?"

"What?"

"Ha," she said jumping back onto her own bed, "just kidding. Now you are in the nuthouse and all, I thought you must have some pretty good secrets."

Kate turned her back on Kylie then. She had no idea what was going on. This woman was crazy. Kate just wanted to sleep. She needed to sleep. Forever. She closed her eyes.

"I was just kidding kiddo. Get it? Kidding kiddo." She laughed.

No response.

"Oh, my goodness. You really are just a kid, aren't you?"

"No. I am not," Kate turned on Kylie then. "I am not a kid." And she told Kylie all her secrets then. Well, her only secret. The secret *you* don't know about yet. Although you may have guessed. You probably have. But guessing isn't knowing and how can anyone know anything for sure?

"This is *my* secret," Kylie said and flipped her hair back revealing a slim red line that that ran the length of her ear. At first Kate thought it was red texta, or lipstick. Kylie moved so close to Kate that she thought Kylie was going to kiss her. Kate turned her head.

"It's disgusting, isn't it?" Kylie said and at that moment Kate realised what the line was. A scar.

"What happened?" Tell me so I can sleep.

"I danced."

"You danced?"

"That's all I did."

Kate's tired mind was catching up. Running past herself sitting across from Mr Guard in his office, breaking the pencil. Past Peter standing in the doorway with Miss Leach. Miss Leach wearing Peter's shirt. The yellow car in his driveway kissing his Mazda. Past herself running down the main street of Beecroft with no one running after her. Sliding in the sludge. Throwing her boot onto the road. Past her father standing in the hallway, stroking the phone. *I'll bring her in now. Thank you for everything.* Her father was on the phone to the hospital before he even saw her bloodied arm. Past the lights flicking on and off in Peter's bedroom. Short, long, short, short, long, long, long, short, long, short. Love. Once, twice, and then stopping in the middle of the third time. The blackness. Her father tooting the horn in the driveway. The smell of the frangipanis outside her bedroom window as she got into the Volvo. The smell of cigar smoke inside the car. The ABBA song. Her mind stopped at Kylie on the bed next to her. In a hospital. Some kind of a hospital. Her pink jellybean. *That's your crime. You must be crazy letting some bloke do that to you.*

"What do you mean this is a nuthouse? What's going on?"

"That took you a while," Kylie laughed. And then, "Are you serious? You really don't know where you are?"

"I'm at the hospital." No. I don't. And then, "I fell over. Slipped. I grazed my arm," Kate swung around on her own bed to show Kylie. Even as she did the ridiculousness of it dawned on her. "Oh, my goodness, where am I?"

"You are in a mental hospital, Kate.'

"No. I'm not." Denial.

"Yes. You are."

"No. My arm."

"It's just a scratch."

"A graze. It could be broken. I fell on my face. The doctor just wants to check me out."

"Pussycat, I can assure you. This is a nuthouse."

"Then I am in the wrong place. I will ring my father. He will collect me immediately."

"He was the one who brought you here. Trust me Kat. If you go out there now, the nurses will tie you to the bed." Warning. Serious now.

"No. No, no no no." NO.

"Listen to me."

"I want to go home." Jumping off the bed.

"Calm down sweetie. Shh, you don't want them to come, do you? Just tell Jack your story tomorrow. It will all be fine." Don't cause a scene.

"Did you cut yourself? Your face?" Try to kill yourself?

"No, of course not. I'm not crazy."

"What are you doing in here then?"

"I'm seeing Jack. You know. Having sex."

"Pardon? With the doctor?"

"Yes."

Kate started giggling then and soon Kylie joined in and they laughed and laughed, kicking their legs into the air until a nurse came by and shut their door.

"Kylie?" Whispered. "Are you just pretending to be a patient?"

"Not exactly."

"Wait. Wait. Why am I here?"

"Your secret, Kat. Think about it."

"But nobody knows about that."

"Are you sure?" And then Kate remembered Mr Guard asking her about the hotel. Peter ringing her at home to tell her it wasn't a good idea that he went to the party. Her father. The Carrolls hearing her talking to a man.

"Even if they do know, that doesn't make me crazy."

"I know that Honey. None of us in here are. Now stop interrupting. I was telling you about my dancing." Kylie leant over and turned on the bedside lamp. The light was so dim it barely penetrated through the light-shade. Kylie slid from her bed and posed near the door, one leg in front of the other and her back towards Kate.

"I'm a dancer," she said, turning and shimmying towards Kate, her breasts shaking under her nightie. "I'm not a ballerina," she said, "which you may have already guessed."

Kate giggled.

"Nor a tap dancer," she said, lifting her nightie and waggling her cotton-tails at Kate.

The nurse came back to the door, knocking. "Is everything alright in there?"

"Yes," called Kylie.

"Kate?"

"She's asleep."

Rubber shoes retreated from their door.

"I am a cabaret dancer."

Immediately Kate thought of peacock feathers and sequined leotards. She breathed in, seduced by the glamour of it all.

"Do you work in a nightclub?"

"Yes, but that's not where this happened," she said, flashing her scar to Kate. "This happened in prison."

"Prison?"

"I was dancing in there. For the men. At Parramatta Gaol. I was attacked."

"Oh my. Oops, I mean sorry."

"It was supposed to be a scam. A man attacked me, but it was fake. I didn't know that though, so I started screaming and two other guys came to rescue me. But the first guy, he had a knife. He wanted to hurt me. He cut me. He couldn't help himself. He was bad."

"Why was it a scam?"

Kylie flipped onto her bed and lay on her back. She leant her head over her bed so that her face hung upside-down in the empty space between their beds, her hair brushing the floor. "They had it all planned. The guy who attacked me was a murderer. His name's Lenny Lawson. You know those Lone Avenger comics? Yeah? Well anyway he drew all those. The Lone Avenger saved all these girls from kidnappers and murderers, but it turns out the guy who drew them all is a killer. He's famous for raping models *and* shooting schoolgirls. He stabbed one girl to death. She was his model. He was painting her portrait and then he just tied her up, fucked her and stabbed her. She was sixteen years old. He's never getting out of jail. So anyway, these other two prisoners set the whole thing up. Lenny had nothing to lose. He was going to die in prison anyway. So, these other two prisoners, *good* prisoners, you know, got Lenny Lawson to pretend to attack me so they could save me. They would act like the heroes and get out of prison early. But that Lenny Lawson, once he got near me, he couldn't help himself. I could see it in his eyes he wanted to cut me. He enjoyed cutting me."

Kylie flashed her hands at Kate, but it was too dark for her to see. If the lamp had been brighter Kate would have seen the thin white scars around Kylie's slender fingers but no doubt, she would have also noticed the longer, angrier scar on the inside of her right wrist and the matching but not matching one on her left, that curved back into itself like a boomerang.

Kylie lay back onto her bed and hugged her pillow to her chest. Her white teeth glistened like the whites of her eyes.

"He enjoyed me when he did it. He smiled as he cut me. He did it slowly. When I sleep, I see that smile. I imagine he is doing things to me, other things. Things he did to those models out in the bush. Or that young girl that he tied up."

Kate didn't say anything. She imagined Kylie dancing in a feathered headdress, her sequined costume spinning flares of light though the dim prison. She saw a man leap out from the audience and felt his thick fingers grabbing her flesh. She felt the knife pressed to her face. Her scar was evidence that the story was real.

"That's why you're in here?"

"No, that's my secret too, I guess. I don't tell them what I dream. Not even Jack. I was sent to see Jack 'cause I was suing. The whole thing should never have happened. We were dancing in a prison, for God's sake. They should have taken better care of us. They should have had guards with guns pointed into the audience the whole time we were performing. Anyway, my solicitor sent me to see the shrink which turned out to be Jack. We hit it off straight away. He's gorgeous. Simply gorgeous. Too old for you of course. Jack understands me. And the sex! The sex is fantastic."

Kate had never heard anyone talk like this. She held her breath, hoping that Kylie wouldn't stop.

"I was sitting in Doctor Grafton's office, telling him my story and Jack just got up and said to me, *Kylie, what you need is a good fuck, and I am the one to give it to you.*"

"He did not." Disbelieving.

"He did." He did. He says it to lots of his female patients.

The nurse came back and opened the door. "Do I have to separate you two?"

"Shh, sleep," said Kylie. And then whispering, "We did it right there in his office and I can tell you, Doctor Jack Grafton fucks like a dream."

"What is *your* dream?" Kate whispered after a while; half-thinking Kylie was asleep.

"To marry Jack and have a baby," Kylie said instantly. "What's yours?"

"To become the new Ita Buttrose."

"Shit, maybe you do belong in here after all. Don't tell the doctor that whatever you do."

Kate hadn't shared this dream with her other friends. To her speaking of this dream was more intimate than her secrets with Peter. But something about the darkness of the hospital reminded her of school camp. Something about the nurses' rubber shoes making their nightly rounds had lulled her into telling Kylie about Ita. She wished now she had kept it to herself.

Kate laid awake and listened to the sounds of the hospital. Strange moans from another room and occasional footsteps. Screaming? Maybe she was sleeping by then. Maybe she was imagining the whole thing. Or dreaming?

※

White light woke Kate. Kylie was asleep in the bed across from her. Kate thought about her own little secrets that seemed so insignificant next to Kylie's story of murderers and false heroes. The graze on her elbow had turned into a stiff, dry scab that any ten-year-old would be proud of. Kate was ready to go home. She needed to study. Screw Peter, she thought. She'd pash off with Michael Ballins right in front of his face. It was only five days until the final exams started. Then she would be in her future. At last, she would be free to meet Ita Buttrose. Kate stretched her tanned legs the length of the bed. Peter would soon come begging for her. Begging for more of what only she could give. Of what only she would do. But Kate would be too busy to see him. She'd be on her way to Paris. *Au revoir* Peter.

A thin woman came in and put a plate on the table at the foot of Kate's bed and then swung the table up to Kate as if she was an invalid.

"Thanks," said Kate but the woman was gone. There was a silver lid covering the plate and when Kate lifted it, using her left arm to avoid the sting of her graze, she found scrambled eggs with parsley, three fat rashers of bacon, toast already buttered and a rounded scoop of baked beans.

"Yummo," Kate said out loud and then looked over at Kylie, afraid she would have woken her. Kylie didn't move.

A nurse came to the door.

"The doctor is ready to see you." C'mon, no mucking about.

Kate stuffed a piece of bacon in her mouth and climbed down from the bed. She pushed her sleeve down over her graze and tried to hold her arm naturally. She wanted to go home. She wanted to see her siblings. *Jack and Jill went up the hill to fetch a pail of water.*

"Remember, he's mine," came the sleepy voice of Kylie. She sounded like she was drunk. The memory of their bond in the dark of the night before seemed preposterous to Kate. Kylie was just a woman in a bed. Maybe even a drunk woman.

Kate followed the nurse through a labyrinth of corridors, her little hat looked like a paper plane that had landed on her head. The inside of the lounge suit rubbed against her arm forcing her to hold it straight down beside her. She stiffened her right arm so they matched. Hopefully the doctor would just think she walked like that. She kept her hips straight and took little steps. Responsible, mature steps. Kate waited behind the nurse as she knocked on a door.

"In you go," said the nurse, opening the door for her, before padding softly back up the corridor. Kate was left in the doorway looking across a large desk at a man in a suit. His eyes were warm and brown.

"Take a seat," Dr Grafton said in a voice like maple syrup and Kate entered the room and sat, still looking into those eyes and thinking that

148

maybe she could steal her roommate's dream. His sexual appetite clung to him so obviously.

Kate decided not to risk it. She broke eye contact with the doctor and looked down at the speckled linoleum. It looked like the lino in the science labs at school.

"Come in Katherine. Close the door. Take a seat and make yourself comfortable." His eyes on her then. All over her. Kate relaxed her arms. Try to look normal.

She remembered the whites of Kylie's eyes glistening in the dark. *What you need is a good fuck, and I am the one to give it to you.* Kate wondered whether this brown-eyed man would say it to her. She started giggling then, covering her face with her hands. She bit her lip and looked up at the doctor but then the laughter enveloped her again and she could barely sit on the chair she was laughing so hard.

"I'm sorry," she said with tears streaming down her face. All she could think was the doctor saying what you need is a good fuck. And I am the one to give it to you. Peals of laughter. Tears. Hiccoughs. She was lucky not to wet herself.

"Katherine Minola," Dr Grafton said, leaning across the desk towards her. "I have been waiting for such a long time to meet you. Why do you think you are here?"

Like a slap in the face Kate was sober again, but then as she started to speak giggles and snorts escaped from her.

"I have a graze, but it's nothing. Kylie says this is a nuthouse. She said… lots of things. I want to go home. Can you please ring my father? He will come and get me." Act normal. Don't flirt. Don't make *that* mistake again. Above all else, hide the love bite. Kate held her hair at her neck with her good arm.

"I don't think it's a good idea for your father to see you at the moment."

"Mum is in hospital. She just had twins."

"She will be going home soon."

"Oh really?" Breathless. "I need to get home."

"Your mother needs her rest."

Kate breathed. She looked at the doctor. He smiled back at her.

"Listen to me, Kate, your father is quite distressed. He feels as if you have run riot behind his back while your mother has been in hospital. He has heard reports, whispers, and accusations."

"None of them are true."

"Oh, I know that. As soon as he told me the stories of your neighbour, of your principal… or teachers, anyway, stories from your school. I knew they were just stories." See how he works? That's all I'm saying. Just remember I warned you!

"That's right." Relieved.

"Katherine," the doctor said. "I am sorry all this has happened to you. Your father has been left alone while your mother has been in hospital. He is not judging the situation to the best of his ability. I'll speak with him. I've known your father for years. I know how to talk to him."

Kate looked across the desk at the doctor. He leaned back on his chair and rested first one foot on his desk and then the other one, on top of the first. Kate thought he looked slightly sexy, in a forty-year-old man kind of way. She trusted him. What a silly girl. But she wasn't the only one. Not by a long shot.

"Thank you so much. My HSC exams are on next week. I need to go home and study. I have a maths practice exam, a practice essay for English and one for French, plus a practice test. I have to figure out how to remember the trigonometry formulas in maths and I have to re-sit a science test. Also, we are having an end of year party next Friday. I have already made my dress. I just need to hem it."

"You sound like a very clever girl. Listen, when do your exams start?"

"On Wednesday. They finish on Friday next week."

"Five-days-time?"

"Yes." Five days until freedom.

"And what do you hope to do after school Katherine?"

"Call me Kat." Oops. Don't mention Ita whatever you do. "I want to be a journalist."

"Kat. I like that. Very original. I can see you are a young woman with a lot of potential."

Kate giggled again. She couldn't help it. She was only seventeen after all. Seventeen-year-olds giggle a lot. Despite how close they are to being adults.

"Listen Kat. I have a little proposition to make to you."

Oh no, thought Kate. What you need is a good fuck and I am the one to give it to you.

This time she didn't giggle. Instead, she held her breath and bit her tongue.

"I think you need a rest. Your mother is just about to come home with two crying babies. They'll prevent you from being able to study. Your mother will be irritable, and your father will be grumpy. I'm not saying anything against your parents, this is just a difficult time for them."

The doctor paused, and Kate remembered her mother lying on the hospital bed looking like a balloon too many days after a party. *Ah, Kate! Don't touch me.* She remembered her mother's still swollen fingers pushing her away.

"You need to be able to study in peace. These five days must be very important to you. Why don't you stay here for a few days? Relax. I've heard that you get on well with your roommate, but she will be in therapy for many hours each day. Why don't you take this opportunity to stay here where everything is calm? I can ask your father to bring in your schoolbooks."

"But I want to see my siblings." Her tongue caught on the esses. Her lisp was natural now. She was almost Ita.

"Of course. They will come to visit you. Your father can bring them in whenever you want." Maintaining eye contact.

"Wait a minute." said Kate. "You know I'm not crazy, don't you?"

"Crazy? You?" said the doctor. "Listen, I think you have been under a lot of pressure with your HSC. I think that some people have been making inappropriate gestures towards you, which must be hard for you to deal with." By this time Kate was crying and Dr Grafton smiled. Gotcha.

"Listen Katherine," he said. "The world has changed a lot since your parents were young. You are a beautiful young woman. You have needs and desires that are entirely natural. What you need is a good rest. I can provide that for you."

Kate cried some more, wiping snot onto her mother's lounge suit. She enjoyed the burning sting of her grazed elbow as she bent it.

"Katherine," said the good doctor, "you look so tired, exhausted even. Let us look after you for a few days. We will deliver you home well in time for your exams. You will feel refreshed, relaxed. You will return to your life ready to take control." Warm eyes. "The food is good here."

"Yes," was all Kate could say between her tears. "Yes, yes," and for some reason she was relieved that she would return to her room with Kylie, all mint walls and cotton blankets rather than her own room, raped of everything she had loved. Without Teddy.

A nurse appeared at the door. She was a different from the one who had brought her here. Fuzzy hair escaped from under her hat, but she seemed to know where Kate belonged and took her back to her room. Kylie was gone, a dishevelled blanket left behind like a skin she had outgrown. Kate was relieved. She didn't feel like talking and she didn't want Kylie to see her girlish tears. As Kate climbed up onto her bed, she remembered that she hadn't shown Dr Grafton her arm. She covered herself in the blanket and stared at the wall.

Kate thought about Peter waiting for her signal. Good, she thought. My lights won't flash tonight and he won't see me. He won't know where I've gone. He can try to find me and he can worry. She hugged her pillow to her chest. Just a couple of days to rest and then she'd return to school, her hair washed and her face relaxed. She'd blitz the exams. She'd send the manuscript of her *Afra* magazine to Ita and Ita would ring her and say, "Don't waste your time at university. I started working when I was fifteen years old. You either have it or you don't, and you obviously have it. Come and work for me. No not for me, with me. I will be your mentor. To tell you the truth, I need your advice about a few things. A young person's perspective. Get an apartment in the inner city. You will never look back."

A nurse came in with a cup of milky tea and two biscuits. This is great,

Kate thought. She bent down over the bed and reached into her bag for the *Cleo* she had bought the day before. Her tea went cold on the bedside table. Kate ate the biscuits and flicked through, looking at the dresses. She stopped short on one page. There it was. Her party dress but strapless. Cinched in waist. Pornographically short. I'm one step ahead of you Ita, she thought.

A nurse came to collect her cup.

"You didn't drink your tea." Accusation.

"Oh no, I forgot." Disinterested.

"You should drink it. It will help you relax." No mucking about.

"Oh, that's okay. I'm fine. I'm just…" Kate closed the magazine. Maybe the nurse would think *Cleo* wasn't appropriate.

"Here," said the nurse, moving closer to Kate's bed and picking up the cup. "Drink it now." Now.

"It's cold." Hiding the magazine under her blanket.

"I'll make you another cup."

"I don't really like tea." Admitting to her non-adult ways.

"It's important that you drink it. Before your treatment starts."

"Oh, I'm not having any treatment. I am just here to relax for a few days. Doctor Grafton is a friend of my dad's." Sweet smile.

"Well, you have to drink something." The nurse whispered then, as if it was their little secret. "How about a nice cup of warm milk with honey?"

"Yes please." Relieved.

Kate read an article on how to have the best legs. She memorised the steps. Hair removal. Buffing and moisturising. She would be ready for Kate Noble's party. Kate leant back over the bed and pulled her scrapbook out of her bag, opening the cover and running her fingers over the title. *Afra.* Not long to go now.

The nurse returned with the cup of milk. Just warm. She stood next to Kate while she drank. A large blob of honey stuck to the bottom of the cup and Kate stuck her finger in and then licked the honey off it. The nurse smiled.

Kate waited for the sounds of the nurse's footsteps to get swallowed up by the other strange, animalistic sounds of the hospital. Kate imagined other patients in pain. She pulled the *Cleo* out from under her blanket and put it inside her scrapbook, just like she had when she was reading *Wuthering Heights* in science class. That was before Mr Mason had become their teacher, of course. He provided enough distraction for the whole class. That was true whether you hated him or not.

Kate started reading an article called *The Awful Truth about Office Affairs*. Lynn and Phil: She was a designer and he was the executive vice president of a sportswear manufacturing company. They fell in love. Kate's eyes started to blur. He fired Lynn. They fell in love. He fired Lynn. Kate rubbed her eyes. He fired Lynn. The letters on the page started to run together like mascara in the rain. She was a designer. He fired her. They fell in love. She saw a bat. She saw a butterfly. She saw two humans leaning into each other: kissing. Kate should have pinched herself to see whether she was dreaming.

Kate lifted her heavy head. Hair was growing on the walls. The same golden hair that grew on Peter's arms. She wanted to get out of bed to touch it but her body felt heavy. Carefully Kate drew up her left sleeve and rubbed her fingers along her weeping scab. She felt nothing.

She called out to a nurse. To someone.

"Hey, hey." Kylie's face was next to her.

"Hey, where were you?" Stroking Kylie's beautiful face.

"I've been here the whole time."

"I feel really quite strange."

"Really quite strange. Wow you really are a North Shore broad aren't you."

"I feel weird. My legs feel lovely."

"Don't worry." Kylie's enormous head towered over Kate's. "They probably just gave you something to help you relax."

Kate looked for her empty cup, but it was gone. Somewhere in her distant memory she remembered the nurse standing there while she drank her milk. But that was so long ago. Maybe when she was five. Before any of this began. She knew this, but her tongue had grown large and lazy in her mouth. Her shoulders felt wonderful. Kylie's head vanished. Kate rolled over in her bed to look at her. Kylie was asleep in her bed. Kate knew then as she looked over at Kylie in her white cottontails, that everything would be okay.

"Kylie? I love you Kylie," Kate said and slept.

The Book of Dreams

Kate

I was in the backyard pressing my palms against the trunk of the ghost gum. It felt like the skin of my grandmother. Something kicked my stomach and Bert Newton was staring at me with his big round moon-face grinning right out of the television. Something kicked me in the thigh. I pushed back but the thing kept wriggling next to me. Two smiling babies were grinning at me with big round moon-heads. They were Bert Newton's babies. I held their hands. I thought they were mine but then I woke and remembered they were my brother and my sister. Mum came in.

"Which one is this?"

"Jason." Exasperated.

"And Millie!" Remembering.

"Yes."

"No, that's not right. What's her real name?" Tangled words.

"It's Amelia. Millie for short."

The babies grinned up at me, showing off the twin teeth in their bottom gums. One started and the other one stopped. They were so cute. I tried to pick one up and smell the baby smell of its head.

"Be careful. Give her to me. They are still very fragile."

Maybe they were but their smiles weren't, or their waving arms. I waved back. Maybe I slept. It's hard to tell. The difference was imperceptible to me. At some point I ended up in my bed. Colourful blanket. That's all I could think. Colourful blanket.

I laid like that until my clothes became twisted around me and my sweaty hair clung to the back of my neck. My grandmother had crocheted the squares in the blanket because the label read *Made with Love by Nanna*. I pulled the blanket around me and imagined Nanna's arms reaching around to cuddle me. Her purple veins and blotchy skin melded into the purple wool. I lay feeling comfort, perfectly warm, the mattress the perfect amount of softness. Everything floated in a haze behind my eyelids in a perfect poppy-induced delirium.

Nanna's arms became Peter's arms, and I remembered him then. Strong. I breathed in the chalky smell of him as I lay in his arms. I giggled at the ceiling because I had a man in bed while my mum was watching Bert Newton in the lounge room. I could hear the mower outside and imagined the sweat glistening on Dad's bald head as he hunched over the lawnmower, oblivious that I had my lover in bed with me. It must be Saturday. I opened my eyes and Peter's arms melted into the pillows. My wardrobe door was open and a slip of blue satin was poking out. I remembered making a dress the same blue as my eyes. I remembered Kate Noble's party.

I must have the flu. That's what I thought then. But no flu would keep me from Kate Noble's party. Her party was the beginning of my future. The end of school. There was no time left now between me and my career. Between me and Peter. I had to go and see him.

I swayed a bit as I stood up. Dishes from food I didn't remember eating sat on my bedside table. I could hear a baby crying a long way away. I thought it must come from a neighbour's house and wondered who had a baby. I walked on pin and needle feet to my wardrobe. When I opened the door further there was my dress. Finished and hemmed. A thick row of pale blue lace had been sewn to the bottom. I stroked the blue satin between my fingertips. Peter's favourite colour, on me. I thought about the ocean.

In the bathroom I locked the door, letting the shower run while I took off my clothes. Steam billowed off the shower recess and fogged up the mirror. *Kate loves Peter* I wrote in the steam. I rubbed it out and watched as more steam came to cover up my secret. *Peter loves Kate* I wrote this time and circled it with the most perfect love heart, rounded and plump.

A sour stench came from my body. I smelled the sickness of my grandmother the last time I had seen her. She was in the hospital, her beautiful face yellow and sunken. I looked down. My body was disgusting. I slid open the shower door and grabbed my father's razorblade out of the cabinet. Thick, dark hair was sprouting from my legs. I checked my underarms and the pelt of fur there frightened me. In the shower I smoothed conditioner over my legs then made tracks with the razor. Blood trickled down my calf and circumnavigated my ankle. I washed my hair; shaved my pits.

"Katherine, are you alright in there?" Nervous.

"I'm having a shower." Obviously.

The lock turned and Mum was in the bathroom holding a bread-and-butter knife in her hand, the way she had done when I turned twelve and started locking her out.

"Mum!" Go away.

"I just wanted to see whether you were alright." Eyes on my breasts.

"I'm sick Mum. I feel really weird."

"Yes, but it's going to be okay now. My goodness, you've lost a lot of weight."

I looked at a fresh patch of pink skin on my arm. The scab must have fallen off. I felt woozy then and gripped onto the soap holder as dark splotches blinded me.

"Mummy, I need to sit down." Help me.

"Here, let me get a towel."

Mum grabbed my wrist and pulled me out of the shower, covering me in a towel. She led me to the corner of the bath to sit down.

"Neil!" she called out to Dad.

"Mum! I'm naked."

"Sorry," she said. "Let's just get you back to bed."

"But Mum. It's Katie's party tonight." I was sure of that. My dress was ready. It's Saturday. Dad was mowing the lawn.

"You need to sleep."

"I'm not missing that party for anything Mum." I mean it.

"Okay Kate. Let's just get you back to bed." Like she had talked to her own mother when Nanna was so old that she had forgotten who we were, and we'd have to bribe her with a Cherry Ripe before she would let us sit next to her in the nursing home.

"I'll be alright."

I let Mum steer me back towards my room. She gave me a gentle shove and I fell on my bed. I hugged my pink teddy and the towel fell away from me. Mum backed towards the hallway.

"I'll just get you your medicine."

"What medicine?" What medicine?

"The doctor prescribed it for you Kate. You don't remember? You've been in hospital."

"What?" I tried to sit up but there was black fluff behind my eyeballs.

"I'll get your tablets."

She backed into the hallway.

"Mum!" I followed her, holding onto the doorway. "What day is it? Mum! My exams!"

She was in the lounge room. The kitchen. I followed. There was nowhere left for her to go. Not outside.

"Neil!" she called for Dad again. "Neil. Come quickly."

Dad appeared, and I realised I was naked. I covered myself with my hands. One covered my public hair, the other flattened my nipples to my chest.

"She is clearly not better." Mum's voice was rising. "Look at her. She's naked. She is very agitated, Neil. She has cut herself! This is what the doctor warned us against if we brought her home early."

"Dad. Go away Dad. Go away!" Screaming.

"Let me help you." He moved closer.

"Go away!" A guttural scream the Carrolls would talk about for years.

I stood naked in front of Dad. The room was spinning. I forgot my exams. I forgot my shower. I had no idea why I was in front of my father in the kitchen with water dripping off me. I heard running water but when I looked out the window it wasn't raining.

Dad's fingertips were squeezing my elbow, gently then harder and harder. He held my putrid body as far from his own as he could and pulled me back to my bedroom. In the doorway he gave me a shove and I danced across the floor and landed on my bed.

I cried. I was scared. What was going on? Dad pushed the crochet blanket so it covered my disgusting body and the woolly hairs stuck to my damp skin. Mum pushed a glass of water into my hand and opened her fist like a flower. The tablets inside were pink and white and speckled like a sparrow's egg. I heard the shower running and wondered who was in the bathroom.

"Here," she said. "Take these."

"What are they?" The room was running around me. Lap after lap.

"They are good for you. They will help you relax. You have been very sick in hospital."

"What's wrong with me?" I remembered when Kate Noble had had appendicitis in Form Two and the scar that I wondered about that she would never show me.

"It's very low down," Mrs Noble had said, indicating her daughter's crotch with her perfectly manicured hand.

Mum whispered, "Don't worry about it now." This will never be discussed again.

I held the tablets in my hand and lay back on the pillows. The blanket itched so I threw it off and looked down at my nakedness. My body felt unfamiliar, as if it belonged to someone else. I tried to swallow the tablets but one of them got stuck in my throat. The bitterness of it tasted familiar. I remembered warm milk and honey. I remembered squeaking shoes and the taste of orange juice in the back of my throat. I saw pubic hair floating like confetti in the air. I laid in bed with the water covering me and just the islands of my breasts poking up. Mum came in.

"Oh, Kate," she said and covered me in a sheet. It was liberty print. "Are you alright Darling?" her voice started to blur like she had a mouthful of honey. Maybe she had drunk warm milk and honey too.

"Yes, I'm still going to Kate's party. I'll be fine."

"Kate. You aren't going anywhere." I opened my mouth like a baby bird and she fed me more pills. I swallowed them dry.

When I woke my room was dull. My dress was beckoning from the wardrobe. I felt better. It must be time to go.

"It's the wrong night," said Mum.

"It's Saturday." Sure of that at least.

There was something odd about the atmosphere of the night. I felt it as soon as I put on my dress. It zipped up too easily. My hair hung limp and I had to flip it upside-down and tease it to get some body into it. Just like Mum did. My makeup sat on top of my face instead of blending into it. I stared at my face in the mirror. I saw my mother staring blonde-haired and blue-eyed back at me. I put on more makeup. I knew that everything was wrong, but I didn't know what everything was. My makeup tightened my face like a mask.

Mum hovered shadowy behind me, the skin on her neck as limp as her hair. Softly, "It's not the Saturday you are thinking of though."

I remembered my HSC. I couldn't remember doing my exams. I realised I hadn't turned eighteen yet. I was in the lounge room. It must be two weeks early for the party.

"Oh."

"Oh." Echo.

Dad was in the hallway. Moving but silent.

"It's all wrong!"

I ran to the kitchen and looked out the window at the Carroll's jacaranda. One branch had reached hopefully over the fence and dribbled its petals into our yard. Bright green leaves were starting to poke through the flowers.

"We were given a tree like that when you were born. The matron gave one to all the parents when they took their babies home. That's why there are so many jacarandas around here. We kept it in a pot for three years until we moved here, but as soon as we planted it into the open ground it just… fizzled."

Mum talked. Dad hovered. Someone turned the kitchen light on and the tree disappeared. I could see my parents' reflection in the kitchen window. Mum was ghostly and pale in her dressing gown. Dad's face hung around the doorway. It looked like he had no body. Like he was the floating head of a ventriloquist's doll. Who was controlling him?

Mum kept talking. She talked fast. I got confused. I had imagined sitting for my exams so many times. Had I, or hadn't I?

"Katie Noble got a new car for her graduation. You know what the Nobles are like. All money and no sense." Forced laugh.

I turned. "We haven't graduated yet."

Dad shuffled his body into the kitchen.

"Yes, well, it was going to happen soon enough. Her parents knew what the end result would be. All that private tutoring." Nervous laugh.

I ran out of the kitchen with the screen door slapping back at the house in my wake.

"Katherine!"

"Kate!" Echo. No one came after me. I could hear babies screaming.

*

I stopped at the foot of the driveway trying to muster as much decorum as I could in my party dress and bare feet. Kate Noble's house was hidden from the road by a huge hedge. I looked at the house, all red brick and stained glass. It was so similar to my parents' house but so much bigger that it made my place look like a model for the real thing. There was a pale-yellow MG in the driveway with its top down, ready to go.

My brain felt like fairy floss and I had to whisper out loud so I could hear myself. But my thoughts melted before I could remember them. I am at Kate Noble's house. I am at Kate Noble's house. I am at Kate Noble's house. I already knew that though. But there was something else. Something I didn't know. I sucked air into my mouth as I started up the drive. Cool grass caressed my bare feet as I skirted the car. The red leather seats looked warm and inviting. I imagined climbing over the door rim and falling to sleep deep in that red leather, but I forced my eyes to stay open.

"This time I will stay awake." I whispered new rules to myself.

I rang the doorbell and listened as the chimes echoed through the house.

"Katie," Mrs Noble called back down the hallway as soon as she opened the door, and then, "Sam, go and get your sister."

"You bought her a car? Already?" What was happening to me?

"Samuel, call Katie." Polite smile. Urgent eyes.

Sam stood ogling me from halfway down the hallway. He was pale and freckly as if he did not belong in the Noble household at all, except for his arrogance, which he had twice as much of. He needed arrogance to make up for his ugliness.

Sam stood still, ready for the show. "Kate, Kate's here," he flung back over his shoulder, laughing at his old joke.

Kate Noble appeared in the doorway. Her hair was short like a pixie.

"You've cut your hair. Oh, my goodness. When did you do that? Oh, my goodness. It looks. It looks... great." My mouth was dry.

I ran my fingers through my own hair then but those locks I had always been so proud of now seemed superfluous. I slowly tucked strands of hair behind my ears. Kate Noble laughed.

"You look just the same." One eyebrow raised.

"Why wouldn't I?" I didn't. I wasn't the same.

The telephone rang in the hallway and Mrs Noble walked backwards to answer it. Watching me.

"Come on, let's talk," Katie said and grabbed my hand and we ran together over the lawn to the special place where we had rolled like puppies as children. A kookaburra laughed at us from a telegraph pole and we laughed back up at it. Laughing felt safer than talking. Still holding hands, we sat carefully on the grass. Neither of us wanted grass stains on our outfits. Katie was wearing a white pantsuit that made her look more glamorous than my cheap blue satin. I tucked my skirt into my lap, aware that Sam and Mrs Noble were watching from the front porch, recording the event in their memories so that they could each re-enact it for their friends the next day.

We stopped laughing although the kookaburra continued. Kate Noble picked a purple flower from the lawn and stuck it in her hair. It matched her eyes. She looked like a fairy. I tried to do the same, but the flower fell from my hair.

"Here, let me," Katie said, turning me around and putting flowers in my hair.

"My cousin goes to some posh school in the country," said Katie. "You can't walk on the grass. They say it's sacred."

"The grass is sacred? That's crazy."

"Yes, except for jacaranda season. Then the girls, and the girls only, can sit on the grass under the tree."

"On the sacred grass?"

"Yes, but they can only sit under the tree if they have a violet ribbon in their hair, so it matches the jacaranda flowers."

"No way." I wondered if Kate could hear the thickness of my tongue. I felt like I was drunk in front of my parents.

"Yes way."

"I'd just put a flower in my hair. The old bat teachers wouldn't notice the difference."

Kate turned me back around.

"Teachers aren't all old and blind." There was a fluttering smile on Katie's lips. I was glad of my long hair then, easy to hide behind. But Kate Noble doesn't need to hide her boldness behind hair. Her purple eyes looked straight at me. "Were you pregnant?"

"What?"

"Katie!" called Mrs Noble. She was watching from the verandah, listening to everything even from that impossibly long distance away.

Katie jumped up and skipped towards her mother in one fluid motion. I stayed under the tree, watching them as they negotiated outside the still open front door, being careful not to look in my direction. I needed to sleep. I lay flat on the grass and looked up at the pink sky.

"Come on," Katie called as she glided back towards me, "Let's go for a drive. Away from our audience." Whispered.

I allowed myself to be pulled up and I followed my friend on tiptoe to the MG.

"Get in," Katie said with all the authority of being born a Noble.

"Why do you have it already?"

"Early," said Mrs Noble, suddenly beside her daughter. "That's right Katie, darling, isn't it? Daddy decided to surprise you before the exams." Mrs Noble looked her daughter in the eye. "Didn't he darling?"

"Sure. Let's go," Katie said as she pulled keys from her trouser pocket.

"Katherine," said Mrs Noble. They stood facing each other. Same height. Both slim. Both beautiful with eyes like the sea. But Katie was not going to be defeated. Not today, with her short hair and her car keys slung casually off her finger like a man. Her breasts were high, while Mrs Noble's breasts laid flat against her chest. Deflated and defeated. She didn't stand a chance, although she did make one more futile attempt. "Do you really think this is appropriate? Katie, you know what I am trying to say Katherine, don't you?" Wheedling like a child. Roles reversed. We climbed into the car while Mrs Noble's nervous hands fondled one earring. Nanna said it was not a nice habit to have.

"I'm just going to show her the flat, Mum," said Katie, already reversing down the drive, not looking behind her and running over the inferior purple of the agapanthus. It's okay. Those things can survive anything. My mum refused to have agapanthus in her garden. She said they were for old ladies who couldn't bend down to pick flowers anymore. For a moment I felt superior to the Nobles. They may be rich. Kate Noble may be beautiful. Her parents might buy her a car for finishing school—something that the rest of us had to do, car or no car. But her parents had ordinary old agapanthus in their garden. Old lady plants. Graveyard plants. I laughed out loud. Kate screeched the car around the corners, laughing with me.

"I can't believe they gave you the car early."

The car spun around a dozen bandy streets, but Katie Noble didn't answer me.

"Were you pregnant?" she asked again.

I looked at her.

"I mean," she said looking at me instead of the road. "Were you pregnant with Michael Ballins' baby?"

A siren sounded as Kate bumped over a gutter on the next turn. A police car was behind us. Kate pulled over to the curb.

The policeman walked to the driver's side door. He looked like Mr Carroll.

"That's some pretty interesting driving there, young lady," he said, standing above us, looking at our legs. Katie's were outlined in linen but mine were bare to the upper thigh. I noticed that my tan had faded. My legs looked yellow.

"There was a dog. I swerved to avoid it." Those sapphire eyes could get away with anything.

"I didn't see a dog, but I will take your word for it this time," the policeman said. "Drive carefully. You wouldn't want to upset your parents now, would you? You are driving a very beautiful car."

"Never," said Katie, looking him straight in the eye. "That's the last thing I would want."

"I'll be keeping an eye out for you from now on." The officer said it like a promise.

We watched him walk back to his police car; his stride stiffened by our laughter. Katie waited until the police car took off in front of us and turned down a side street to wait for its next victim.

"What a boring job. How would he even know whose car this is?" said Katie, ruffling her hair in her hands.

"I didn't have a baby," I said as Katie wrenched the steering wheel. The car veered and felt like it might tip. I closed my eyes and when I opened them, we were on the road heading towards the Harbour Bridge and the city.

"I didn't ask if you had a baby. I asked if you were pregnant."

"I'm not pregnant!"

"*Was* pregnant."

"Oh." You remembered your mother saying that sometimes things happen. You remembered something about borrowed money. Who said that?

"You've lost a lot of weight."

"I've been sick. Who said I had a …a pregnant." We both laughed then. "Half of them."

"And the other half?"

"You went mental and had a lobotomy."

I was the only one laughing as Katie screamed over the Harbour Bridge. I had to hold my hair down with both hands. "Look at all that," Katie said, taking her hands off the steering wheel and gesturing towards the city. I imagined Ita Buttrose in one of the skyscrapers, making choices and giving orders.

Katie was looking at me, but I forgot what we were talking about. I stared upwards at the struts of the bridge arching over our heads. It is the arch of the bridge that holds it up, not the stone pylons. We learnt that in science.

"I don't get it," Michael Ballins had said. "It has to be the pillars. Or the whole thing would fall down."

But I had understood. I held my head back and looked at the arches above me and felt them pulling, keeping the road beneath us in place. I looked at the navy sky though the bars of the bridge, looking for birds. The bridge curved over our heads like the diagram of an ecosystem with that bug that gets eaten by the frog.

"So… what do you reckon will happen to everyone?" I screamed into the wind.

"Oh, I can tell you that. Sue Golding will go to medical school and marry a doctor before she finishes and become his receptionist. But she will still act as if she knows more than the doctors. The other Sue will become a teacher and end up just like Miss Fance. Frances will get engaged to Michael Ballins because they won't be careful in the bedroom." Katie gagged on her own finger and pretended to retch over the side of the car. The MG slid across lanes until we were inches from a mustard-coloured station wagon. The driver honked her horn, her middle-aged face screwed up in anger. Katie stuck her fingers up right in the woman's face and moved her car even closer until the woman had no choice but to let us have the lane, her horrified lips spewing silent curses at us.

"Little Michael will join the air force to prove that he is big now." Katie winked at Kate and gestured to her crotch. "Like we hadn't noticed."

I looked at her for hidden signs of despair, but Katie was concentrating on the road. "Which is fine because I need to have at least three serious affairs before I even think about getting married."

I laughed. It was as if all Kate Noble's snobbery had been cut off with her hair and she was carefree and happy. It made her even more beautiful. But then who drives a convertible without gaining a couple of points in attractiveness?

Katie raised one eyebrow then and said coyly, "And the rumour will be true. Mr Mason will have to move schools because he has been found to be liaising," she spread that delicious word out as far as she could, li-ay-sing "with none other than (she beat her fingers on the steering wheel for effect) Miss Leach."

"Oh, but that's not true. It's such an old rumour anyway." Straight face.

"It's a fact now kiddo."

Katie slowed down just enough to fling a two dollar note into the hand of the toll collector and then accelerate before he could give her change. She cut left over four lanes before pulling over. Cars tooted as they were forced to rearrange themselves in the wake of the MG. I looked behind us then for the policeman, but he hadn't kept his promise.

"See that?" said Katie, pointing to a skyscraper over the other side of the bridge. "The one away from the other buildings."

"You can't stop here—you're nuts."

We both laughed this time. We had never gotten on so well.

"That's where I am going to live next year. It's called the Blues Point Tower. My flat is number 58, facing the water. Two bedrooms. I can see everything from up there. The Opera House. The Harbour Bridge. If I am late to catch my ferry, I can see it coming."

"Fantastic! I am sure you will get into law."

"Oh no, I've decided to do journalism. Daddy bought me the flat to congratulate me. I have to share though."

"I'll share it with you."

"I'm sharing with Sue Golding. She's doing medicine at Sydney Uni."

"You don't know that yet."

"Kate. Christmas has been and gone. Our results are in. Stop playing with me Kate. Where have you been?"

She was right. Of course, I knew that. The babies were smiling. The jacaranda flowers had fallen. I knew I hadn't had a baby. I wrenched the car door open and started walking back over the Bridge, away from the city. I watched the Blues Point Tower, bobbing its ugly head over the other side of the bridge. No footsteps came chasing me, and this time I didn't expect them.

Katie reversed up next to me and had to keep driving backwards to keep up.

"I was never pregnant," I threw at her, realising too late what that meant I was admitting to.

"Get in Kate," she said. "Come on. I'll take you home."

"I'm not going home."

"Where are you going then? I'll drive you."

"No."

I wanted to run to Blues Point Tower and up all the stairs until I found flat number 58. I wanted to open the door and go inside and lay down on the bed and sleep. There was never enough sleep.

Katie was still reversing alongside me. My car door was still open and flapping like the wing of an injured bird.

"Are you going to someone's house?"

"No."

"Are you running away?"

"Go away." Katie's voice in my head was stopping me from grasping at memories that were sliding around in my brain. I would remember something for a moment and then forget it. I knew I had forgotten something important. What was it?

Luckily Katie didn't argue for long. I knew her heart wasn't in it. She wanted to drive her new car and show me her new flat. That's all she wanted from me—a witness to her dreamy life. I turned my head away from Katie. She couldn't go back any further anyway without running over a toll collector. I was now free to think. I remembered things, but I couldn't choose what to remember. I remembered Peter. I remembered my exams. I knew the periodic table of the elements and the parts of a flower. I knew the genus of a mouse and how to calculate sin, cos, and tan. I knew that just the smell of orange juice made me vomit. I knew that history was a bunch of times and dates that were only relative to the present day in context. I knew that pubic hair could float through the air as gently as a dust mote. I knew that Peter never loved me, or he would have come and rescued me. I knew that Ita Buttrose didn't go to university. I knew *The Crucible* was about betrayal. I knew that I had missed out on turning eighteen and I had missed my HSC exams because I was lying in a hospital bed with so many drugs being pumped into me that my legs melted.

I leant against the balustrade and hung my heavy head over the edge of the bridge, staring at Kate Noble's view of the city. Two gulls screamed and fought in mid-air. One of them turned downwind and plunged towards the water, flapping its wings as if it had lost its grip on the air. I imagined living in Blues Point Tower overlooking this grey reflection-less water. I looked at the Opera House with the ferries running towards it and away from it as if they too couldn't decide whether it was ugly or beautiful. I imagined running to catch a ferry to my office in the city. I would meet with Ita Buttrose and we would plan the next edition of *Cleo* together, moving photos around, selecting and rejecting. They say that looking at water brings peace, but all I could see was restlessness in the choppy water. I thought I would like to live with the water endlessly shifting around me. I could watch that water forever. Just that and nothing else. Time wouldn't matter then. Not ten days until exams or four weeks until Christmas. I stayed there until the light had almost all been sucked out of the day.

"Hey. Get off there."

I turned and a man was behind me, a toll collector in his vest. There was another person. And another. Someone held a camera up and flashed my face with arrogant light. I hid behind my hair.

"Put that away," a man yelled to the woman holding the camera, and then so softly I had to strain to hear him above the wind. "It's okay, love. Just step down from there."

I laughed then but Katie was gone and there were no kookaburras there to laugh with me. The camera flashed again and a policeman grabbed my arm and a red blanket was thrown around my shoulders even though Katie had said it was after Christmas. The light flashed once more, and the police covered my face in the blanket like a criminal and I was in the back of a police car with grey vinyl seats and the police didn't pay the Harbour Bridge toll. I guessed they must be exempt.

"Kate." The policeman knew my name.

"I wasn't doing anything." Nothing.

"Your friend called us. She said you were very agitated. She is worried about you." About herself.

I assumed they were taking me home, so I sat in the back seat and closed my eyes, letting the blanket fall off my face. If I pretended to sleep maybe they would stop talking to me and I would have time to figure everything out. I was wrong.

The police car pulled up in front of Ferriby Private Hospital. I knew that because I read the sign. It didn't look like a hospital. It looked like Granny's cottage from a fairy tale. There were white roses growing in the front garden. Why did I recognise this place? A man came and opened my door. It was Dr Grafton. He leant in to talk to me. I remembered him and almost jumped up to hug him because I was so happy that I remembered something as last. But then I didn't. I stayed in the back seat of the car, hugging the blanket around me, tighter and tighter the more he talked.

Dr Grafton stopped talking. He got into the police car and sat beside me. He was wearing an evening jacket and bowtie. He didn't say anything and for a moment I wondered whether the police would escort us both to a ball. But the police stayed outside, and the doctor just sat, and I just sat, and I knew that sooner or later I would fall asleep and they would have me then.

I kept my eyes as wide open as I could. They couldn't make me go in there.

"I wasn't trying to jump, you know."

"I would be very surprised if you were."

"Why?"

"Women don't kill themselves it that way. They use pills."

I was a woman. I must be eighteen now. I was a woman, but I knew I was not that kind of a woman. I remembered Kylie then. I remembered Mum stuffing my mouth with bitter pills until the edges softened on the world. I wanted to sleep. I needed to sleep, but I kept my eyes open.

"I missed my HSC." Accusation. "Why did you keep me in there so long? Why can't I remember anything?"

"You were in hospital because you've been sick."

"I missed my birthday." I sounded like a petulant child. "I missed my exams. I missed out on university."

"You are not well enough for university, Kate."

"I'm fine. There's nothing wrong with me."

"Kate, the police just brought you to me." I looked out the car window at the policemen smoking next to the hospital sign. One of them kept tugging at his moustache and I wondered what he was thinking about. "Your parents are worried. They didn't have any idea where you were. They said you just ran off into the night with no shoes on, no money. Your mother is hysterical. You were climbing up the railing of the Sydney Harbour Bridge."

"You said you believed me. I was never going to jump."

"I do. But Kate, I must ask you this. What were you thinking about when you were leaning over the bridge?"

"The water. I like the water."

"What do you like about the water? What were you thinking?"

I wanted to swim. I wanted the water to go into my ears and clean out my brain. I wanted to swim down until the daylight was so far above me that the world looked green. I had nothing to say.

"So, you see my dilemma, Kate?"

"I know what it looks like but I'm fine. I didn't do anything."

"Kate, do I need to remind you why you were brought here the first time?"

"My sleazy neighbour?"

"Falling in love with an older man. Having an inappropriate relationship with him. I think you did this because you saw this man as a father figure. As for your neighbour. Your neighbour may have been enticed by the behaviours you were displaying."

"I wasn't displaying anything."

"Katherine. You call yourself Kat. What's a man supposed to think?"

I wanted to kick him then, to punch him in his smug doctor's face. I looked at the police waiting under the hospital sign, finishing off their cigarettes. The one with the moustache stubbed his butt out under the toe of his boot and crushed it into the ground. The other took a long final drag and looked over to the car to see if I was still sitting there. I was. I should have run then. Slipped my seatbelt off silently under the cover of the blanket. Worked my body over to the door closest to the road. I thought about it. I looked at the neighbour's houses for the gardens with the thickest bushes. Somewhere to hide. I could have done it. Slapped that doctor's smiling face and then run while the police were still wondering if they had time for another cigarette. Having nowhere to go should not have stopped me. Sometimes I think about Ronald Ryan, the last man hanged in Australia. Why did he go so calmly to his death? He should have run. Kicked and screamed. Sure, he would have died anyway. They would have caught him in the end, but without a fight there was no chance at all. I was thinking of Mr Mason in science class saying, "I expect you all to act like the mature young adults of Beecroft Secondary College." I was sitting on the edge of the bed while Peter pulled on his jeans saying, "Kate, you are so beautiful sometimes I forget how very young you are." I remembered that, and I forgot to fight, and forgetting to fight was the worst thing I could have done. I should have tried. At least I should have tried. But I was worried that the police would drag me inside in front of everybody. I was worried about where to go. I was worried about causing a scene. I wanted to be an adult. I looked at the white roses glowing in the garden. A lonely pigeon was scratching around in the grass. The pigeon made me think it couldn't be that bad. But that's just because I didn't remember.

"Come into my office and we'll have a little chat."

The black fuzz floated in front of my eyes again as Dr Grafton helped me out of the car. He held my arm like a gentleman escorting me to a party and we walked together into Granny's cottage. I could have escaped even then. I could have slipped out of his loose grasp and ran while the police were pretending not to watch us. Pretending not to look at my long, yellow legs. Maybe I could have made it. I should have fought. But instead I walked inside on the arm of a monster. And that was how I ended up with round two of Slumber Therapy.

"Oh no. I have their blanket still."

"That's okay. We can return it later."

*

As soon as I was in Dr Grafton's office, I told him everything that had happened. He must have been used to deciphering words from crying patients as my sobs didn't seem to put him off.

"Here," he said, "have a look at these." He pulled a series of pictures out of his desk drawer and came to sit on the couch close to me. His suit pants rubbed against my freshly shaved leg. The fabric was silky. They must have been much more expensive than my father's serge suits. The pictures he showed me were like those I painted at kindergarten when I was three years old, where the teacher folds the paper in half and it makes a butterfly: all pretty colours. Except these pictures were all black ink.

"What do you think this one looks like?"

"A bug." Is that right? Dr Grafton nodded imperceptibly and flashed another card at me.

"A moth?" He nodded again, his face blank.

"And this?"

"An umbrella." What was the right answer?

With each card the doctor rotated his body on the couch. His knee pressed further into mine. I put the red blanket between us. Maybe that was the wrong thing to do. The doctor stood up and moved his office chair opposite me and started again. He flashed another card towards me and then another. They blurred in front of my eyes and the ink bled across the page. I wanted him to stop but he thrust another picture at me. Again. and again. Pushing me and pushing me. I thought he would never stop. I counted the pictures.

"A bug." Eighteen. I already said this.

"A horse's head." Nineteen.

"A flower." Twenty. I needed him to stop. Now. I'd had enough.

"Two colourful fish. Kissing." The doctor's face didn't move although the picture was black and white. It is as if he had expected this. As if I had played right into his hands.

"Well, Kate," he said finally as if the pictures and my answers had told him nothing about me that he didn't already know, and yet everything. Even things I didn't know about myself. I pulled the blanket back over me.

Dr Grafton raised his eyebrow and looked at me with his warm, brown eyes. "What do you think I should do with you?"

"I just want to go home." I thought of my bed with Nanna's warm blanket.

"Where is home? Is home with your parents?"

"No!" Sudden realisation. "Not anymore."

I cried then, and the doctor reached his hand inside my blanket. He stroked my hair as if it was still beautiful.

"How do you feel right now?"

"Tired. I want to sleep. I want to wake up and find that none of this has happened."

The doctor stood and held out his hand. My eyes blurred again as I stood up and he held my elbow to steady me. His arm was around my waist. I leant into him. He felt warm. Warmer than the blanket that dropped to the floor as he walked me out of the room. Why did I go with him? Was it simply because I didn't want to go home? Back to my parents and two new siblings that grinned like the Cheshire cat whenever I looked at them? Back to a place where I had failed my HSC by default? Where Peter didn't love me? I wanted to forget all that. Again. I wanted the walls to grow hair as blonde as the sun and my legs to melt into oblivion.

But that is not why I let the doctor lead me back to the room of sleep. I really wanted to go to Peter's place. I wanted his strong arms around me. I wanted him to fuck me again—just once more so that at least I would know this was the last time. So at least I knew that the salty taste of his sweat was there as he strained to make me come. To perform just for me. One more time. I knew that if I left here, I would go straight to Peter's and he would reject me again and I would not be able to handle that rejection a second time. So I let Dr Grafton take me back to the room at the end of the hall and when I stood in the doorway and looked at the bed it felt like home. Dr Grafton was behind me, guiding me through the doorway, holding my forearm.

And then retreating. Using me as a shield. A crazed woman was charging towards us.

"Miss Mitchell," Dr Grafton said, his voice as stern as Mr Guard's.

"Call me Kylie!" she screamed, her face too close to his and her body floating somewhere behind, like a ghost.

The doctor almost ran back up the hallway then, shoving me into the doorframe on his way.

"Go then. Fine." Kylie threw her pillow. It landed at my feet.

I remembered her. I remembered my secrets and hers. I remembered her long brown legs. Dancer's legs. I remembered her face. The face of home.

"Kylie, it's me! I'm back!"

"What were you doing with him?"

"What? Who?"

"Don't act all innocent with me." Her Farrah Fawcett hair was all messed up. She shoved her face in mine. "Jack of course. Was he treating you?"

"We were just looking at pictures."

"Well, he's mine! Leave him alone." Screaming. Pushing. Her hands were against my hips, shunting me backwards. Her eyes were red balls.

"I just got here."

"Didn't take you long then, did it?"

"Kylie, don't you remember me? It's Kat. I'm not stealing Jack."

"Don't call him Jack, little girl."

A nurse grabbed Kylie by the shoulders and shoved her back into the room. I was surprised she didn't resist. Her arms went limp as soon as the nurse touched her.

"Sorry," a nurse said to me. "Miss Mitchell has developed an obsession with Dr Grafton. We will find you another room."

A needle. Kylie turned to liquid and the nurses poured her onto the bed.

"No, it's okay. She knows who I am now. We are friends."

"Heaven help us." Rubber squealed on linoleum as the nurses left the room. Their words floated back at me from down the hallway.

"That Kylie Mitchell needs to go home."

"She can't go home. She's a mess."

"Well, she wasn't a mess when she got here but she's certainly a mess now."

I climbed onto my bed and stared at the smooth painted wall.

"I'm pregnant you know," Kylie's words were the half-sung, half-spoken words of a drunk person. "I'm having Jack's baby. Not even his wife has done that. That means I am the one. I am his and he is mine. Crazy, isn't it? You couldn't win Doctor Grafton off me if you tried. Neither can anybody else. He's gonna leave his wife and we'll get a little place and we'll live by the sea and have water babies that can swim before they can walk. Maybe they'll be born with tails. They'll be mermaids. And Jack and I will get married and he'll give me a pink pearl ring straight from an oyster shell."

Her words slurred into nothing and I imagined babies with mermaid tails swimming with angel fish. I waited for them to bring me the drink that made my legs feel lovely and hair to grow from the walls. But they didn't come, and I fell asleep anyway, comforted by the stiff sheets. I woke hearing Dr Grafton's voice in my room. I peeked through my eyelids and saw him bending over Kylie. He was still wearing his evening suit with his bow tie.

I know this really happened because they didn't give me any medicine that night even though I wanted them to and waited for them patiently like a good girl. I wanted those speckled sparrow's eggs. So much. A nurse came in. Maybe she had some pills for me now. Pink pills like the ones that Mum gave me. Pink pills that make my legs dissolve into a tail so that I can swim underwater. I already knew I could breathe underwater. I started to sit up so that I could swallow better. My sheets rustled.

"Shh." Doctor Grafton didn't sound like a doctor now. But he was. I knew that at least.

"Kat can't hear anything. She's doped."

I was not sure why Kylie said that. Maybe she thought I was. Maybe she didn't know otherwise. But maybe she did know. Maybe she knew I was awake. Maybe she wanted me to hear. I held my breath. I listened then. I listened because Kylie wanted me to.

Kylie moved and her sheets sounded like the static on television after the programs have finished. The static I always heard when I fell asleep on the lounge while I was studying. While I was waiting for my parents to sleep so I could sneak over to Peter's place.

"You are too emotionally disturbed to have a child, Kylie." Doctor Grafton didn't even whisper.

"But it's *our* baby. I can love it at least. That's more than what a lot of babies get."

"It's not a baby, darling. It is just a few cells." Calm. Insistent.

Kylie sobbed as Doctor Grafton helped her out of our room. Her dancer's feet were soundless as if she didn't exist. Hear no evil.

Later Kylie came back with Doctor Grafton and another woman. She was as floppy as a rag doll and drawled out words to me, but I couldn't understand her. I pretended to be asleep like a child who wants to be forgotten so she can stay up late. The woman and Doctor Grafton stayed and soon Kylie stopped mumbling and her breath was low and soft. I peeked between my eyelids and the doctor was next to her bed. He was still wearing the suit, but his bowtie was gone. His hair was rumpled and there was fear in his brown eyes. Was Kylie going to die? Doctor Grafton watched Kylie sleep as if he was afraid that she wouldn't wake up. As if he was willing her to wake up. I wondered what had happened to her. I waited for them to leave, to go to the toilet, but even this they did in shifts so that someone was there. Someone was always there. I remembered Mum's voice. *Sometimes things happen.*

"Kylie," I wanted to call. "Hey, are you okay?"

They finally left, and I listened to their footsteps recede. I heard a door. I heard nothing.

"Kylie." No answer. "Kylie!" No breathing. I wondered if they'd left me in a room with a dead person.

I threw my pillow at her body and it bounced off, landing with a thud on the floor. I held my breath, squeezing my eyes shut. I listened for her breathing but I couldn't hear anything. Slowly I pushed the blanket off and slid off the bed. My bare feet splatted onto the floor. I was no dancer. I tiptoed over to the other bed like a child. I heard it then, Kylie's thin breath whistling in and out. In and out. In and out. I looked at Kylie's face. It was bruised. One eye was swollen and purple. Her lips were large. No one was worried that Kylie would die. Doctor Grafton wasn't worried that Kylie wouldn't wake up. He was worried that she would. I needed to learn to keep quiet.

*

I didn't know why it took so many days for them to bring me the medicine. The little pink pills that I knew I would never get if I dared to ask for them. The pills that I knew would somehow stop the twitching and the sweating. The pills that made my skin itch at the thought of them. That taste in my throat. It felt like forever. When they finally put me under, I welcomed the oblivion. Who could ask for more? Death without dying and lovely, lovely legs.

"Put these two together. They are thick as thieves." The sound of nurses with their squishy, rubbery soled shoes.

Ferriby Hospital was bigger this time. There were more beds. Rows of sleepers hibernating from the world. It was peaceful. I woke and I fell. Woke and fell. I went along with the ride like I was floating on a cloud. It felt familiar and I knew that I had done this before. I knew that this is where I belonged. Where I was meant to be. I was a child of the sky and I knew how to deal with pain, and love.

"Now Katherine." Doctor Grafton's voice.

"Call me Kat."

"Kat. Like a pussy cat?"

"Yes, like you know, meow." I didn't know what I was saying.

"Like a pussy? Do you know how to purr Kat? Or do you need someone to teach you?"

Then Kylie was next to me with the squishy rubber shoe brigade. She was naked and the nurses were hovering, fat and then thin like they were in a funhouse mirror. I grinned at them. I tried to think about Peter, but I didn't care. I wasn't worried about him. I wasn't worried about Miss Leach. She could suck Peter's blood and I would be happy for them. Genuine happiness. All I could feel was love.

I saw the nurse wiping blood from between Kylie's legs. From that secret place my mother could only whisper about. I was a child in the bath and my mother was handing me a face washer. Don't forget to wash in between your legs. Her face turned away. Her nose wrinkled. I remembered Kylie saying she was pregnant. Now the nurses were wiping and wiping at blood. They shoved a towel there, but it soaked through. More nurses came. They were like molecules connecting together faster and faster. The linoleum swirled around their knees, and their feet became buried in the foam of the sea. Disintegrating.

I tried to sit up then, but my lovely legs wouldn't move. The baby. Something was wrong with the baby. Sometimes things happen. Kylie sat and swiped at her leg with her hand, covering it in blood. *You are too emotionally disturbed to have a child, Kylie.*

"Where's my baby?" *It's not a baby Darling. It is just a few cells.* The patients in the other beds didn't move no matter how loud Kylie screamed.

"Get Doctor Grafton." Squishy shoes ran.

They ran back.

"She isn't pregnant. She's hallucinating." Doctor Grafton's voice.

"Look at her breasts. Her areola are huge."

Kylie was shaking her head from side to side. Her hair was wet and matted across her face.

"I've got a baby. Jack stole my baby."

More squishy shoes.

"Doctor Grafton says she's hallucinating. It's just her monthlies."

A hyena scream that didn't end. I closed my eyes and stayed in bed like a good girl.

"Doctor Grafton says to put her in deeper!" Now. Hurry.

Squishy shoes left and when they came back Kylie's scream was sucked back into her and sealed inside. I sat up. Squishy shoes came, and a nurse pushed me gently back onto the pillow. I was five years old, asleep behind the sofa. I could hear my parents searching for me, and I smiled in my sleep. Thank you, squishy shoes.

*

My sleep became strange and my dreams were full of hands. Mr Carroll's octopus-hands were on my chest pressing down. I tried to wake up, but layers of sleep and layers of blankets were holding me down. The pale green cotton hospital blanket was tucked in so hard I couldn't move my feet and the red police blanket kept covering my face no matter how many times I pushed it away. Nanna's blanket lay on top of them all, but its colourful wool had started to unravel, and the loose ends were twisted all around me. The more I struggled the more the veins of wool wove around my wrists and trapped me in the bed.

But I was not alone. Thick fingers were touching me. Thick fingers were kneading at my breasts and twisting my nipples. Shoving at my legs, pushing them apart. Thick fingers were trying to get inside me, but they didn't know where to go. I tried to sit up and the hand was gone but then slapped across my mouth. I could smell myself on his hands, sour and strong. I was quiet, but someone was screaming. I woke up.

"Help me. Oh, please God, help me. Please untie me. I want my baby. I can't hold my baby. They have tied me up. Help me. My baby will fall off. Untie me. Please. I need my arms. I need my arms. I need my arms."

Squishy shoes came. Only one set. Squish, squish, squish. Kylie was quiet.

"I need to use the bathroom." That's all I cared about. Kylie was keeping me awake.

"Just do it in the bed. We'll clean it up later."

"I can't do that." I can't do that.

"Everybody does that."

"Well, I simply cannot."

Squishy shoes left then. I tried to hold on. I needed to leave. This was a mistake. I got out of bed, but my legs crumbled beneath me. They were under the surface of the linoleum. I sat on the ground. The lino felt smooth and cool. I lay with my cheek on the ground. The lino floated over my body. It was my blanket. I realised I could swim. I used my arms to swim breaststroke, my shattered tail dragged along behind, dropping shiny blue scales in its wake. When I got to Kylie's bed, I untied the rubber glove pinning her wrist to the bed rail. We would escape together.

"Kylie." I pulled at her arm, but she was asleep. Fast asleep. Dead to the world.

I needed to wait. To wait for her to wake so I could find her father in the undersea kingdom. Warm liquid spread below me, like a carton of milk spilt at the breakfast table, impossible to retrieve. I sat in the puddle of my own piss.

Squishy, squishy, squishy, squishy. Squishy.

I was in bed. Not awake. Not asleep. The walls blurred with blonde hairs and the green of my hospital blanket. I closed my eyes. There was a dull ache in the back of my head. Behind my eyes. I smelt oranges. I gagged. Someone else was in the room. I opened my eyes, white. I closed them, black. Opened to the whiteness of day. Closed, dark nighty-night. I chanted, "White, day. Black, night. Open, closed. Closed open. Open is day. Closed is night."

Squishy, squishy, squishy, squishy. Squishy.

A white shadow said, "Go to sleep. It's night-time."

My thick tongue repeated the words, "Go to sleep, it is night-time." Everything was white.

The nurse injected liquid into a tube stuck in the back of my hand.

"Night-time, yes. It is night-time."

I pissed myself as I fell back through the bed. The liquid stung as I tried to open my legs. I remembered Mr Carroll sweating on top of me in the bedroom with naked silhouettes on the wallpaper. I was covered in someone else's sweat. *Open your legs. Relax Kate.* But I clamped them shut because Mum was right. *It's not very nice to sit like that Katherine. Closeyourlegs.* But they weren't *my* legs because they were stuck together with scabs and pus and I couldn't get them apart. My knees had melded together, and the skin had grown over. Squishy, squishy, squishy, squishy. Squishy. Night, day, night, day, night, day, day, night-light. The night was light.

Iwoketherewassomethingchokingmepullatplastictubesgoingdownmythr oatpullthetubessoftpaddingnursescomingggagginglcannotbreathelwasscream ingcatinthehattrytoopenmyeyesgluedshut.

Squishy, squishy, squishy, squishy. Squishy.

"Relax." I had been kidnapped. Someone was grabbing my hands. I twisted out of their grasp, but I couldn't see. Everything was black.

"Relax Kate." They knew my name. They tied my wrist to a pole at my side. I screamed. I hid my other arm behind my back. I kicked my legs that were stuck together. My knees came into contact with something hard. I should have fought earlier. It was too late to fight now.

"For fuck's sake girl, chill."

I kicked again and there was a weight on me. Hands holding me down. Fingers touching me uninvited.

Squishysquishysquishysquishy.

The weight got heavier on my chest. I cried out and it sounded like possums mating. They stabbed me with something. It felt like a knitting needle going straight through my skull.

I struggled. I screamed. Thin vomit sprayed from my mouth and the needle came. Oblivion. Why didn't the kidnappers gag me? I screamed and waited for someone to rescue me. But only the kidnappers came.

The needle.

Blackness.

I hatched a plan in my dreams. I stayed silent when I woke, choking on my screams. I stayed still, sucking on my vomit and gently edging my hand out of my restraint. My eyelids were heavy. I slept. I opened my eyes, so I could see them. Nothing. My legs wouldn't move. I realised I was in a hospital bed. The bars at my sides were like the metal bars my mother had in hospital. They were protecting me so I wouldn't fall out of bed. I hadn't been kidnapped at all. I remembered the needles. I saw the tubes. It all made sense now. I must have been hurt. Badly hurt. I couldn't feel my legs. I couldn't tell whether I was in pain, but I cried out anyway.

Squishysquishysquishysquishy.

"What's wrong with me?"

"It's okay. It's going to be okay. It's Eva. I will look after you," the nurse said, and I cried. "You shouldn't be here," she whispered and I knew then that I had broken my back. I would never walk again. A needle was stuck into my thigh. I felt that. I smiled. I slept. I woke. I slept. I woke. My back was broken. I fell off the Sydney Harbour Bridge. I jumped. I jumped because I wanted to die. The needle came and pinched me. I smiled. I slept. I woke. I had fallen out of Katie's car. She was going too fast around the corner and a dog ran across the road. Katie had to swerve to miss it. The car crashed. I broke my back. The policeman that looked like Mr Carroll came and looked at my legs. Up and down. He winked. The needle came. It stung. I smiled. I slept. I woke. I tried to move. There was a great weight sitting on my chest. Massive chunks of rock that broke my ribs.

I remembered Peter. I loved him. I wouldn't be able to dance with him at Kate Noble's party. I would never walk again. I made a choking noise.

I'd had an accident of some sort. I was sick.

Squisyshoescamerunningtobringthecreepingblackness. I laid in my envelope. I never wanted to wake up.

I woke. I called out. Nothing. I choked. Nothing. I wiggled my toes. I could wiggle my toes! I looked down at my feet and realised then that I was naked. I was ashamed and tried to cover myself. There was no blanket. I felt wetness between my legs and reached down. My hand came back with shit on it. Cold yellow shit. There was orange juice and vomit in my throat. I pulled at the tubes in my mouth with my shitty hand, so I could scream. I slept.

Squish, squish, squish, squish, squish, squish, squish, squish. I woke. My eyes were slits. The room was dull. Perfect for sleeping babies. In the bed next to me was a naked man. His shrivelled penis was trying to hide in his pubic hair. There were naked bodies on beds, lined up like cars in a car park. They were dead. I could smell piss and vomit and fear. It smelled like the night I wanted to forget. I could hear screaming but the bodies lay still with tubes down their throats. There were rows and rows of beds. What did they want us all for? I climbed over the metal railing on the side of the bed and fell to the floor.

Squishysquishysquishysquishy.

"We are just putting you back into bed Katherine," they said.

"You are very sick," they said.

"We'll look after you," they said.

"Don't worry," they said.

"Just relax," they said.

"It's going to be okay."

The needle pinched. I smiled and in that beautiful moment in the warmth of oblivion I believed them. But none of their voices sounded like Eva.

*

Bugs as persistent as a child woke me. I tried to brush them off my arms until I realised they were crawling under my skin. I clawed at my arms. I could see the lines they made under my skin. I tried to peel it off with my long nails but that just drove the bugs deeper into my flesh. I needed to escape. There was a phone on the table next to my hospital bed. It was red and shiny, just sitting there waiting for me to use it. I couldn't believe that I hadn't noticed it before. I picked up the receiver and it felt cool and heavy in my hand. I rang Brad the Chesty Bond man. He was lying on my parents' bedside table at home waiting for the phone to ring so he could answer it before Mum or Dad. I didn't know why I hadn't thought of it before. It was so simple. Brad the Bond's man would come to life and be my lifesaver.

"Hi Brad. It's Kate."

"Hey," he sang. "What's up, buttercup?"

"I need your help."

"Right on. Just let me put on a clean Bonds singlet and I'll be over in a jiffy!"

Brad was standing next to my bed, blocking the sunlight from coming in with his huge chest. He took my breath away.

"You were fast."

I kissed his papery lips.

Someone was on the bed with me. I couldn't tell if it was a man or a woman. Fat spread out from their thighs and flattened against the bed like a wet witch that had melted into a puddle with eyeballs and a hat—her bones disintegrated. Flesh kept swelling until I was crushed up against the bars at the side of the bed. I couldn't breathe.

A nurse came. Her shoes didn't squeak. It must have been Eva.

"We need to transfer this one right away. He's gone completely yellow. Ring Doctor Grafton again."

"I tried. He won't come. His wife said he's up a ladder."

"Ring her again. Say it's urgent this time."

"It was urgent last time." Soft soled shoes.

Soft shoes again.

"I rang Hornsby Hospital. The matron said she is sick of getting Ferriby's mistakes. She said, what are you doing down there?"

"How rude."

"What sort of an attitude is that?" Squishy shoes peeled the yellow man from me and wheeled him away.

*

I woke. I felt orange juice trickling down the back of my throat. I gagged. I was in kindergarten. Four years old. There was a bowl of cut-up fruit on the table. I had to eat one piece before I could go outside and play. This was the day Murry Murphy tipped red paint all over my dress. The teacher tore it off me, her fingernails gently grazed my body from my thigh to my armpit as I held my arms up over my head. I sat in my underwear in front of the other children's mean four-year-old eyes until the teacher came back with a dress from the office.

Squishysquishysquishysquishy.

The sensation of the new dress against my skin was unfamiliar. It smelt different. I liked that feeling, of not being myself. That's why I chose a piece of orange from the bowl of fruit. I usually chose banana. Sometimes apple. Never orange with its seeds and white pieces of pith that were impossible to remove.

I slept. I woke. I was in a dormitory like on school camp. But this was no camping trip. There was a skeleton girl parked next to me. Stiff hair stood up in a tuft between two hipbone mountains. She wasn't real. Shiny skin stretched across her like a blanket. There was a steady rise and fall of the cage holding her heart. A vein ticked in her neck. Tick-Tock.

Tick-Tock. Shutupshutupshutup -Tock. Tick-Tock. Tick-Tock. Tick-Tock. Tick-Tock. Tick-Tock. Tick-Tock. Tick-Tock. Tick-Tock. Tick-Tock. Tick-Tock. Tick-Tock. Shutupshutupshutup -Tock. Tick-Tock. Tick-Tock. Tick-Tock. Tick-Tock. Tick-Tock. Tick-Tock. Tick-Tock. Tick-Tock. Tick-Tock. Tick-Tock. Tick-Tock. Tick-Tock. Tick-Tock. Shutupshutupshutup. Tick-Tock. Tick-Tock. Tick-Tock. Tick-Tock. Tick-Tock. Tick-Tock. Tick-Tock. Tick-Tock. Tick-Tock. Tick-Tock. Tick-Tock. Tick- shutupshutupshutup. Tick-Tock. Tick-Tock. Tick-Tock. Tick-Tock. Tick-Tock. Tick-Tock. Tick-Tock. Tick-Tock. Tick-Tock. Tick-Tock. I was dreaming with my eyes open. I wanted to sleep.

A yellow strap held my right wrist to the metal railing at the side of the bed. My bed was soggy from the piss and shit that had been left to go cold under me like an unwanted meal. I tried to sleep. I remembered running. I was strong, and my bare feet smacked onto the footpath. The muscles in my legs sang as I moved them; my hair followed the rhythm with a muted flagellation on my back with each stride. But it wasn't me running. It was the nurses. Their rubber feet thwacking against the linoleum.

SquishsquishsquishsquishSquishSquishsquishsquishSquishsquishsquish squishSquishySquishsquishsquishsquishSquishsquishSquish. Shutupshutup shutup.

"She's just a baby. She's thirteen years old."

"Doctor Grafton's notes said deep sedation."

"I gave her the standard."

"Did you even look at her? She's anorexic. She's probably barely over five foot tall."

"I gave her the standard."

SquishsquishsquishsquishSquish. Shhhh.

"There was nothing in the book. Just this. Problems with her parents.

She isn't eating with the family."

"Are you telling me that you gave this girl that dose of drugs based on a scribble on the back of a manila envelope?"

"I didn't know."

"Let's get her out of here. She needs to go to Hornsby Hospital. Now. Do you want another one to die on us?"

"Stop it. Transfer the patient. Now."

I blinked and the skeleton girl was gone. The bed was empty. The nurses were gone. I was magic. I had wanted to stop the noise. I had wanted them all to go away. I had simply blinked my eyes and they were gone. The noise went. I slept. The yellow strap holding my wrist gave me magical powers through the metal posts of the bed. My head was full of fairy floss. The Cat in the Hat was sitting next to my bed eating fairy floss. His sticky hands were touching my legs. He slid off the bed and I rolled over just in time to see him swim away. I saw a fish. And then another. One red. Another blue. And I knew exactly what the Cat in the Hat was up to. I lay on my bed and watched the fish swim around the beds in schools with no teachers. I reached my fingers over the bed into the warm water. There were too many fish to count and they changed colour as they swam, turning red then blue. Red then blue. Red. Blue. Red. Blue. Red. Blue. Red. Blue. Red. Blue. Red. Blue. Red. Blue. Red. Blue. Red. Blue. Red. Blue. Red. Blue. Red. Blue. Red. Blue. Red. Blue. Red. Blue. Red. Blue. Red. Blue. Bubbles erupted from their mouths forming a cage around The Cat in the Hat. He was trapped but happy. I smiled, knowing that he was safe.

When I woke up the bed next to me was still empty. The skeleton girl had left behind a brown, watery stain. I could see the outline of a head and then an indistinct blob. It looked like a map of Australia. I looked for Tasmania, but it wasn't there. Tasmania was missing. The skeleton girl must have left this map as a message just for me. My brain hurt trying to figure it out.

squish-squish-squish-squish-squish-squish-squish-squish-squish-squish

Two tubes hung from my nose. I tugged at them but was afraid to pull too hard in case my brain came out like an Egyptian mummy. I needed to rescue Kylie. I was naked. I would have to steal clothes from someone's clothesline. That was my plan. The window between our beds was open. I climbed off my bed and slid towards it.

squish-squish-squish-squish-squish-squish-squish-squish-squish-squish

I hid amongst the beds. Then suddenly Brad's hand was in mine. Shh, he put a finger to his lips.

"Come on, Princess," he bellowed. "Let's blow this joint."

"Shh," I whispered. "They're coming."

Squishysquishysquishysquishy.

Brad was standing next to the window. The moonlight was shining into the ward and I admired the silhouette of Brad's muscles as he slid the window open. He winked. I was at his side. The breeze floated through the window and flicked the hair from my shoulders. Brad watched as I shook my head so that my hair cascaded down my back. It was beautiful again. He put his hands around my waist and I smelt the musky smell of him as he lifted me onto the windowsill. There was a flyscreen. Soft shoes came towards us. They stopped. I froze with Brad's arms holding me steady and I could feel the warmth of him. Outside the garden was a silver and white fairy tale. The footsteps moved away. I punched the flyscreen and it tipped into the garden, still attached at the bottom ledge. I held onto the window frame and lowered one leg into the garden. The thorns of a rosebush clawed at my leg and I felt the heat of blood. I imagined my red blood painting the white roses just like in *Alice in Wonderland*. The flyscreen let go of the window. It was too loud.

"Run!" yelled Brad.

I was straddling the window. One leg was scratched but free in the outside air. The other was stuck on the window ledge.

"I can't leave you."

"Run, Buttercup. I'll catch up to you," Brad said as he flipped my other leg from the window ledge. I stood there then, with him on the inside and me on the outside.

"Go," he whispered. He was starting to ripple in the breeze. I ran then, before he disappeared. I could hear the sound of cars swishing along a road like a song. I was running towards the sound. The road was busy. Freedom road. I was running for my freedom. For Kylie. The night air licked my glorious skin. I was naked but I didn't care. I didn't need Peter or an HSC mark. I was a person and I was free.

A car stopped next to me, a dark green hatchback. A woman wound down the window.

"Where are you going?"

"Home."

"Jump in and I'll take you."

"Beecroft," I said as if she was a taxi driver.

I closed my eyes so that she couldn't see that I was naked. She drove, but not for long enough. She parked in front of a house. There was a sign. *Ferriby Private Hospital.* I looked at the driver. She was wearing a nurse's uniform. Doctor Grafton was waiting on the curb for me. He draped the red police blanket around my shoulders like a skin as the nurse helped me out of the car.

"You are a bit of a silly girl for running away, aren't you?" There was comfort in his eyes.

"No, I'm not." I sounded like a child, so I had to let him take me back inside.

*

I was in a different room. Sitting in a recliner. I was not in bed where I was supposed to be. I looked around the room. Nothing was where it was supposed to be. Waists hung off the edges of chairs. Breasts dangled into coffee cups. I could see my future.

My blanket protected me from their laughter. One of them looked at me.

"What are you in for, lovely?"

I didn't answer. They thought they were so clever but none of them had a red blanket. They turned to each other and nodded and looked and smiled at each other, winking behind their hands when they thought no one was watching. Playing murder in the dark. I snuggled into my blanket. Nighty night.

I woke and fell, woke and fell. There was mud on my knees and splinters in my fingertips. Peter was in a bed next to me. I stood up and scraped the splinters across Peter's sleeping eyelids. Tears of blood poured down his cheeks. More and more of it until his face collapsed in on itself. But he didn't wake up. His fingers twitched so I squeezed them until I heard his bones being crushed like the bones of a bird. And then I started putting stones on his chest. The room was full of rocks and I piled them up on his body. But Peter just kept saying, "More weight."

When I woke my sheets were wet and cold. Peter was gone and the rocks were gone. I realised it was a nightmare. It had all been a nightmare. I had not missed my HSC. Peter still loved me. There were still ten more days until freedom. The stress of the exams must have been playing tricks on my mind, causing bad dreams. I was lying on a beach in the warm sun. I must have fallen asleep. The sand was as white as a bleached bone. The sea unbelievably blue. There was silence. Even the waves licking the shore at my feet were soundless.

"I just need a little rest," I said. Doctor Grafton was lying beside me in a white dinner-suit and red silk tie. A slight breeze had unlocked a strand of hair from his coif and it hung languidly over his brown eyes, as if it too were relaxing. Doctor Grafton led me to a plane waiting on the beach. A cluster of guards watched us. They were fingering their rigid guns, ready to protect me.

"Let's blow this joint." I looked at Doctor Grafton then and realised he was really Brad. He had come to rescue me. He took off his suit coat just like superman and stood in front of me in all his tanned glory, wearing his white Bond's singlet.

Brad's teeth gleamed in the sunshine. They shone out against his bronzed face and nothing could go wrong. Nothing at all because when I looked at him his little-boy cheeky smile lived on top of a man's body that could help me run away and wreak vengeance on my captors. Brad was going to rock me and hold me when I got back to his kingdom. I would find the castle of my dreams with the drawbridge open and I would enter my sanctuary.

The moat would be filled with electric eels hiding below pink waterlilies. Doctor Grafton would come after me. Mr Guard with his pencils, and my parents with the police. Even Peter would try to find me. They all would. But the drawbridge would be closed. Big brass locks would keep me in. I would live in a tower made of bubbles. But I will want to go out. I will want to play. I will want to swim in the moat with the pink waterlilies. That is when I realised that Doctor Grafton must die for me to be free. I needed to summon Brad to kill him. It would have to look like an accident. Like something had gone wrong. Or like he had done it to himself.

Arms reached up through the bed and pulled me down. I could hear someone breathing under the bed. Music was coming from below. Another man came past my bed. Not Doctor Grafton. I told the nurse I saw him again. The man with the thick fingers.

"That's just your mind," she said. "You're not well yet. Hold still."

I did what I was told like a good girl. The good girl that I was. I had learned my lesson. My knees burned from where the nurses pulled them apart. *Keep your legs open, love. Relax, love. That's not a very nice way to sit Katherine.* I didn't scream when my skin was torn off in chunks. I was quiet. Just like a good girl. Closeyourlegs. Keep your legs apart so they don't seal back together again. Keep them closed like a good girl. Everybody wants to be a good girl.

"Again," he said. "Again, again." But my legs hurt and Istillfelt sleepy and I wanted to lie down and thiswasnogood. I thought about my HSC. Why wasn't there a subject called Love? My brain was dissolving as fast as fairy floss, leaving the sickly-sweet taste in the mouth of my memories.

"It's going to be okay, Kate. Just relax."

I swallowed the lie and I couldn't move. I didn't want to anymore. All I could taste was orange juice congealing on my tongue. I was standing next to the playground with somebody else's dress chafing my skin. I was chewing and chewing and swallowing but the flesh of the orange just wouldn't go down. I gagged. Four-year-old mouths were chanting, "You're still eating. You're still eating. You can't eat outside. We're gonna tell." But I was wearing the spare dress and I was not me, so the kids didn't scare me at all.

I felt weird and drunk and stupid. My brain didn't remember what I was thinking a moment ago. I didn't know how I had gotten into the car. I felt like an old lady—soft and saggy with spongy teeth. My parents' house wavered before my eyes like an apparition. Dad drove right up the side of the house to the kitchen door. He got out of the car, but I just sat and stared.

Dad held my elbow and steered me into the house. I was on the lounge. I could hear crying coming from up the hallway and angry voices coming from the kitchen.

"Look."

"Too early. Again. Remember what happened last time?"

"Skeleton girl."

"Treatment not finished. Doctor's advice."

"Go back. Take her back. I can't deal with this and the twins."

"You'll manage."

I tried for a while to piece everything together, but images kept floating out of my mind and I forgot that they were ever there. At some point Mum came and sat next to me, her legs long and lithe like a memory. Dad was silent while she explained everything to me. But I couldn't understand her. I heard, "Look, look, the wallpaper is yellow oh feelthebreeze can you see that skeleton she's a skeleton now dancing in the breeze of her treatment that went out the window in a few days comfortable couch baby crying and anotherone against the doctor's advice crying toosoft softbreeze the dancing curtain of days in a few days the curtain can dance back to the hospital with Kate allwrappedup like a skeleton."

But if I wrote about what happened over the next few weeks like that, you'd get tired of reading and the whole point of me writing this is so that you will read it. Also, I'm not one to delve too far into a past. I prefer to view it like the reflection in a mirror. Something that I can see but not reach

194

out and touch. Touching the past can be dangerous. It can make you crazy. Wake up! Come on. It's daytime. I haven't finished telling you my story yet.

The Book of Secrets

Jack

We were in a formal dining room and we were all drunk and the usual things were said regarding suicide. Jack did not believe in suicide, of course. Everybody knew that. He often said that only a man in a burning building with no arms or legs has the right to commit suicide. Not that any of us *believed* in suicide. Indeed, it was against our professional judgement. But in our profession, you can imagine, suicide was a topic of much debate, especially between the main course and dessert. It mostly came up when the women were out of the room. We let our wives take our emotions into the kitchen with the dishes and discussed suicide while they organised dessert.

Someone invariably said, what about terminal illness? What if you were in pain and would die in a month anyway? Why not?

It was hardly an original argument and it met with the same old rebuttals. I refuse to bore you (and myself) with them here. I am sure you can imagine what was said.

On one particular occasion a woman plopped a Pavlova in front of us and said that if one of her children died, she would kill herself immediately.

Oh, those lovely would-be conditionals. Such a ridiculous assertion was met with, doesn't that depend on which child dies? What about the others? You have to remember that this was in a time when only child families were a rarity.

Jack then gave a little speech that floored everyone. Personal experience and stories always win an argument over statistics. Especially at a social gathering. He might have encountered more resistance at a medical conference, but that is not where these conversations took place. People on the whole do not care about statistics. They care about stories. Stories can change the world.

On this particular occasion, I forfeited the Pavlova, as it had Chinese gooseberries on it. A ridiculous fruit to mix with cream. To save the host the embarrassment of me scraping the fruit off and leaving it on the edge of my plate, I feigned fullness. Such indignities did not bother Jack, however. I watched him shove the fruit deep into his mouth and wash it down with wine. He had to empty the glass to do the job properly, but he replaced his empty glass on the table with a flourish and said, "When I was studying in Montreal, we were shown a film of a case study of a man who had been very badly burnt. He was in constant pain for months and begged to be allowed to die. They filmed the man at this time and he was screaming in pain. His lips and nose had been burnt off. His face had literally melted. The pain was unbearable. There was nowhere left to take skin grafts from."

At this time the idea of spray-on skin was science fiction. Jack took another gulp of wine before he went on. He was drinking rather rapidly by this stage of his life.

"This poor man's scarring was horrendous. He begged to die for months and I swear to God that if I had been the doctor on his ward at the time, I would have increased his morphine loading just slightly. It wouldn't have taken much. Not much at all. Even his own mother begged his doctors to do it.

"The end of the film showed him a few years later. He was hideously ugly. No one wanted to employ him, and his injuries prevented him from taking part in day-to-day activities that the rest of us take for granted. Yet he was married. A woman had found it in her heart to love him. The pain and the relentless itch had not gone, I am sure it was there every time he looked in the mirror, but nevertheless he had found a wife who for some reason genuinely loved him. He was happy. They made a family. They had a house. What more could a man want? His suicide would have made all this impossible, yet at the beginning of the film it seemed like death was his best option."

Jack always won the argument in the end.

Kate

There is something I didn't tell you about when I went back to Ferriby, when they didn't put me under straight away. This is not a confession or a clumsy attempt at a plot twist. Why didn't I tell you sooner? I prefer not to think about it. It's embarrassing. I guess that's why. Why am I telling you now? I'm not sure. I am not even sure that I will. I will write it down but there is nothing to say I won't rip this page up as soon as I write it. Maybe I will burn it and you will never know about it. Only I will, and it is under these conditions only that I put this part of my life in writing at all.

A nurse came for me one night. I know it was late because I could hear the other nurses smoking and gossiping softly in the corridors.

"It's time for your appointment."

I thought they were coming for Kylie, so I pretended to be asleep. Kylie was lying in the bed with her back to me. Her bruises had faded and they weren't watching her so closely anymore.

"Kate, wake up. Doctor Grafton is waiting for you."

I thought of the pink pills as I let the nurse help me out of bed. "Get dressed," the nurse said. I turned my back on her and changed back into my party dress. I couldn't find Mum's leisure suit, so I grabbed the red police blanket that was still on the end of the bed and put it around my shoulders like a cape. I followed the nurse's shoes as they squeaked along the hallway. The lino was cool against my bare feet. The nurse took me outside where a taxi was waiting for us. It was dark. I felt dizzy and leant against the car while the nurse instructed the driver through the open passenger window.

"This patient needs to go to our Macquarie Street rooms. Doctor Grafton will be waiting for her there. Just drop her off in the usual spot."

The nurse helped me into the back seat and closed the door. The houses we passed melted into each other, but I knew I was awake because the vinyl seats were cold under my thighs.

I tried to catch glimpses of the houses hiding behind hedges. I wondered what would happen if no one trimmed them and they grew so tall that the people became trapped inside for centuries. I imagined I had a large blade that would cut the tops off all the hedges as we drove past. I would stick them into the tyres of the cars next to me. The taxi sped towards the Harbour Bridge. We were going into the city! I undid my seatbelt and bounced into the middle seat so I could look up at the archways through the front windshield. Then I slid over to the other side of the taxi, trying to catch a glimpse of the Blues Point Tower.

"Hey, stop moving around back there," said the taxi driver. It was like he was a nervous dog after that, watching me in the rear-view mirror. I covered my legs with the red blanket because his teeth shone with too much saliva. Then Blues Point Tower appeared and I imagined standing up there in Katie's flat, looking down on the cars going over the bridge. I wondered whether I would be able to see the difference between an ordinary car and a taxi from up there. I imagined standing at her living room window and doing a perfect swan dive into the harbour.

I enjoyed the ride through the city to the night-time glamour of Macquarie Street, with its important buildings filled with empty lights. Doctor Grafton was on the footpath waiting for me, wearing a tuxedo jacket with a white bowtie the same colour as his shirt. He leant forward and looked at me through the window with his inviting brown eyes, unlike the wolfish eyes of the taxi driver. He opened the car door and watched me get out. I held the blanket around my shoulders like a shawl and pretended the doctor was taking me to a show at the Opera House. Maybe Ita Buttrose would be sitting next to us in the audience.

"This way," beckoned Doctor Grafton after he'd paid the driver.

I followed him into the foyer of a large building. The doctor smelt like wine and musky cigarettes.

"After you," he said, indicating a flight of stairs.

I started the climb and the doctor followed. He was right behind me. Too close. I went faster but so did the doctor. I could feel his knees coming in behind mine. I stepped up two steps at once and almost fell.

"Careful, steady there," laughed the doctor, holding me by the waist.

We continued up the stairs like that with him holding my waist and I could feel his dinner suit against my back. We got to a little landing and the receptionist's desk was empty. I don't know what I was expecting but for some reason it surprised me that no one was up there. The doctor peeled the blanket off me and laid it across a chair in the waiting room. I followed him through a doorway into his office. It was even more stylish than his office at the hospital, with leather-bound books lining the walls and the biggest desk I had ever seen. There was a huge glass jar on his desk and I swear it had a brain floating in it. Even Doctor Grafton's telephone was shiny, and I wondered whether he hired somebody just to polish it or whether it had been polished by his smooth, soft, doctor's hands.

The doctor reached for my shoulders then and pressed me backwards onto a leather couch. His hands stayed on my shoulders as he dropped right to his knees on the carpet in front of me. For a moment I thought he was going to propose.

"You know why you are here now, don't you?" said the doctor. And then I did. *What you need is a good fuck, and I am the one to give it to you.*

I sat up.

"I have to go," I said.

The doctor laughed.

"Oh Kate," he said. "You are being very immature."

I tried to stand up, but his hand rested on my shoulder like a warning.

"Your curiosity will keep you here, Kate." His eyes made my cheeks feel hot.

I twisted away from his hand and pushed at his wrist as he came at me again.

"Stop acting like a spoiled child," said Doctor Grafton. But I didn't care what he said. I ran back out to the bare waiting room and down the stairs and out onto the street. I stood there. I had nowhere to go. The doctor was behind me and I knew I couldn't run. I turned and stared him down. A streetlight shone onto us like we were on a stage. He was holding the police blanket in his hands and walked towards me like I was a cornered animal.

But I stood my ground and glared at him. The doctor was close enough to grab me but all he did was put the blanket back over my shoulders. That's it. That's all he did. He really was a gentleman. It was an anti-climax really. Silently Doctor Grafton beckoned a taxi for me to go back to Ferriby. I sat in the front seat this time.

Jack

I do remember one particular occasion. It must have been later on in the 70s and Jack was seeing the beautiful Nancy Collins. She wasn't just one of his flings, you know. She played hard to get by refusing to live with him.

"She says she can't study with me around."

Jack could turn anything into a boast. Nancy was studying business or some such thing. Not very ladylike but that did not bother Jack. In fact, I think he rather liked it. And, of course, they eventually did move in together, once she had created that need for it in Jack by refusing him for so long. Ah, women are so cunning, and men are so simple. For those women who figure us out at an early age, the world is their oyster.

It was the early 80s. Jack left his wife and moved with Nancy Collins into a terrible, rundown old terrace. For once I thought it was Jack who had been conned. Real estate agents are the masters of that art. I can tell you, whoever convinced Jack that place was a 'renovator's dream' was a true artist of what in Australia we love to term as bullshit. I hate to be so crude, but this is the only word to describe this situation and sometimes I like to go with that old adage, "If you are thinking it, you may as well say it." It is swear-words used without thought that should be the real crime. Well, I have thought long and hard and the only word I can think of to describe that slogan on the For Sale sign—*renovator's dream*—is bullshit. And Australians are supposed to have built-in bullshit detectors, so go figure. It needed bulldozing, not renovating, but Jack was convinced of the value of its character. I have never understood the lure of character myself. To me, a house is a house. A marital bedroom, one for each child and one left over for guests and hobbies, as well as my study of course. For me houses are a practical endeavour and ornate balustrades do little for my emotions.

Not so for Jack. And as I said before, this is when I began to worry about him. Not because he bought the place, or was attempting to renovate it, which was foolish enough in itself, but that he began cutting in new doorways. When I went to visit him, it was the second time I'd seen the house.

It had been improved. The joy of living within each other's skins gave the place an aura of happiness that created nostalgia in the peeling paint. Nancy had given the place that womanly touch. I don't know how they do it. Some women could live in a tent and make it feel like the most romantic place in the world. They simply place a doily here and there, and a house becomes a home, so to speak. Not that Nancy's taste was old-fashioned. I looked around at the modern furniture and all it made me feel was old, and I realised that Jack looked old too. His jowls were sagging like a bulldog. But the energy coming off him was of a man half his age. He became a young man to match Nancy. I guess in vigour they were well matched. No one could ever deny Jack Grafton his vigour.

"Come into the kitchen," Jack said. Everything looked different. Light shone through a large opening cut into the back of the house.

"Have a drink." Jack handed me a glass of white wine, as it was still early in the day. He knew how to treat a guest even in the midst of a disastrous renovation.

Despite the extra light showing off the flaws in, well everything, the place had acquired a kind of potential.

"That new window has made a remarkable difference."

"I did it myself," said Jack, which I did not doubt. He took me out the back to show me the window he intended to fit into the space. It was a trim, aluminium affair with louvered glass and I thought at that moment everything would be fine. The court cases against Jack were dragging on but they were held up by imbeciles who had no understanding of our profession, or of Jack himself. Manslaughter of a patient is such a ridiculous allegation to make. As soon as the judge got his hands on this mess and looked at the matter through an educated eye, not the hyperbole of the press, then everything would be straightened out. I was sure of that, and Nancy had obviously given Jack a new lease on life.

Kate

Don't talk to the fuckers. That's what I yell to myself inside my brain where no one can hear it. Don't talk to the fuckers! And I deafen myself. I feel sorry for them sometimes. The new ones fresh out of university trying to make a name for themselves with their big-beaded necklaces and lopsided haircuts. University should teach them that lopsided haircuts are not a good idea for anyone trying to help people with lopsided brains. But the ones that really drive me nuts are the ones that have had so many sad cases sitting in front of them—worshiping them—saying you are the only person that has helped me. They think they are little gods. They surround themselves with losers and it makes them feel smug when they go back to their middleclass houses in their middleclass suburbs with their middleclass husbands and children with perfect teeth. They think they have the power to change the world—starting with me. The smugness oozes out of their well-meaning smiles. But I'm not going to play their game. They haven't met me yet. But I know them. They are all the same. I know what they are going to say. And it's all bullshit. If I complain about the food, they will ask if I want to volunteer in the kitchen. If I say I'm bored, they will suggest I participate in the craft lessons, sitting around a table making ugly homewares like a retard at the sheltered workshop. If I say I wanted to go home—that would be the worst thing to say—then they would just drag up all that shit again. All the things I've done wrong. All my addictions and suicide attempts.

I know what will happen if I mention leaving. The woman will pause. Take a deep breath. Tuck her lopsided hair behind her left ear and fiddle with her necklace. Push up her glasses for emphasis. For fucking emphasis! As if the words aren't enough. "How will you support yourself?"

I am going to get angry. Of course I am. I never used to be like this. They would love me to say that. They want to pinpoint the exact moment I went mad, like the climax of a bad movie. They don't want to hear that my treatment made me go mad. I was fine before this. They don't believe me so I don't say it anymore. I don't say much anymore.

I know what you are thinking, I am mad because I don't speak. And if I am mad now then surely I always was. It is simple. If I speak, I must lie. "Yes, this room is nice, with the tree outside the window and everything."

"Yes, I am so lucky." Go away and leave me alone.

"The food is good here, better than the last place." Go.

"The doctor seems to understand me." Just go. Fuck right off and close the door behind you.

"No, Mum, I don't mind that you didn't get a chance to visit me last weekend because you were out with the twins and thank you so much for showing me your new dress, sapphire blue, *my* favourite colour. It matches our eyes."

I guess it doesn't really make me angry anymore, this fake politeness. But I am bored with it all. The things I have to say are really enough to make me sleep. "Yes, what a lovely spring day." I'd rather say nothing at all.

"It wasn't the dreams that scared me the most," I made the mistake once of telling some fuzzy-haired therapist with crystals in her waiting room— crystals for fuck's sake. I told her about the rats. I'm not sure why. Perhaps it was the crystals. They disarmed me for a second. I wasn't prepared for her tie-dyed clothes and the smell of incense. She looked like she drank a bottle of vodka every night just to erase the thought of us all. But she did catch me off guard.

"They kept me asleep for months. When I was awake terrible things happened. Rats ran across the walls and the ceiling. They climbed up the beds and I couldn't move. I screamed and screamed but no one came. I didn't even know if there was any noise coming out of my mouth. A rat ran up my leg and it had huge balls that dragged across my skin until it got up to my stomach. Its huge claws scratched at my breasts and then it bit me on the neck."

The woman leant forward then, and her loopy earrings swayed back and forth like a child's swing, hypnotising me. Her droopy earlobes showed her age.

I went on, "It drank my blood and the spit right out of my mouth while

I screamed. I could smell the filth on it while its balls hung off my chin."

She told me this never happened. The nurses told me a million times. It was all in my mind. I had imagined it. I had hallucinated it. I was having a psychotic episode. But I can still feel those heavy balls dragging across my stomach. I can smell that creature paralysing me. It happened to me, real or imaginary. *They* made it happen.

I shook my head then. It was the only thing I could do. I couldn't stop shaking my head and the tie-dyed therapist had to resort to giving me the pills that she had been keeping from me for days. She handed me a cup of water and her earrings kept swinging but I couldn't open my mouth in case I swallowed the rat. The woman shoved them into my mouth and held it shut until they were down. I kept scratching gouges out of my chin, but the rat was gone. My throat felt hard and I could feel the rat's fur on my tongue. Even though it had never happened. And I thought—I really am crazy. I am as crazy as fuck. So now I prefer to keep my mouth shut.

But I kept going to see her. I don't know why. Her name was Di and that's what I call her. On paper at first and then one day I said it. "Di," and she smiled at me with her whole face, jumped up from her chair and hugged me, giggling like a schoolgirl. I was trying. I really was. There was still time, Di told me. Time for university. Time for an awesome job working with Ita Buttrose. "Oh Honey," she'd say because that's how she starts all her sentences. "Oh Honey, you lost some time, but you didn't lose your intelligence."

I realised then she was right. She told me about bridging courses to get into university and even gave me a brochure one day.

Once I started talking, I just couldn't stop. But only to Di. Not to anyone else. Not the woman behind the reception desk: all fake nails and fake smiles. Not the bus driver on my way home. Not even Ben who I live with. We don't need to speak. We have other ways of communicating.

I got off the bus just around the corner from our house. The sun was warm through my cardigan so I knew it would be my birthday soon. I was sure that when I arrived home Ben's bedroom door would be open, welcoming me. My mouth felt warm from the words I had spoken. But I was careful. I hadn't told Di any of my secrets. I didn't tell her about Ben. I just talked about Ita and university and she gave me a notebook and a pen so I could get used to taking notes from the television. The notebook had an elephant on the cover. Di showed me how to draw up columns for who, when, what, where, and how. My homework was to watch the news and fill it all in. I fingered the notebook as it dragged on the corner of my canvas bag. I walked past the house on the corner with the black cat with the tiny ears that sunned itself on a rock next to the letterbox. I bent down to pat her, but she ran down the side of her house. She did the same thing every day because we didn't trust each other yet.

Our house was next. It was really Ben's and mine, but other people lived there. I didn't like them, but Ben said they are good for me, for my socialisation. I disagreed, but I didn't tell him that.

It wasn't so bad once they knew I didn't want talk to them. Lisa was okay. She was fat and smelly and lay around all the time in front of the television or in her room with the door open. I could see her when I walked past on my way to see if Ben's bedroom door was open at the end of the hall. If it was open then I was allowed in for sex. Every time I checked I turned my head just enough to see her in there spread out on the bed like Jabba the Hutt. On hot days I could smell her on the way past, like a warm tuna sandwich. But she didn't try to be my friend, so I almost liked her.

Kate

Secret number 1. You have probably guessed it wasn't as simple as that the night the nurse sent me to Doctor Grafton in a taxi. I had to prove to him that I wasn't the child he thought I was. Remember him telling me I was being immature? Well, I showed him. I stood up right then and there in his office with all his fancy books and his shiny polished telephone. I unzipped my dress and let it fall to my hips. There is nothing childish about that. I kissed him full on the mouth and let him pull back on my hair so that he could bite me on the neck. I let him shove me back down onto the couch and I opened my legs willingly. I wanted to show him that I was as mature and worldly as other woman. Or perhaps I was just curious, as he said. I imagined watching us from above with my blonde hair fanned out on the couch like a halo and the blue of my wide-open eyes matching the blue of my dress. But the doctor scrunched his eyes tight shut and just pushed and strained. I licked the sweat off his forehead as he came.

"There are three things necessary to have a happy life," my doctor said as he zipped up his fly. "To eat in style, to drive in style and to fuck in style." Oh doctor. Do tell me more.

He drove me back to Ferriby then in a little sports car. The hospital food wasn't always great but that night I had at least done the other two. I hoped the nurses would see me returning sitting next to Jack, but the fuzzy-haired nurse at the front desk was busy writing something when we walked past, trying not to look. Jack stayed in the corridor when we reached my room. He gave me a few of those little pink pills. I swallowed them without water. "Dessert," I thought as I leant into the fuzz.

Jack

We started off having a great time in Jack's half-finished kitchen. The window held no glass. The breeze came in to tickle our chins and the papers floated half off the table where we sat. There was an air of camaraderie between us, not that it had not always been that way, but I guess our bonds had deepened due to those infernal legal matters.

It was a day like any other. We both drank a little too much. Our wives were not there to keep us in check and so we laughed like hyenas about one of the nurse's hairy chins. It seemed so funny at the time and I realise now that it was because we were both avoiding a certain topic. Kylie.

Eventually my stomach rumbled, and I stood to leave. Jack stood with me.

"Just come and have a look at the spa before you go," he said, gesturing up the hallway. The spa looked like it had been dumped in a spare bedroom, with pipes leading to nowhere. There was a bunch of wires circumnavigating the walls, held on by electrical tape.

"I've moved my property around a bit," said Jack. The room was moving a little uncomfortably in front of me, so I headed back to the kitchen to sit down. Jack sat too.

I gestured to the glassless window. "You most certainly have," I said. Hyena laughs again.

"I mean legally. I have backdated some documents to before the Royal Commission started, but only you need to know that." Jack winked.

"Why would you do that?" I had had enough suicidal patients to know the signs.

"Oh, come on. You know what they call me. The Mad Doctor of Ferriby."

"Jack, that's what you call yourself!" More hyenas.

"Yes, well. The problem is, I think it is catching on. I thought it was best to change the name of my properties into Nancy's name."

"Nancy's? Are you crazy?"

"Apparently I am." If a laugh could be a sentence the hyenas died off mid-laugh like a thought only half said.

"I put property in my daughters' names also."

"Jack," I said, leaning back in my chair. "It isn't going to get to that."

"They've locked me out of my own hospital."

I thought he was going to cry then. In all our years together, through the split with his wife and even Kylie's suicide, through all the trials and the patient deaths, Jack had never cried. His eyes looked spongey.

"I need to go to the bathroom," I said. To my relief I heard Nancy's voice in the kitchen before I returned. Jack was back to his jubilant self and had poured me another Scotch, for it is inevitable that wine must give way to Scotch at some point on afternoons such as these.

As the afternoon melted away, I began to see the charm of the place, and the charm of Nancy was undeniable.

"Nature calls," said Jack and I watched him bumble up the hallway in a zig-zag fashion, as if the walls had apposing magnets that were pulling him towards them.

"Thank you." Nancy looked relieved.

"For what?" Young women are so lovely in their sincerity.

"Jack looks so much more like his old self."

"That is due to you, my dear. And this place." I laughed.

Jack came back then, and Nancy turned from me and I could see for a moment what she would look like when she got old. I knew then that there was trouble in paradise. It had not taken long.

"Darling," said Jack in his best radio presenter's voice. "Come and join us for a drink."

"Oh, I was just going," I said, picking up my keys.

"You aren't driving." Nancy was such a child.

Another Scotch appeared in front of me along with a plate of cheeses and pâté.

"At least eat something first," said Jack, and of course I obliged.

I am not sure how it happened but the next thing I knew Jack was snoring on the lounge and I was alone with Nancy. She may have been four decades younger than Jack but at that moment she did not look it.

"Can you come over on Monday night, between six and nine?"

At first, I thought she was propositioning me. Especially when she smiled, touched my arm and said with raised eyebrows, "Perhaps every Monday night?"

"Ah well," I said. Do not get me wrong I am not a prude and am easily able to maintain myself in the presence of a beautiful woman, even a beautiful younger woman. Being a doctor, these kinds of propositions are not uncommon. Yet of course being Jack's girlfriend put her off limits.

"Jack is my friend." Stoic.

"Yes," she removed her hand from me and I knew then that I had gotten the wrong idea and that she knew. Luckily, she was going to pretend nothing untoward had happened between us, which of course it hadn't.

"I have to go to class on Monday nights. It is nearly exam time and I don't want to have to withdraw now. But I worry about Jack being alone."

"Monday nights." I was stalling for time. "Worried about what?" The unspeakable.

"You know," she said. I did, and I was not in the mood to pretend I didn't so Nancy would spell it out for me.

I picked up my keys.

"Mondays it is," I said to her. "Monday evenings are generally rather dull. I may as well spend them here."

"Thank you," she said. "But don't let him know I spoke with you. Just drop in. He hates the idea of me arranging babysitters."

I realised then.

"That's why you invited me over here today?" Women are so cunning.

"It is."

I took the opportunity to hold her soft wrist.

"I will come over every single Monday. I will watch him in the bathroom. I will use some ruse or another. I can be inventive. Perhaps we can play cards together. It will become our hobby. Don't you worry."

I am not sure whether Nancy was grateful for my promise to her or simply happy that I let go of her wrist. (I would not have touched her like

211

this on any ordinary occasion, but an afternoon of drinking and a damsel in distress does certain things to a man, as you probably well know.) Anyway, those extra years lifted off her face as she waved at me from the doorway. Living with Jack would have to add at least a few years to a woman at the best of times, and these were not the best of times. But she didn't insist on my not driving, which had been my sole intention when I gave that little spiel. You see, men can be cunning too.

Kate

Sometimes writing this makes me feel feelings I don't want to feel. Sad and mad and all things bad. Ha! Sometimes I think why, oh, why am I writing this crap today? Di told me it would help the bad memories leave my mind, but she didn't tell me I'd have to relive them first. I should be sleeping in a bed that smells of wine and love. All cosy with the bedspread pulled up to my chin.

Well, the bed should at least smell like wine. Love is another thing entirely, which you probably know more about than me. But I sit here, and I write, and I imagine who you are, reading this. Sometimes you are a teenager, full of life and hope and living off peanut butter sandwiches and gossip at lunch-time. Sometimes you are a forty-year-old woman, reading this naughtily while your kids are at school, hiding from the housework. Sometimes you are retired, enjoying your old age much more than your youth because you can read all day in front of an open fire, smoking your pipe. You are old, but I make you remember what it was like to be young. I wonder whether you hate me for that. I wonder what each of you thinks of me.

Because this is not a diary. This is not something that I will tie up with a string and lock in a drawer because I am too embarrassed for someone to read it. I am writing this to be read and so I imagine you all while I am writing. I really do. Maybe you think I really am crazy. That doesn't matter. That's your choice. I didn't write this to convince you of my sanity but to let you know what happened to us. To lots of us. Some of us were not crazy when we were put under Slumber Therapy, but most of us were crazy by the time we got out. Some of us left with a whole lot more nightmares to add to the hallucinations and psychosis we had already experienced. Some of us became permanently brain damaged. Some of us died as fluid filled our lungs and we drowned in our own phlegm. Many of us killed ourselves. Most of us ended up bitter and confused for the rest of our lives. A lot of us became addicted. Most of us cannot work. At least one of us was murdered.

I would like it if you did like me, though. You don't have to be my friend, but perhaps you could smile when you think of me, occasionally, over a cup of tea. I really like that idea—as if I am someone you used to know. I think about you a lot these days, but the more I think about you the more I wonder whether you would still like me if you knew my secrets. Some of them are little. Some of them are big. Some of them don't matter at all. You already know about that night with Doctor Grafton where I fucked in style, drove in style, and sucked pills into my mouth straight from his hand. And you are still here. But one of my secrets might make you throw my story across the room in disgust. Because I have lied to you. Or at least I haven't exactly told you the truth. But I will now. I promise. But then I wonder—are you ready for this? Am I?

I can't decide and so I am leaving the decision up to you. I have left this part sealed in my *Afra* magazine, just like the sealed sections of *Cleo*. But don't get too excited. That doesn't necessarily mean it is about sex. That just means it is private. So, you don't have to read it. You can keep these pages sealed. Chaste. It's up to you. You can read it now if you like. I kind of hope you won't. But I kind of hope you will—and that you will still like me anyway.

My biggest secret of all? I gave it away right at the beginning if you had been paying attention. So why didn't I just say so? Why did I lie? Lying is an act of survival. I lie so that people will still like me. I thought you would have guessed. I left you enough clues. He was my science teacher.

I paid attention in all of my classes. Did you pay attention?

Remember the mosquitoes on the very first night? Night one. Peter knew so much about carbon dioxide. This is the twist in the tale. Of course, you would have figured it out.

I don't want your sympathy to evaporate. In science in my first year of high school we put some water from Bondi Beach in our flask and evaporated it over the Bunsen Burner until a thin film of salt was left. Our science teacher wore socks pulled up to the knees and sandals of an infant. We were more able to pay attention to the science before Mr Mason came with his honey skin. This teacher told us something about Gandhi in India and a fairy tale that made salt seem like Turkish Delight that Edmund was desperate for in the Lion the Witch and the Wardrobe. I was surprised at the amount of water it took to get that small scraping of salt. But when I wet my finger and licked it through that salt—the taste of it in my mouth made me believe in those fairy tales. So I hope there is a shadow of sympathy left for me, like salt on a petri dish.

But I am avoiding my secret here, aren't I? You already know I was taken away for having sex. Well not just that, but for liking sex.

So here is my Secret Number 2: Peter and Mr Mason are one and the same.

I thought he loved me. I really did. But the excuses started soon enough.

I have to do some marking. I forget how very young you are. I have a staff meeting.

Jack

Each Monday when I went to visit Jack, he looked worse. He'd given up smoking but that only meant that he had swapped his chain smoking for continuous drinking. He had become fat. He looked morose, but I convinced myself that he wasn't depressed. His hair was always coiffed. He always wore well-pressed shirts. He never became one of the tracksuit wearing greasy-haired characters of despair I have seen walking into my office for the last thirty-odd years.

What concerned me more were the doorways. Nancy seemed nonplussed by these but each time I visited, which was weekly I will remind you, Jack had cut another doorway into their house. Once he even answered the front door to me with a circular saw in his hands.

"Come and have a look at this," he'd say, and a new doorway would have appeared so that the bathroom could be entered by both the kitchen and the lounge. Nancy was constantly moving the furniture around as her wall space contracted. This is what bothered me the most. I am a man, of course, but the trajectory my life has followed has not allowed me to know enough about carpentry to recognise what is safe and what is not. Of course, I have heard of supporting walls and such things, but I had no idea whether Jack was cutting through these or not. The look on his face when he showed me his new doorways though, that childlike look of delight, prevented me from ever asking him. I do not blame myself for that. I am a psychiatrist. If the walls came tumbling down one day, it was hardly my fault.

On this evening, though, Nancy answered the door.

"In the kitchen?" I asked her by way of greeting. Our familiarity had reached such comfortableness.

"Shh," she said. "He's sleeping. I'm not going to college tonight."

"Okay, I'll go." To tell you the truth my wife had made the most succulent corned beef that Sunday, with white sauce, which was my favourite. She always made enough to eat for a week, and as it was only Monday, I was keen to head home. White sauce, which she would make fresh each night, was wonderful hot, even warm, but cold was another matter entirely.

"Please stay," said Nancy, and it was her hand on mine that convinced me.

In the kitchen she poured my Scotch. She remembered the ice, two fingers of Glenfiddich, and a splash of hot water straight from the kettle, just the way I like it. I looked at Nancy then, her broad honest face and nurturing brown eyes and knew that she could make a man very happy. I knew Jack's decline in temperament had nothing to do with her. I wondered how low he would have sunk without her.

"Jack is going to kill himself," she said matter-of-factly. "He's just waiting for an opportunity."

"We won't give him one." Simple as that.

"I cannot babysit him 24 hours a day."

"Yes, you can. We can." I drank. "He'll be better when the Royal Commission finishes," I said, full of temporary conviction. Perhaps it was denial. I looked at Nancy, "Jack would never do that. He doesn't believe in it."

I couldn't bring myself to say that word: suicide. At work, of course, it rolled off my tongue with regular monotony: suicide, suicide attempt, suicidal tendences, fantasies involving suicide. But never in relation to Jack.

"Did Jack ever tell you the story of the burnt man?" I asked her.

"I've heard all of Jack's stories." I have to admit to you, that despite her beauty and her obvious love for Jack, Nancy's tone then made me like her a little bit less. She clearly did not realise that Jack's stories were parables for life. But then, she was still so young.

"We went to Linda's for dinner last night," Nancy said. "Jack was off his face. He was drunk, but that wasn't all. Who knows what he'd taken, but he was all over the place."

"I can hear every word you are saying in there," came an announcement from the lounge room. "None of it is true, my friend. She is making it all up. Every word."

I jumped at the chance of leaving Nancy in the kitchen all sulky and over-dramatic; traits of the female species which cause men to run a mile. The number of times I have had overdramatic, sulky women in my office with their big, sad, cow eyes and tales of woe that surpassed any physical beauty they possessed. They wondered why their husband got a mistress. I sympathised of course, but sometimes I wanted to shove a mirror right in front of their self-righteous faces and say, "Look at that! No, it's not the wrinkles around your eyes. Guess again. No, it's not your thin lips. Try again, third time lucky. No, it's not the shape of your bloody nose, excuse the French."

Ah, women like that, they never understand. Fake breasts and noses and they still wonder why their husbands leave them. Cooking classes won't help you, love. Just stop being such a whinger for five minutes, will you? Greet your husband with a smile and he will be much less likely to stray.

But alas, once more I digress. Where were we? I wonder whether perhaps I digress from the urge to avoid telling you what happened next. You can guess. Jack passed away. We all know that he killed himself. That he washed down a handful of Tuinal with a can of beer in his car. That is no surprise to you, so why am I telling you this little tale at all? To make sense of it for me? For you? Who knows?

For better or for worse I joined Jack in the loungeroom. By the time I got there he was asleep again. His hair was mussed and his skin grey. He had bare feet. I had never seen Jack with bare feet.

Nancy must have followed me from the kitchen. "He's asleep."

"What happened to his hand?"

"He cut himself with a knife last night when we went to Linda's for dinner. The cut is deep. I know now he can do it. He will do it." She sounded tired, like a first-time mother that doesn't realise that one baby is nothing, who should be mustering her reserves for when she has four of them and stop counting her hours of sleeplessness. There is simply no point in that.

It wasn't long after the suicide of Kylie Mitchell. Only a few months, probably, because there was still all that fuss going on about all the money that she left Jack in her will. You can imagine that suicide was a raw subject for him then. He always used to tell us the stats. Men do it this way and women do it that. Men kill themselves violently, in front of trains and jumping off cliffs. Or with guns in their mouths. Women are so much more peaceful about it. That is actually what he said. Making suicide seem almost graceful for them, like men simply had two left feet.

Women use pills, mostly. Or gas themselves in their cars. I don't believe these differences are due to grace but due to courage. They say only a weak person kills themselves, but I disagree. It must take a brave man to jump in front of a train or to put a gun inside their own mouth and pull the trigger. Even a woman must be brave, I guess, to end her life with vomit spilling from her mouth after an overdose. They are the brave ones, not us. We choose to kill ourselves slowly with alcohol and cigarettes. We have all grown up knowing the difference between right and wrong, heaven and hell. Whether we choose to believe, it is there inside us, and only a brave person plans their own funeral.

After Kylie killed herself, I thought Jack would tell the story of the burnt man. But he didn't.

Kate

I sat in the courtroom and watched Doctor Grafton on the stand. He wore a white suit and a silk tie, but the flesh from his cheeks had fallen into pools on either side of his chin. I wasn't listening to the lawyers; I was just watching my doctor and remembering the smell of him and the way my legs felt, fuzzy and yummy after he cupped my chin in his fingers and fed me the pink pills. My skin itched with the thought of it and I felt nauseous. I couldn't concentrate. All I could think of were those pink pills that I love—and hate. I looked at five things quickly to distract me, like Di taught me to. The ceiling, a wrinkly neck, the grain of the wooden pew that rippled like a wave in front of me. And Doctor Jack's silky tie.

Jack started talking. "It is not such a strange phenomenon as you suggest that all the Slumber patients received electroconvulsive therapy. The two treatments went hand in hand and produced some very sophisticated results. Our centre specialised in giving ECT. This is the reason, and the only reason, that our patients received shock therapy. That is the service that we provided and that is the reason patients came to us."

I understood my nightmares then. The flashes of pain. I realised then where they came from. The pulses of light and the agony of knitting needles being forced into my eardrums. I stood up. Right there in the courtroom. Everyone looked at me. Doctor Grafton looked at me. I knew he recognised me. He recognised my blue party dress. So did the others.

The gavel hit the desk.

"Would the woman in the public gallery please sit down?"

But I couldn't. People were talking. They stared at me. I opened my mouth, but no air went in or out.

I stepped on handbags as I pushed my way out of the pew. I stepped on toes without apologising and ran. The guard opened the door and I crossed the road into Hyde Park and walked back and forth. I flung myself to the ground but that didn't help anything and all I could see were the flashes that had torn my memory apart. I stood. I walked. I flung myself to the ground again. And again. I sat and watched ibis come and poke their long, curved beaks into the garbage bins as if cold McDonald's tasted better than raw fish. Birds with no shame at all.

I could see the courthouse from where I sat. I watched as a man walked across the road, his eyes scanning the street, this way and that. Even from there I could see that his suit pants were cheap. His shirt still had the square creases from the packaging. He found me by the time he reached the edge of the park and smiled like we were old friends. I knew his smile was a lie. I don't have any old friends. I sat on my haunches like an animal, ready to spring away from him as he reached into his jacket pocket. He held a packet of cigarettes out to me, an exchange for letting him sit next to me. I didn't care that I was so easily bought.

I sucked the smoke deep into my lungs. I wanted to say, "That is the best thing anyone has ever given me." But I think he knew.

We stood on the corner and watched the circus across the road as the courthouse finished for the day. We watched the media throng surrounding the expensive suits of the doctors and the lawyers and the cheaper shirts and ties of the crown witnesses. We watched the nurses in their flat shoes even on their day off. I wondered which one of them was Eva. Cameras flashed in the dusk.

"Why don't you testify?" He drew on his cigarette as if it wasn't him who had spoken.

I sucked in another lungful and let out the smoke in two dragon blasts from my nose. Please don't look at me. Not at my pinned eyes.

"Then your voice can be heard. It is hard, but we will look after you."

I smoked my cigarette right down to the filter and I would have smoked that too if I could have. I buried the butt under some dead leaves just like I had done at school.

"Look," he said. "I don't want to pressure you."

He offered me another cigarette then and we smoked together. I turned so I didn't have to watch Doctor Grafton's white suit shining like a beacon on the courthouse steps. The homeless ibis were much less offensive to my sight.

"I have been trying to get here for seven years," he said, indicating the courthouse. "Don't turn your back on us. I am like the oldest child who has broken the parents in. No one believed me. Not even my own lawyer. They thought I was crazy. That I'd made this stuff up. Now is our chance."

I looked at him then.

"I know it happened to you too. I'm right huh?"

I smiled at him then and that's all it takes for people like us to become friends. We don't need words with all their lies and implications, double meanings and treachery. Just a smile in exchange for another cigarette.

"I won you know," he said. "Grafton was found guilty of assault and battery, false imprisonment and negligence. I got money. You could get money too. Enough to set you up somehow. You are only as crazy as he made you."

*

He came to visit me in my flat. He came in for a cup of tea. He made it. I fiddled around feeding Bertha her seed, then he came out of the kitchenette and handed me my cup. My flat was brown except for Bertha. Her droppings and seed husks littered the floor while she scuffled around the bottom of her cage searching for her favourite seeds. All native budgies are green. People have bred all the other colours: yellow and violet and blue and white. Yellow came first through a genetic mistake —they're even in the wild sometimes. They don't last long though. Too obvious to predators. But Bertha was safe with me even though she squawked a lot—that is what female budgies do.

We drank, and I stared out the window through all the flats and all the houses to the bush where Jack Grafton killed himself. Flies laid their eggs in his eyes before the police found him. That made me happy.

Jack

Some people's stories you wish you never knew. Some conversations you wish you had never heard. Indeed, that happens when you are a psychiatrist and fathers tell you about sodomising their sons. You wish you had never heard it. You wished they had told someone else, not you.

I was at Jack's house the night he rang his daughter. Of course, within our circle everyone knew that Jack was sterile. It was due to childhood mumps, which is why none of us ever believed Kylie Mitchell's story of her unborn child being Jack's. If Jack hadn't been sterile plenty of women would have been around to prove it, and children too, no doubt. It was not a case of blame the wife for the lack of offspring, if you know what I mean.

It was Monday. Jack and I were drinking Scotch. Nancy was there drinking Champagne when Jack leapt up from the table and grabbed the phone off the wall. Nancy rolled her eyes as if these lunges of epiphany were common-place, but I had a sinking feeling and I was right.

"Sussana? It's Daddy," said Jack. "I have to tell you something Darling."

I knew what he was about to say. I knew it all and I should have jumped on Jack then and ripped the phone from the wall, but my Adams's apple swelled to the size of my throat and I couldn't speak.

"Is your sister there? Don't worry. You can tell her Darling."

Nancy stood up then.

"Jack!" Nancy wrestled him for the telephone. Jack shoved her. I stood. Nancy tried again, and Jack shoved her again. I hovered. I was ready to step in if anything serious had happened. Don't get me wrong. Susanna must have been speaking.

Nancy was crying but Jack had spun around and around until the curled telephone cable wrapped him up.

"Susanna. You are adopted."

"Oh shit-fuck. Oh my God." Nancy sunk to the table then.

I would have stopped him, but the words were already out. There was nothing any of us could do. We all knew the twins were adopted, of course, but the twins had no idea. Then again, I guess it would have come out sooner or later. That is why Jack told them. I am sure of that now. He wanted to protect his girls. His wife was very angry about it, but then wives can be like that, as you may well know.

Jack

There was all this hoo-hah at the Royal Commission about that young girl who tried to jump off the Sydney Harbour Bridge. She was the longest sedated patient ever, either here or overseas. Jack must have won that bet in the end. I remember sitting in the witness stand. I think it was the third week of the hearings and I was tired. Everyone was tired. We'd all had enough, and the prosecution was using this tiredness to their advantage. They were trying to manipulate us into saying something we did not mean. They were ready for us to slip up.

I would never lie under oath, of course, but there are ways of describing situations that cast a different light on the unfolding of events. On this particular day Jack was not giving evidence. Instead he sat with his legal team wearing a grey suit and sunglasses. I could tell by his general demeanour that they were getting to him. I was sitting in the witness box while this lawyer-type paraded up and down before me in that disconcerting manner they must teach at law school. They all do it, parading up and down as if the court room is a stage. It is enough to put one off their game completely. They are professionals at unnerving people. This fellow buttered me up first with questions about my relationship with Jack Grafton, which as you should know by now, I was proud to answer.

"Yes, we have known each other since medical school. We are both members of the Royal College of Psychiatrists."

"Yes, we socialise together."

"Yes, we have been to one another's houses and have a personal relationship that extends well beyond the usual relationship between colleagues."

"Yes, I would consider us to be good friends."

"Yes, we share intimate details about each other's personal lives."

"Yes, we are confidantes *as such.*"

"No, there was never a competition held between us as to how long we could keep a patient sedated. A patient would be sedated for as long as was necessary to complete their treatment."

As I said there was all this hoo-hah about the girl who tried to jump off the Harbour Bridge.

"I am afraid that I have no memory of this girl."

"I am aware that she was sedated for over three months, but this is only through the media hype about the situation. I have no memory of her being at Ferriby."

"Although she was there for three months?"

"Yes, that is correct."

"So, let me see if I understand this correctly. Doctor Jack Grafton, with whom you admit to being good friends, to whom you admit to not only having a relationship that extends beyond the usual relationship of colleagues, whom you admit is your confidant, left you unaware of a girl who was a patient in Ferriby for over three months? You say you were unaware of this girl's existence, either through the general observations of a professional, or through the conversations, the many, many conversations you must have had with your fellow psychiatrist, friend and *confidant* over this period of time."

"I have no memory of this girl."

"Well, perhaps I can remind you. This *girl's* name is Katherine Minola. She was a healthy seventeen-year-old girl when she was first put into an artificial coma but turned eighteen during the time she spent unconscious. I do believe that this makes her a woman, and not a girl. During a subsequent Slumber treatment, Katherine Minola lost almost half her body weight and her knees became stuck together from bed sores, a complaint that any well-trained nursing staff would have been able to avoid. This *girl* would have been easily recognisable by her long blonde hair, especially if you walked past her bedside on a regular basis. I put it to you that you must have been aware of this patient's presence."

"I have no memory of this girl. Let me remind you that I never worked at Ferriby Private Hospital. Any patients discussed would have been in a peer review context."

"So, you deny any knowledge of her existence?"

I despise it when an educated man begins a sentence with a conjunction.

"I have heard of hundreds of patients at Ferriby Private Hospital. I cannot be expected to remember them all."

"Even such a beautiful, young woman, left lying in a darkened ward, naked?"

"As professionals we are used to seeing nudity. We do not allow ourselves to see a patient in the manner to which you are inferring."

"What do you think I am inferring?"

I looked at the prosecutor. His suit was impeccable. His hair was carefully slicked back over his crown. I could tell he had an anal fixation. Some Slumber Therapy would not have gone astray on him. I bet he drove his children mad.

"What do you think I am inferring?"

I would have told him, but his question was overruled. Apparently, it was too argumentative. That would not have stopped me. Let me argue anyway. I would have said that I had no sexual interest in my patients. I would have told him that and I would have meant it too. I am not the kind of necrophiliac scoundrel he was inferring, and while I objected to the question, I would have loved to have answered it nonetheless.

"This young *woman*," he stressed the word as if he had not already made that point several times, "contracted pneumonia and had to be taken to Hornsby Hospital in a seriously ill condition. She eventually recovered, physically at least, but I must let the courtroom know," the show-off bastard gestured around the room then said, "that to this day, upon waking up from her *slumber*, the sleep that was *supposed* to reset her brain, Katherine Minola has barely spoken another word. She cannot work. Obviously, there are some flaws to this treatment. This woman nearly died, and she has woken up unable to speak."

"Firstly, you cannot announce flaws to the treatment based on one patient's unfortunate experience."

"I am not planning to." He smiled then, for the judge and for the audience seated in the pews, like ignoramuses at Sunday Mass.

I turned to the courtroom and explained it to them. "Unable and unwilling are two very different scenarios." I asserted. "This girl was put under Slumber Therapy for a mental disorder. Her waking and not speaking is a psychological matter, not a physical one."

I wondered who was advising this fellow on his medical knowledge. Pneumonia cannot be contracted. I was going to wax lyrical about this as well but caught myself just in time. Pointing out this lawyer's errors was not necessarily going to win me any favours. Instead I said this, "You are talking about a *young* woman who was caught attempting to jump off the Sydney Harbour Bridge. If she had succeeded, she would most likely be dead. That is the reality of the situation. A dead young woman. Slumber Therapy saved her life."

"You are assuming that death and Slumber Therapy were the only options available to this young woman. No further questions."

Kate

I never tried to jump of the Harbour Bridge. That is the truth. I just wanted to get out of Katie's car. I just needed to think. I needed to be left alone. I still had my dreams. I just needed to remember what they were.

But I have tried to kill myself. When I finally got home after my second Slumber Therapy it was coming up to Easter. One morning I pulled open the cutlery drawer and found Mum's small vegetable knife. The one with the wooden handle. I remember sitting out on the back steps, balancing the knife between my knees like a tightrope. It wouldn't have taken me much to slice into myself. I could even take the drugs so I wouldn't feel a thing. But then perhaps the point of killing yourself is to feel something before you leave, even if it is pain.

I imagined Mum coming home from up the street with the twins and finding my body deflated on the steps like an old party balloon. I stood up and went back inside, putting the knife back into the second drawer in the kitchen, along with the potato masher and the eggbeater and my mother's other tools of the trade.

I knew Mum would be home soon and the silence would be decimated by the twins' squealing and screeching. Happy or sad they sounded the same to me. I hid in my room before they arrived. It wasn't the thought of them, or even the thought of them finding me that stopped me from slashing my wrists. It was the fact that I wasn't twenty-four years old yet. Kylie was twenty-four years old when she killed herself. I had to beat her. I had to survive longer than that. It was a game I was playing with myself. That was all.

Jack

That Kylie Mitchell has a lot to answer for, if you ask me. Jack was fine before she killed herself. As I've said before he may have been a lady's man, but he always pursued his women with the most gentlemanly aplomb. His own wife stayed loyal to him until the end, although they no longer lived together. And then there was beautiful young Nancy. Jack gave her a pearl ring and a Siamese cat, and he gave the exact same present to Linda Pascal, although they were separated by then. The kittens were from the same litter and the two girls even became friends. The current lover and the past love—friends. Imagine that! This was not the work of a womaniser. Jack was simply a gentleman who happened to love women.

Kylie wasn't like the others. I could see that from the start. She was a dancer of sorts, if you can call that type of cavorting around dancing. She had the legs for it. Jack was much taken up with her, or with her legs, at least. I can't say I blame him for that either. She had a lovely set. Yet this woman didn't belong in our world, even as a lover. She didn't understand our rules. She became clingy and dependant on Jack. It was very uncomfortable at times.

Jack was still living with his wife at the time, and he was seeing Linda, who was also his receptionist. Life was complicated enough without Kylie turning up at all the wrong moments to ruin everything.

I remember one time we had all decided to go camping. My wife at the time did not like camping, so her mood desperately needed to be lightened. We met at the hospital and Linda was sitting in the passenger seat of Jack's new Jaguar with a scarf around her head and large sunglasses on. Her looks were always been a little bland and horsey for my taste, but at that moment she epitomised freedom. She looked like a movie star.

Then Kylie arrived and saw us all leaving.

"I'm coming too," she insisted. Jack tried to talk her out of it. He took her aside and said this and that. Kylie must have loved the attention being diverted away from Linda's movie star status and I am sure she played on that, making it impossible for us to leave without her. Taking her was a big mistake. She made Jack's life hell for the entire time we were away. The first night Jack spent with Linda. They were seeing each other after all. They'd even held dinner parties together. She was his substitute wife of sorts. But Kylie got so jealous. She seemed to have no idea of her position in the pecking order, not only in Jack's world, but in society in general.

Why am I telling you this? I guess so that you can understand where I am coming from. So that you know Kylie's death was not Jack's doing and such a fuss should never have been made of it.

The most upsetting aspect of all this is that I gave Jack a bottle of claret when he adopted the twins. It was not any old bottle of wine. It was a fifty-year-old bottle. Jack decided to save it until they turned twenty-one. It wasn't just that he opened it before their birthday, but it should have been drunk to celebrate something, not to mourn the loss of someone. Especially someone like her.

"I went over to her flat after Kylie was gone," he told me on one of those Monday nights, "and I drank the whole thing. The whole bottle in one go, and I was so upset I didn't even taste the stuff. I was going to kill myself, right there and then, but I was too pissed even to do that."

Jack wasn't joking either or being melodramatic. He would have killed himself then, I was sure enough of that. He had tried, and he had used a gun too. I sometimes wonder what would have happened if he had succeeded that day, if the gun he had tried to fire at his own head had not missed, leaving the bullet in Kylie's wall. I wonder if that would have made me an accessory after the fact, having supplied the wine.

Sometimes I think it would have been better if Jack had gone that night with that good quality claret in his belly and died a man's death, as much as suicide can be, at the hand of his own gun. It would have saved him the woe of the manslaughter trial and the embarrassment of the Royal Commission. He lived a little longer, true enough, but if he had died then at least he would not have died with a bottle of beer in his hand, washing down pills like a woman. He would have killed himself in response to the death of his lover, an understandable enough reason. As it was, he was forced into his death through the hounding of the media. Jack fell on his own sword, so to speak. I honestly think he had just had enough of everything. When I saw him last he looked extremely tired. He really just needed to get away from it all and have a rest. To this day I am saddened by the demise of that bottle of claret.

Women are all the same. Either they complain about having too much sex or not enough. From the Greeks to Freud the womb has been blamed for woman's inherent irrationality. Freud really knew it was the vagina. Freud was too polite. The Maoris knew the truth of that monster—the toothed vagina. Even without teeth it can chew up a man and spit him out. Like a wild animal it has to be fed with care and if you lose control of it the result is madness, both for the woman and for those struck down by her evil power. That is what Kylie did to Jack.

Kate

Where am I now? I didn't testify. How could I? There was no way I was getting up there in front of everyone and being forced to tell my secrets. I didn't want to answer any of their questions in a court room. Stand there as a witness while they threw a lot of words at me. But I did go back there. I sat on one of the wooden pews like I was at church and listened every single day to what they had done to me. Men were on the stand. Women were on the stand. It didn't matter because our stories were the same. They told my story for me. I didn't need to repeat it.

I heard it all. The things they did to me that I knew and the things that I only learned about then. I saw Doctor Grafton come and go with his beautiful suits and his warm brown eyes, genuinely surprised that his patients were unhappy with him.

So yes, I got my money too. I'm not telling you how much. It's none of your business. They call it compensation, but how can you compensate for lost potential? For a life that never got started because a teenage girl was silly enough to fall in love with someone she shouldn't? Beecroft definitely missed the 70s that I recognise from the television. A pity too. I would have loved all that peace and flower power stuff. Free love. Huh. Obviously, that's what got me into trouble, a decade after the 60s were supposedly swinging and the pill was supposed to have changed our lives.

So, what did I spend my money on? Surviving. I live in my little flat that sits in the middle of other little flats. It's no Blues Point Tower, but outside I can hear the birds screaming at each other in an old liquid amber. Every spring I watch the mynahs tossing chicks out of other bird's nests. Sometimes I watch television. I watch *Neighbours* and *Home and Away*, the eternally interesting lives of teenagers who instinctively do what they rest of us are too scared to do.

Each year I look out at the liquid amber naked in the winter while I freeze in my little flat. I keep my oven on with the door open to keep warm. In the summer the sun heats my bedroom and cooks me inside. The trees are my calendar. I don't need any other. There is a jacaranda next-door. I chose my flat because its branches hang over the fence and dribble purple flowers onto the ground. When those flowers start to bloom, I know it is my birthday. Then the green leaves grow up on the trees and my purple flowers fall into a carpet on the ground. From the moment those flowers bloom until the moment they are replaced by the green leaves, I consider it to be my birthday. It stretches my birthday out. Sometimes it lasts right up until Christmas if we have had a cool spring. But it doesn't replace the birthday that I lost. I have stagnated at seventeen. No longer a schoolgirl and never an adult. I read books about lives that were interrupted by poverty or abuse. They give me hope. I read the biography of Ita Buttrose. And Richard Branson and Macpherson Robertson. I read them as if they are a map showing me how to get to my future. But then the unease of leaving my little flat arrives and I turn on the television.

I have another secret for you. Perhaps you think this whole thing is childish enough. In this case skip this secret and leave me just this one piece of dignity. But I have offered it to you anyway. I have done the right thing. I never know which one you will judge me for, but I can't seem to stop now, so here it is. I still read *Cleo* magazine. I flip through the articles on careers and motherhood and imagine myself at work, my desk surrounded with framed photographs of my children, golden-haired and smiling. I read the editor's notes and practice her words in front of the mirror, pushing my hair about this way and that.

Jack

We had no other option in the end. We had to admit Jack for Slumber Therapy. This proves we all believed in the treatment. Oh, physician heal thyself and all that codswallop. Jack had sunk so low. What else were we to do? We admitted him under the name Jack Lee. The nurses knew who he was, of course, and it embarrassed them as he was nursed naked along with the rest. ECT and Slumber Therapy to reset his brain. What else could we have done? We had to keep him sedated, even before he arrived at Ferriby. He could never know where he was. Where he had been. But it all went wrong. It all went so horribly wrong.

It wasn't long before we were all crowded into Jack's empty office, drinking to get drunk. Everything was gone. The brain in the jar that had sat on his desk was gone. So were the files and the photos. I had never been in Jack's office without him there and I am sure I was not the only one who felt like a trespasser. His desk was still there, too heavy to move, and I felt the need to stand on it then. My motivation was clear. I was taking a stand for Jack. I stood on that desk and everyone raised their glasses. His friends were there. There were still many of us. Nancy was there and so was Jan. I raised my glass in order to toast a wonderful man.

"Doctor Jack Grafton," I began, "was the top student in both cardiology and psychiatry at Sydney University. He studied with the most eminent psychiatrists in his field around the world, from Europe to America. On his return he opened the ground-breaking new…"

"This is a wake not a bloody résumé!" They were right, of course, but the interruption made me angry.

"Come on, Brian, get off the desk." Hands reached up to help me down. My glass was refilled before I could complain. I took a deep drink. Ah, the cheap Scotch was rotting my mind as well as my guts.

Let me introduce myself then. I guess it is about time, although, by now you know some of my nastier habits, such as drinking cheap Scotch, albeit from a Royal Doulton lead crystal decanter. I am sure by now you have gleaned my medical credentials also. But a formal introduction is something that up until now I have avoided. My name is Brian Lockwood.

It is not that I feel guilt. I have no reason to feel guilty. Of that I am absolutely sure. Trust me, I have tortured myself enough over the question of my possible guilt that I know for certain I am guilt free. This is not due to a lack of sympathy for the Slumber Therapy patients. I feel sympathy. But more than that I feel shame as a person who has lived, and no doubt will die soon enough, unable to repair the reputation of my friend and colleague, the much-esteemed Dr Jack Grafton. I have attempted to set down the life and times of this wonderful man, but I have nonetheless been unable to show him as he was. I read back over these pages and see a flamboyant caricature. A coif of hair out of proportion and swooning women all grinning madly back up at me. Forgive me for how my lack of skill as a writer has presented him to you in this way. The story I had wanted to tell of Jack was subtler. I hope that the image of the man I knew is perhaps camouflaged between the lines of this ramble. I hope you have not given up on me or I am like a mouse shouting in the desert with no one to hear. You see? I can write a pretty little simile when the mood takes me. But is it enough for me to know that you are still there?

Perhaps Jack's voice is disguised somewhere in the stories I have told, between the dynamite in a Leichhardt backyard lighting up a jacaranda tree and his desire to find a physical cure for the stale porridge of a sick brain. Somewhere amongst all that chaos there is a man who was my friend.

Kate

Sometimes I stand naked in front of the full-length mirror that hangs on the inside door of my wardrobe. I look at my naked self after I have a shower. My body is still fine. Childbirth has not stretched and distorted my figure. My breasts have softened but my nipples still point optimistically upwards. My stomach is still flat. My thighs still have the diamond gap between them that Peter wanted to see the whole world through.

Hanging in my little wardrobe is the blue satin dress with the pale blue lace still attached to the hem to protect my modesty. Sometimes, during my birthday, I put this dress on. It still slips easily over my hips and zippers from the waist. I put on my party dress and go and sit down on the purple carpet of fallen jacaranda blossoms that nature has provided.

I speak then. To the birds waiting for the stale bread I have saved for them. I am their mother and I say all those motherly things. "Share with your brother. Stop fighting. You've had enough, you can't possibly want any more. Eat up. Come on now, if you want to be big and strong."

When I speak to the birds, I lisp like Ita. I don't want Mother Nature to find out exactly who I am. I watch two magpies fighting on the grass while the mynah birds watch. The mynah birds don't care. They have already chosen the best pieces for themselves. The foolish magpies are scared of them.

I stand up and one of the magpies runs away from me, not concerned enough to fly. The other stops to look me in the eye and sings. Its song is so beautiful, whistling up and down. I tear up slices of devon and toss them into the air. The devon never gets the chance to hit the ground before the magpies swoop it up. I feed them just so I can have my own private choir. Magpies look old when they are juveniles, all grey feathers as frizzy as my own is becoming. They will turn black and white by the end of the summer, but there won't be as many of them by then. I sit again and watch my magpies wrestle in the dust while a crested pigeon takes the scraps. I wonder what it would be like to be grey and wrinkled in youth and then grow and bloom into adulthood with unblemished skin and fine silky hair and all the wisdom in the world.

Acknowledgements

This project would look very different if it wasn't for the expertise of my supervisors at the University of Newcastle, particularly David Musgrave, Hugh Craig, and Keri Glastonbury, for their knowledge and their capacity to provide support and criticism in unison. Without the financial support of the scholarship program the writing of this book would have been impossible.

Many of the staff at the University of Newcastle provided invaluable services that made my research both fun and fruitful. The library staff at the Ourimbah campus were particularly supportive. I would like to thank Julie Mundy-Taylor, research librarian, Anthony O'Brien, teaching librarian, and Fiona Neville, liaison librarian, for being literary detectives.

I would also like to thank Puncher and Wattmann, especially Ed Wright, for taking a chance on my first book and giving me practical and thoughtful editing advice.

On a more personal note, I would like to thank my fellow writers from my writing group *The Galloping Abs*. I would especially like to thank Libby Lovell for recounting high school in the 1970s, including euthanising and dissecting mice.

I have also really enjoyed the reprieve and social support provided by the HDR Coffee Club. Fellow post graduate students Rebecca Poynting and Karen Dimmock have discussed everything with me from cutting the wings off a bird to giving artistic advice, all over a cup of hot chocolate.

My friends have been fantastic at leaving me alone except when I need them. Tasha Ward and Margo Mannix have been my own personal cheer squad throughout. Special thanks goes to my partner Christopher Jones for being the biggest critic of my "turgid" writing but helping me format it anyway. Special thanks to Joplin, Claude and Spike for finding the trampoline and handballs so entertaining, learning to use the microwave, and supplying me with kisses and cuddles on demand.

I would like to thank my parents, Pam and Maitland Vertigan for distracting me with various dramas so that I could keep my priorities in check. Finally, I would like to thank my sister Anne Vertigan for inspiring me but also for holding a bottle of Scotch ransom until I finished this book.